THE DUKE'S CARRIAGE WINDOW

THE ROGUES OF DEVIL'S SQUARE

BOOK TWO

LAUREN SMITH

This book is for Lori and Meredith. Lori has been a bright start of support and friendship for me these many years of writing. The heroine in this book is inspired by and named after her daughter Meredith. Happily ever afters always exist as long as readers like you keep turning the pages!

1

Meredith Montague's heart was breaking.

She held her Uncle Benjamin's hand as she watched his chest rise and fall in shallow breaths. All was quiet in the bedchamber of Burton House, the residence that she'd called home for the last five years. Dusk had settled in over the wild gardens beyond the windows of her uncle's room.

She had seen death before, with her mother when she'd been fourteen. But even now, at nineteen, she was still not used to the creeping, foreboding presence of *the end*. It was not frightening, but it filled her with a quiet, choking despair. She couldn't stop death, not even to save someone she loved.

"Meredith," her uncle rasped. "There's a letter in the top drawer of my desk... in my study. You must take it to my nephew in London."

"Your nephew?"

"Yes... Darius, the son of my elder brother. He is the Duke of Tiverton."

Meredith had heard about Darius a few times, but Uncle Ben was a very quiet, reserved man when it came to his family. He had been close with his elder brother and had not taken his death well. It had broken her uncle, just as surely as his death would break Meredith.

Uncle Ben's blue eyes were still clear enough that she saw he was making every effort to convey the importance of the matter.

"Darius is a good man... I've asked him to take care of you, as I have done... I have asked him... to find you a husband."

Her uncle coughed, and she went to fetch a glass of water for him. He lay back in his bed with a heavy sigh. She didn't want to upset her uncle, but she had to understand what he intended for her.

"Darius... Darius must take me in? I cannot stay here?"

She wanted to stay at Burton House with its sunny rooms and splendid old white and blue china teacups, and the comfort of the quiet world here did not frighten her. This was her home. Uncle Ben was her home.

"We both know you cannot stay. I have left a provision in my will that Harry *must* provide you with travel money. But Harry... makes rash decisions. He will not handle the money and land well... But you... I can protect you in the way I cannot protect this house...and sending you to Darius will protect you."

Harry, Uncle Ben's only child, was a wild, reckless

gentleman that Meredith didn't trust, or like. He was the sort of man to kick a dog when the poor beast got in his way.

"I understand," Meredith said softly.

"You can trust Darius, my dear..." Uncle Ben closed his eyes. "Go... find the letter now and I will rest."

She didn't want to leave him. Part of her feared that if she stepped outside his bedchamber, he would slip away without her having a chance to say goodbye.

He gave her hand a gentle squeeze. "Go on now, Meredith. I promise to be here when you return."

It took every bit of Meredith's strength to let go of her uncle's hand. She paused at the door to look back at the kind, old man asleep on the bed. His illness had ravished his once handsome looks. This man had been a father to her more than uncle.

But in truth, he wasn't even her uncle. Not by blood.

Her mother Mariah had once been in love with Uncle Ben, but she had chosen another man in the end. Her mother had lived for only a few years with the man who had sired Meredith. She couldn't even remember what he looked like, only that he had left them penniless when he'd returned to his wife and then he'd died shortly after.

Uncle Ben, newly widowed himself, had taken pity on them and paid for a cottage by the sea near Fraisthorpe Beach on the eastern coast of England, not far from the village of Burton Agnes.

When her mother had died, Uncle Ben had moved Meredith into his home. The last five years had healed her and given her new life and peace. For a time, it had been the same for Uncle Ben, until the illness struck him down.

Now she was to lose her uncle and the peaceful life they had shared in this lovely, old house. There were to be no more morning rides across the estate, no more long walks to the village for midday luncheons. No more visits to the tiny bookshop to buy books that she and Uncle Ben would read and discuss over dinner.

Her mind played over a thousand things that would come to an end once he was gone. It was as though her own life was ending, and it was. This version of herself, the Meredith of Burton Agnes, would be gone forever. She would become someone new, a woman living in London with a stranger, a duke no less.

The idea was terrifying. This duke would have no time for her and certainly no need of her. He would have his gentleman friends, likely a wife, perhaps even a mistress. Uncle Ben had never mentioned Darius being married, but he so rarely spoke of his nephew except to express regret at some terrible quarrel they'd had a few years ago.

Surely, being saddled with her would upset any decent man. Despite her uncle's assurances, she couldn't envision a future where her very presence wouldn't outrage a powerful, influential duke. She was a bastard, a nobody. He would dump her onto the first free man he could convince to marry her, wouldn't he?

Meredith's chest tightened with a fierce ache and she swallowed hard.

She drew in a deep breath, trying to still her racing

heart. She didn't want to end up like her mother. She would find a way to save herself. Choosing the wrong man, the wrong life, and having it end all too soon. She wouldn't let that happen.

"Miss Meredith?" A soft voice disrupted Meredith's thoughts. She turned away from the bedroom and found Mrs. Todd, the housekeeper, standing beside her. She hadn't even heard her approach.

"Good evening, Mrs. Todd," she greeted wearily, and hoped she wouldn't burst into tears again. The poor woman had been Meredith's only shoulder to cry on since Uncle Ben's health had taken such a steep turn for the worse.

Mrs. Todd sent a worried glance toward Uncle Ben's closed door. "Is he...gone?"

"No, he is sleeping. I am to retrieve a letter from his study. Will you watch him for me?"

"Of course, dear." Mrs. Todd entered the bedchamber and sat in the chair that Meredith had just vacated.

With the assurance that her uncle was not alone, Meredith went downstairs to her uncle's study. The room smelled of tobacco and old books, two scents she'd come to cherish for the warm memories they created. Shelves full of so many wonderful stories made the room cozy despite its enormous size.

The desk was covered with a mess of papers, but Meredith ignored it and opened the drawers. After a bit of searching, she found what she was looking for. A letter bearing the Duke of Tiverton's name and address in

London. She tucked the letter into the pockets of her skirts before she exited the study. As she moved to close the door behind her, she bumped into someone.

"Oh! I'm terribly sorry I—" She gasped as a large hand closed around her waist as she turned around.

"What were you doing in my father's study, Merry?" The nickname grated on her ears.

Harry St. John stood in front of her. He was dressed fashionably in striped trousers and an overflowing style of cravat that matched his carefully coiffed hairstyle. If she were honest, Meredith thought it all made him look very silly. He was a decently handsome man with dark hair and eyes, but it was those same eyes which reminded her to never trust him. They were locked on her with an upsetting intensity.

With a careful slide of her hips, she dislodged his hand from her body. "I was just seeing to something for Uncle Ben." She didn't mention the letter. She didn't trust Harry.

"Oh? May I help?" He sounded sincere, but Meredith didn't trust the sharp look in his dark eyes.

"No, no thank you, Harry. I've seen to it already. When did you arrive?"

"Just now. I received a letter from the butler a week ago saying my father was unwell." Harry gave her a pointed look. She hadn't written him with the news, but the butler had. Clearly, that fact displeased him. But Uncle Ben had not wished for Harry to be here and had told her not to write to him. Meredith wasn't about to cower before Harry for doing what Uncle Ben had asked, no matter how much she bristled at his unspoken accusation.

"Have you seen him yet?" Meredith asked, knowing he had not, but she tried to distract Harry, who was moving his hand toward her hip again.

"I will, when I am ready," Harry replied. "First, I believe *we* have things to discuss."

"We do?" she asked, clueless as to what he thought they would need to talk about.

"Yes." Harry opened his father's study door and ushered her back into the room. He closed the door behind him and remained in front of it, blocking her way out.

"My father has paid for your upkeep since you were a child. First with your mother at that little cottage, and now here."

Meredith didn't argue, but wondered where this was going.

"Once my father is gone, you will become my responsibility." Harry leaned back against the closed door. "I will be quite content to allow you to continue living here, of course. But I require something in return to justify the expense of your lodgings and meals."

"Oh Harry, I couldn't stay. I—"

He cut her off. "I understand that you were a pleasant companion for my father. You could be a companion to me as well. Of course, I would require things from you that my father did not." He caught her wrist, jerking her toward him. "I am so very lonely, you see."

To her surprise and utter horror, Harry tried to kiss her.

She only just managed to pull back enough to avoid his lunge. "Harry!" She almost shouted his name as she shoved against him with her free hand. "Let me go once. *Please!*"

Harry's eyes darkened and his grip on her wrist tightened.

"Meredith, be reasonable. You are a very pretty girl with no name and no money. How else do you expect to survive? You will only be used by men, it is your fate. At least I am honest about my intentions. I am offering you a way to stay in your home, to keep your belongings and your life here. All you must do is welcome me into your bed."

Meredith jerked her arm free. "I will not be used by you or anyone," she warned. "Now get out of my way or I shall *scream.*" The footmen of the house would come to her defense, even if they might suffer consequences for it. Harry was not exactly a favorite among them.

Harry seemed to weigh his choices before he stepped away from the door. But as Meredith rushed past, he snatched her arm again, even harder than before.

"When he dies, you will be mine," he hissed in her ear. "No other man will take you in without a payment of some kind. *Think on that.*" And with that, he released her.

Meredith fled back to Uncle Ben's room. Mrs. Todd took one look at her and hastily got up from the chair to close the bedroom door so they could speak alone.

"What happened?" she asked in a whisper. "Your face is red, child."

"Harry. He..." Meredith's voice had become shaky, and she felt sick to her stomach.

Mrs. Todd's tone grew sharp. "He hurt you?"

"Only my arm." Meredith winced as she held out her wrist, which was already bruising.

"Tell me everything he said and did," the housekeeper insisted.

Meredith explained about the letter in the study and Uncle Ben's wish to send her to London to Darius, who would take her in. And then she explained how Harry had found her leaving Ben's study.

"We must pack your things at once. I won't have you hurt on my watch, child."

"But I cannot leave Uncle Ben —"

"You won't. But I want you ready to depart the second he passes." Mrs. Todd said. "I shall see to everything."

Meredith nodded and sank warily back in her chair at uncle Ben's bedside. She yawned and laid her head down on her bended arms just to rest for a few moments.

"Wake up. Wake up, child." Mrs. Todd's voice pulled Meredith from the depths of dream. The room was dark except for a single lit candle. Uncle Ben lay still in bed.

She reached for her uncle's hand, which was now still and cold within her own. No... he'd passed away while she'd been asleep.

"He's gone, child. Slipped away a short while ago. You were so tired, I didn't have the heart to wake you. But he knew you were here with him. That's what matters."

Meredith stared at Uncle Ben's face in the candlelight. His features had relaxed and his eyes were closed. The pain that he ravaged his face for weeks was gone at last.

"Did he...suffer?" she asked.

The housekeeper wiped a tear away. "No child. He was looking at you while you slept. Then he smiled, and then after one last breath he was simply...gone."

Meredith covered her mouth with the back of her hand to stifle a sob. She leapt out of the chair. The housekeeper pulled her into an embrace, gently rubbing her back.

"There, there, my dear. It's all right. It's all right."

But it wasn't all right. It would never be all right again. The pain in her chest was unbearable. She wanted to scream, to break a vase or, *anything* to escape the raw inferno of agony that was destroying her heart.

"Breathe, love. Breathe," Mrs. Todd urged. She placed a hand on Meredith's cheek. "You'll survive this, my dear."

Meredith managed a nod, but she didn't agree. She was dying inside.

"Say your goodbyes to him, and then we must get you out of this house."

Meredith had almost forgotten Harry's threat. There was no time to waste. She bent and pressed a trembling kiss to her uncle's forehead. Her tears fell upon his waistcoat as she straightened and frantically wiped at her eyes.

"I have you packed, Miss Meredith. Joseph has the coach waiting. He will take you to the stagecoach down the road. I have secured your passage all the way to London. If you need to rest, you can stay in a coaching inn along the way, and the passage will still be good the next day."

"I have a bit of money ..." Meredith began. She'd been saving her pin money.

"I found it and tucked it into your reticule which is with your valise. Be quick now. Master Harry is still asleep. I want you long gone before he wakes. There's no telling what kind of ideas will get into his head."

They hastened downstairs. The house was still quiet and dark. It was a few hours until dawn. Not even the servants were up and about yet, except for the groom, Joseph, who waited for her outside by Uncle Ben's coach.

Meredith hugged Mrs. Todd. "Thank you."

"Write to me when you reach London now, or else I'll worry." The older woman gave Meredith one last hug. Then Joseph helped Meredith into the coach and they were off.

Half an hour later, Meredith was inside the crowded stagecoach that would take her to London. She clutched her reticule tight and gazed out the window at the approaching dawn. The farther she got away from the place which had been her home, the more she was both forlorn and relieved. She'd left behind her only friends and Uncle Ben, but at the same time she had escaped Harry.

She replayed that moment in the study over and over, trying to understand what had made Harry think he could treat her like that.

Harry had never tried to hurt her before. He spent very little time at Burton House. He was ten years her senior and often carousing in London, according to Uncle Ben, but when he came home to visit, he had always been polite. He had never tried to do what he had just done. Not that Meredith had ever trusted him. Mrs. Todd had instructed Meredith to be wary of men she did not know well and included her warnings by saying that even Master Harry was not always a gentleman. Mrs. Todd clearly had known something Meredith hadn't about Harry.

When the coach stopped to change horses, Meredith stretched her legs and asked the driver how much longer it would take to reach London.

"From here? Five days, miss," the man replied as the grooms checked the harnesses of the new team of horses that were set to replace the old team.

Five days from Yorkshire to London… It already felt like a thousand years.

BY THE FOURTH NIGHT, MEREDITH DECIDED TO USE THE LAST OF her money to pay for a proper bed at a coaching inn. She had not changed clothes or bathed since she'd started, and she smelled of horses, sweat, and the stable yard.

After she was assured that her passage to London would be valid the following morning, she went inside the inn and spoke to the innkeeper. There were a few spare rooms left, and she paid for a dinner and a breakfast.

"If you want to make the morning stagecoach, I'll have a maid rouse you," the innkeeper said.

"Thank you ever so much," Meredith replied. "Could you send dinner up to my room? I am quite tired and afraid I shall fall asleep."

The innkeeper seemed to take pity on her. "Of course, lass. Go on up."

She took the key the man gave her and climbed the creaky stairs to the rooms above the taproom. Her room was only two doors down. Her limbs had grown heavy, as though weighed down by stones. She had barely slept in the last four days. She had to keep an eye on her travel case every time they stopped to make sure no one stole it, and couldn't risk missing getting back on the coach whenever she needed to relieve herself.

She opened the door to her room and dropped her case on the floor. With a few dragging steps, she collapsed face down on the bed's feather tick mattress with a groan. She wasn't sure how long she lay there before a noise behind her forced her to roll over.

A maid, no older than her, balancing a tray on one hip, was trying to close the door behind her as she entered the room.

"Sorry miss, for waking you, I mean. I have your supper." The maid closed the door and set the tray down on the table by the bed.

"Thank you," Meredith said as she climbed out of bed. "Does it cost extra to have a small bathing tub brought up?"

"Only if we're full it would, but we aren't full tonight. I'll see if the lads can run up a tub with some water," the maid replied.

"Thank you. I haven't bathed in four days," Meredith confessed.

The maid gave her a sympathetic look. "Eat up, and I shall send the lads up soon."

Despite her weariness, Meredith devoured the stew and

mopped up the remnants of the soup with a thick chunk of bread she'd been given. She wrapped the extra wedge of cheese in a handkerchief for tomorrow's journey.

Shortly after dinner, two young men carried in a copper tub and filled it with hot water that was still steaming before they left Meredith alone. The tub was not large. All she could do was remove her clothes and stand inside of it. Shivering as the water cooled on her skin, she used a cloth to wipe herself clean of the dust and sweat of the last four days. Dark bruises marred her arm where Harry had manhandled her. The spots were tender to the touch, but she felt a little more like herself now. Once finished, she put on a clean chemise and crawled into bed.

Sleep came instantly, but not without dreams.

"Please, Merry, be a good girl and stay quiet." Meredith's mother whispered. She led Meredith up the stairs to the beautiful stone manor house. Her mother's face, finally free of tears, was still splotchy as she knocked upon the door. It was close to night-fall. Meredith didn't like the dark. The dark held dangers that every five year old instinctively feared and she pressed herself tight against her mother's leg, fisting her hands in her skirts.

The door opened and an elderly man stared at them.

"May help you, madame?"

"Please. I need to speak with Mr. St. John," her mother said. "Tell him it is Miss Mariah Montague."

The man nodded. "Step into the foyer and I will speak to the master."

Meredith clutched her mother's hand as they entered the foyer. Candlelight illuminated the tapestries, and she saw a marble bust of a beautiful woman that looked a little like her mother decorating the space beneath the staircase.

"Remember, you must be quiet."

Meredith nodded. She was always quiet. Papa didn't like it when she made noise. He didn't like to be reminded she existed. But that papa had left her and mama.

The elderly man returned. Behind him was another man, younger, closer in age to her mother. He strode toward her mother, and the elderly man quietly left them to speak alone.

"Mariah? Is it truly you?"

"Yes, Benjamin," her mother whispered. "I know it's been quite a long time…"

The man reached up to caress her mother's cheek. "Are you well? I—"The man's gaze dropped when he saw Meredith. "And who is this?" his tone was still gentle, still full of concern but as Meredith looked up into his eyes, she wasn't afraid.

Her mother gently pulled Meredith to stand in front of her. "This is my daughter. Meredith."

The man glanced between her and her mother before he knelt down in front of her. "Hello Meredith. I am Benjamin, but you may call me Uncle Ben, all right?" He then offered her a warm smile. "Are you hungry?"

Meredith glanced at her mother, who shook her head so Meredith mimicked her.

"Nonsense, you both looked tired and hungry. Come into the drawing room. We'll have some tea and something to eat. Then you will tell me what's happened."

Meredith nestled on a settee beside her mother before a warm fire and dozed off soon after she'd eaten. The man's voice was oddly soothing. Her papa's voice had always been distressing to her, but Uncle Ben? He felt safe.

"So it settled, Mariah. You will have a little cottage by the sea. I will see to everything. And you must bring the child to visit me. This house is too quiet since Harry moved to London."

"You don't mind that she is...?" She did not finish her question.

"Mariah, she is yours. *That means she will always be welcome in my home."*

"Benjamin, I can never thank you enough for saving me ... for saving her."

Meredith woke, feeling tears in her eyes. She'd been so young when she'd first come into Benjamin St. John's life, but he had been her hero, a father to her more than anyone connected to her by blood.

Now he was gone. That loss sank in deep for the first time in the last four days and she wept, wept for the loss of someone who'd become her world.

So much had happened so quickly. Ben's illness, his death, and her flight from the house. She could still feel Harry's hands on her arms, squeezing tight. There was no possibility of staying, not when Harry would demand she become his mistress.

What upset her more was how foolish she'd been to think that Uncle Ben would live forever, and she would always have a safe place with him. She'd given no thought to a life beyond that world. Now she was headed back to London to face a new life, a very new and very terrifying world, and living with a man she'd never met.

Her thoughts drifted to Darius, Uncle Ben's nephew... the Duke of Tiverton. As she understood it, he and Uncle Ben had argued shortly after Darius's father had passed away. The fight had upset Ben, but his pride kept him from reaching out to his nephew.

Please let him be kind. Meredith's only hope was that he could do as her uncle wished and find her a good man to marry. She must be content with that if she could find no other fate of her own making. But a woman born out of wedlock with no real family to her name held few prospects.

I must be content. I must. Whatever comes.

2

Meredith tried to calm her nerves as she climbed the steps of the beautiful townhouse on Knightley Street. She had learned that this lovely little parade of homes also went by another name ... Devil's Square.

When she'd arrived in London an hour ago, she had asked the stagecoach driver if he knew where Knightley Street was.

"You'd best be avoiding the Devil's Square, miss. What business takes you there?"

She had told him she was visiting a relative, which was mostly true, given that The Duke of Tiverton was family— at least in spirit. After that declaration, the elderly driver relaxed and provided her with the directions to Knightley Street.

Now, as she stood facing this supposed Devil's Square, she couldn't understand why the driver would have been concerned. The area was lovely, the front gardens well kept, and the homes themselves were in fine condition. It was clear this was a place where wealthy families lived. Based on the driver's reaction when he'd spoken of Devil's Square, she'd expected it to be a rookery of some sort, or some frightening part of the city that would see her dead within the hour simply for trespassing.

She double checked the numbers posted on the gate that separated this house from those on either side. Yes, this was the correct home.

It was built of red brick, and had a neo classical detailing that covered the portico and string courses. The front was covered in wisteria which had climbed all the way up the portico and tiptoed its way to the base of the windows across the brickwork, creating a dazzling water-fall of purple blossoms. Meredith let out a dreamy sigh as she imagined how it would have felt to grow up in a home like this. It was much harder to grow Wisteria in Yorkshire.

Meredith continued to stare at the house. Her heart beat a little faster as she realized her perusal of the house was, in fact, her attempt to stall. She was afraid to knock. Afraid to meet Uncle Ben's nephew. Afraid of everything that would follow. She was quite literally on a precipice as she stood at the top of the steps leading up to the portico. The late evening sun was dipping below the tops of the trees, bathing everything in a dark gold light which made the house feel very warm, very welcoming. But would that be true of what lay inside? Would she have a home here?

Don't be such a peahen, Meredith, you have a spine. Just knock.

She braved the last few steps to stand directly in front of the door. She raised a hand to lift the knocker, but the door swung open before she even touched it. A tall figure barreled out, crashing into her.

She gasped, but as she started to fall back, the person grabbed her arms, holding her steady. A cane clattered to the ground at her feet.

"I beg your pardon," said a deep voice.

Meredith, finally gathering her wits, got a look at the man who had almost sent her tumbling down the stairs.

The man was beautiful. His hair as dark as a raven's wing, and his penetrating blue eyes were so striking that she could only stare at them. He was tall, quite tall, and to lift her head now, to gaze up into this man's face, was pleasant in a way she couldn't explain.

He wore a fine tailored coat of dark green that paired with his buff colored trousers, and they fit him so perfectly she could not help but notice his lean hips and muscled thighs. Meredith blinked as a spark of heat filled her body. This man was appealing in a way she'd never felt before.

She had met a fair few gentlemen whenever she and Uncle Ben had visited the village of Burton Agnes, but she'd never seen anyone like this. He was simply beautiful.

He was also a little frightening, because there was an intensity coiled up within him like a wound spring.

The gentleman's eyes roved over her in a similar fashion, and Meredith wondered, no, *wished*, he was as curious about her as she was of him.

Suddenly recalling her purpose for standing there, she spoke.

"Are—are you Lord Tiverton?"

"Yes," the man replied without hesitation.

Meredith dug into her reticule for Uncle Ben's letter and held it out to him.

Puzzled, he took the letter and opened it, unfolding the pages as he silently read its contents. When he had finished reading it, he lifted his eyes to hers.

"What is your name, child?" His tone was curt, and she immediately rankled at being called a child when just moments ago she had his attention as a woman. What had Uncle Ben written in his letter to change this man's attitude toward her?

"I'm not a child," she said. "And it's Meredith Montague."

"Have you read this?" Tiverton lifted the letter up.

She shook her head. "No, but Uncle Ben said I was to deliver it to you. He said that you would help me find...a husband?" She prayed Uncle Ben was right about this man.

Ignoring her question, Tiverton said, "You traveled all the way from Yorkshire alone?" He glanced around behind her, as if expecting her to have a chaperone.

"Yes, I took stagecoaches and spent the night at a coaching inn last evening. I had little pin money saved up, but I am thankful you are home this evening... I have no money to stay anywhere else."

There, she'd said it. She'd made it clear she was dependent on him. Now she had to pray he wouldn't toss her out.

"My uncle was unable to leave you no money at all?" he asked.

"He tried, but...you see, it was a bit complicated after he died. His will only left a wish for his son to provide me with a home and money at his discretion. Harry said that I should remain at your uncle's estate, and... Well, he demanded I be his companion if I wished to stay. Naturally, I couldn't agree. No matter how insistent he was."

She rubbed her arms, and Tiverton's eyes dropped from her face to her body. She looked down to see the bruises which had started to yellow on her wrist. "He then refused to provide me with any money at all, since it was at his discretion."

Tiverton scowled. She feared she had upset him. Were he and Harry close? Had she made a grave error in speaking so frankly? But it was her way to be open on most matters. She'd never learned to guard herself in conversation, as many ladies were directed to.

"Harry is a bastard," Tiverton said, his tone abrupt. He turned around and opened the door to his home. "You will be safe with me."

A tidal wave of relief rushed through her. She did feel safe. No matter how intense Tiverton was, he didn't scare her, not like Harry had. But her relief was short-lived as his focus dropped to the travel case at her feet.

"I don't suppose you have any decent evening gowns in that small travel case?"

"Only one, but it's a bit out of fashion—"

"It will do. Come inside and change quickly. I'm off to a play that I simply cannot miss, and you shall come with me so we can discuss your situation further." He bent down to retrieve the cane he had dropped.

Meredith gaped at him. Tiverton met her look of shock with a gentle firmness as he straightened up.

"Fear not. You have a home here, Miss Montague. It is only the details that remain to be seen."

She let out a tight breath, her chest relaxing.

"I loved my uncle and will honor his wish to care for you and see you settled in marriage to a good man."

"Thank you, Your Grace."

He ushered her inside where an older gentleman, presumably the butler, met them at the door. Tiverton handed the man his cane.

"Your Grace?" the man inquired. "Back so soon?"

"Ahh, Chelsea, I've had a bit of a delay. This is Miss Meredith Montague...my new ward. She was the ward to my uncle, who I've just learned has died. I need to discuss certain things with Miss Montague, but cannot miss Lady Kentwell's play, so I've decided to have Miss Montague accompany me. We haven't much time. Please fetch an upstairs maid and have her help Miss Montague with her evening gown."

"Er...yes, Your Grace." Mr. Chelsea called out to a passing maid. "Nell, take Miss Montague upstairs to the Seaside Room. She'll need some assistance changing. Please make haste, as she is to accompany His Grace to the play this evening."

She glanced around the beautiful house as the maid ushered her hastily up a grand staircase.

"In here, miss." The maid opened a door and gestured Meredith into a bedchamber room.

Meredith had but a moment to take in the lovely walls painted a rich blue like the ocean with frothing seascapes painted on the walls. It made her think of home, of the little cottage near the beach where she and her mother had lived for so many years.

Then she dropped her valise on the bed, digging hastily through its contents with the maid helping her until she found her favorite dark green evening gown. It was plain, though not unattractive, with embroidered tulips on the hem and sleeves. Nell began undoing the buttons of her evening gown while Meredith unfastened the front laces of her day gown. Soon, Meredith was wearing her evening gown and her travel boots had been replaced with slippers. The maid assisted her with her evening gloves, but when they looked at her hair in the mirror, she winced.

"Not much I can do if you're in a hurry, miss."

"I know, but it will be all right for tonight. Thank you ever so much, Nell."

The maid dipped into a light curtsy. "Yes, miss."

Meredith followed the maid back downstairs, her reticule in her hands. Tiverton watched her approach, and she swore his eyes darkened into a midnight blue with interest.

"Right...well, let's be off. My friend, Kit Hollingsworth, the Earl of Kentwell, is waiting on us." He offered her his arm, and Meredith gratefully accepted it. She felt a bit light-headed after having barely slept in days.

As she curled her fingers around his forearm, she felt the hard muscles beneath his coat sleeve. A flush of heat crept into her neck and face. She had never been this close to a gentleman that she didn't know.

You mustn't think of that. He isn't the man you will marry. He is more like a cousin...a brother. He is family.

But he wasn't. Not really. And a very persuasive part of her mind kept pointing out that annoying fact every time she caught a hint of the light cologne he wore.

A string of coaches waited across the street and Meredith's eyes widened as Tiverton led her toward a group of dashing gentlemen clustered around the first coach.

"Kit, my apologies for the delay." Tiverton addressed the man who was by far the largest and the most intimidating of the group, even though he was well dressed. So this was his friend, the Earl of Kentwell? The man looked as though he had been raised carrying boulders up the side of the mountain, not born to a life of leisure.

"It is no trouble, Darius." The man's eyes then slid to Meredith, who still clutched Tiverton's sleeve.

Her mouth ran dry. Would Darius be judged by these men for having to take her along? There were no other ladies present. She knew all too well that she was a burden in most cases. Uncle Ben tried to pretend it wasn't true, but she was used to people crossing the street to avoid her, or women gossiping behind their fans at the local dances in Burton Agnes. She was a bastard child, a woman with no determined future, and now she was hanging onto a duke's arm like her life depended upon it.

"This is Miss Montague...my uncle's ward," said Tiverton. "She is now my ward, it seems. She's just arrived from Burton Agnes in Yorkshire."

"Your ward, you say?" Kit replied, amusement flashing in his dark brown eyes as he bowed to her. "It is a pleasure to meet you, Miss Montague."

"It is a pleasure to meet you, Lord Kentwell."

One of the of the others in the group spoke up. "Do we all get introductions?" he asked with a charming grin as he stepped forward.

"Yes, but not right now," Tiverton gave a warning look at the other gentleman, who was smiling at Meredith. "We shall be late if we don't leave it once."

Meredith's face was bright red as Tiverton marched her past the other men standing beside Kit, all of whom were staring at her in the most curious way. This was her fault. If she'd only come to Tiverton's home sooner, she might have been allowed time to explain herself and rest at his home, rather than be paraded out like this before a half dozen gentlemen, creating only more questions for her host.

"This is my coach." Tiverton opened the door and slid her hand into his as he assisted her inside. She took the seat facing the front and he sat opposite her. A footman closed the door. The coach interior was lit with heavy glass lamps, casting gold light onto the dark blue velvet cushions, each of which were embroidered with a gold crest bearing a "T" for Tiverton.

Uncle Ben had had a lovely coach, but nothing as fine is this. Meredith was not used to being in the presence of such wealth, but the seat and cushioned back felt like heaven after five days in rattling stagecoaches.

"Now...we have a little time to talk. Tell me about my uncle's death and yourself. It is best to start the beginning."

Darius St. John watched the woman sitting across from him closely. Her gloved fingers twisted in the reticule she held on her lap. He could not fault her for the show of nerves. She'd been through a harrowing experience and he'd given her no time to settle down or rest.

The news of uncle's death was a terrible shock to him, and it had for the moment taken control over his thoughts and he needed answers. Why hadn't he received any news of his uncle's illness earlier? He waited for her to speak and was glad to see steel in her hazel eyes. She'd been through much, but the experience hadn't broken her. Good.

"As I understand it, your uncle was in love with my mother many years ago before I was born, but she chose another, one who did not actually marry her, but instead kept her as his mistress. Your uncle then married another."

"Harry's mother," Darius said, nodding. "She was a good woman, although I did not know her well as she died when I was but a lad." He hadn't known about Uncle Ben's first love, but then, his uncle had always been reserved about his life.

"My father left my mother and I when I was four returned to his wife and within a year he died. My mother was desperate after he left us. She sought refuge with your uncle. He purchased a cottage by the sea and paid for our keep until my mother died when I was fourteen."

"I am sorry about your mother," Darius added quietly. He had lost his own mother young and the loss of a mother left deep scars that never fully healed. "I believe I remember Uncle Ben mentioning you... now that I think about it. I would have met you if I'd only bothered to visit him at Burton Agnes." His heart was heavy with a thousand regrets. He cleared his throat. "And after your mother died?"

Meredith sighed, her gaze drifting briefly away from his face as she glanced out into the darkening night through the window curtains.

"I loved my mother, but it was a relief to come live with Uncle Ben. He welcomed me into his home in a way that I never felt while I was living with my mother."

Knowing his uncle, the man had doted on Meredith. He had a truly kind heart and a great love of company, despite his own quiet manners.

Darius leaned forward slightly. "When did my Uncle fall ill?"

"It was about two months ago."

"Why didn't he write to me?" Darius asked her.

"He didn't believe he was that ill. We simply thought he had a cold, but then it suddenly turned into a steep decline in his condition. The doctors were not entirely sure what made him so unwell, but he passed peacefully five nights ago." Meredith seemed to debate her next words carefully. "Mrs. Todd, Uncle Ben's housekeeper, helped me pack and leave just after Uncle Ben passed away. She didn't want me to stay in the house with Harry, though it would mean missing Uncle Ben's funeral."

"It would have been a very bad idea for you to stay, given what you've told me of that cad of a son of his," Darius finished for her. "So you traveled here at once."

"Yes. I slept little and stayed on the same coach for four days until last night, when I was too exhausted to keep moving. I had enough money for room and board, but left for London at first light, which brings me here and my rather abrupt appearance at your door. I must apologize for any inconvenience my arrival has caused you."

"You are not an inconvenience," he replied softly.

She had traveled for four days without sleep? Darius inwardly cursed. Had he known, he would have let her sleep in his home rather than dragging her to the play tonight. She was doing a fine job of hiding her fatigue, but he could see the weariness in her hazel eyes. And now... thanks to Uncle Ben, she was his responsibility. He didn't hate the responsibility...but he didn't like the limitations. Meredith was the sort of woman that he wanted to pull onto his lap and curl his arms around her as he kissed her and soothed her worries away with compassion and then passion. And he could not do that because seducing one's ward was... even beyond the bounds of propriety.

He took stock of the woman again. Her golden brown hair was a bit unkept, but that was from travel and not inattentiveness. She would be lovely indeed once she was properly dressed and her hair tamed with a brush. Her current gown was not only plain but also tight-fitting. The woman possessed a wealth of bosom that threatened to pop out of the bodice. It was damnably distracting. He appreciated breasts the same as any hot-blooded man, but something about Meredith's bosom proved more tempting than it should. If he wasn't careful, he'd end up no better than his blasted cousin Harry.

"I must apologize, Miss Montague. Had I been more knowledgeable about the circumstances behind your arrival, I would have insisted that you stay at my home and rest rather than accompany me. Have you eaten today?"

"I had a light breakfast this morning and a bit of cheese around midday." She glanced away, embarrassed, but Darius was the one ashamed. He was not proving to be a very good guardian for this woman.

"I'm sorry. I'm not usually such a wretched host." He sighed and dragged a hand through his hair. "It's only that..." He hesitated. He could not unburden his soul to this poor woman.

"Only what?" Damned if those soft hazel eyes of hers didn't send him reeling. She was exquisitely beautiful in a quiet, regal sort of way that held him in fascination. *Timeless*...that was the word. She was a timeless beauty that would have caught a man's admiration in any era. Yet she was here in this moment with him, and he had to remind himself that she was now his ward, and a gentleman didn't seduce his ward. He cleared his throat as he remembered he hadn't answered her question.

"It's my friend Kit..." he began. "He's been gone a very long time. Seven years, in fact. He's only now just returned. His new wife, Suzannah, has painted the sets for the play we will see tonight on Drury Lane, and I wanted everything to be perfect. It's important to Kit, and what is important to my friend is important to me." He was rambling now. He, the cool, collected Duke of Tiverton, had found himself flustered and nervous like a silly schoolboy. "And now with Uncle Ben...I am not myself this evening and for that I deeply apologize for any rudeness I've shown."

"I understand, Your Grace. Friendships matter a great deal. I had only one friend growing up, a girl named Celina. When her family learned I was not Uncle Ben's child, I was deemed an unfit companion. I've had no deep friendships since. You must cherish and protect those you have." Her gaze dropped to the floor. "Grief wounds the heart in ways we can never prepare ourselves for. You mustn't fault yourself for anything done in a state of grief, certainly not on my account."

Darius could not deny the pain in Meredith's eyes and scrambled to put her at ease. "I shall introduce you to Suzannah this evening. She is wonderful and I believe she will not hold the circumstances of your birth against you. You will need suitable friendships and hers will be an excellent start."

"I would like to meet her." She paused and then with a

blush she asked. "And what of the gentlemen that surrounded Lord Kentwell this evening? Are there any among them who I could look to for a possible match?"

Darius hadn't considered this possibility until she brought it up. *Were* any of his friends suitable as a husband for her? His immediate reaction was a violent snarl at the thought. They were honorable men, of course, and true friends. Yet he'd seen how they enjoyed women's company. He could trust Meredith's life to them, but her future wedded happiness? They were the sort of men to offer to keep her as a mistress, not to marry her, not from any fault of hers, but because none of his friends, aside from Kit were ready to settle down. Even Kit's marriage had been quite the shock to Darius, a welcome one, but a shock none-theless.

"No...while they are gentlemen, they are not the sort of men I would set in your path for matrimonial candidates."

"Oh..." Her look of dejection hit him full in the face like a physical blow. Had she formed an instant attracted to one of his friends? She'd only seen them for a brief moment and hadn't even been formally introduced to any of them.

"Not because of you," he hastened to add. "But because they are a bit...wild. You need a gentleman ready to settle down."

And the more he considered any of them, especially the ever charming Vincent or wicked Warren, putting their hands on Meredith, the more Darius's vision turned red. That stunned him. The group of boys he'd grown up with, Kit, Lionel, Vincent, Felix, and Warren, were as close to him as brothers. Yet he would fight any of them if they set their sights on seducing Meredith. Why?

I am simply protective because Uncle Ben was protective of her, that's all. She is my ward. I am responsible for her.

It was certainly *not* because he was reacting to this woman in a way he hadn't reacted to a woman in a long time.

It must be the shock of losing Uncle Ben, he mused. *I'm not acting like myself out of such an unexpected grief.*

The coach stopped and Darius glanced out the curtained window. They had reached the theater. One of his footmen opened the door and Darius climbed out, then turned to assist Meredith.

The moonlight accented her swelling bosom as she leaned down to exit the coach. Darius caught the footman focused on the same distracting sight. With a half-cough, half-growl at the servant, Darius took Meredith's hand and helped her down. They passed by the queuing people outside the theater who were busy gossiping and socializing. Darius spotted a woman selling oranges and waved her over.

"Two, please." He slipped a couple of coins into the woman's palm and was handed two plump, ripe oranges. He gave one to Meredith and kept the other. Her brows rose in confusion.

"Once we're seated, you may eat it. After the play, when we return home, I shall see you properly fed."

"Thank you, Your Grace." An attractive blush lit her cheeks as she clutched the orange close to her chest. Why that made his heart turn over, he wasn't quite sure. This was certainly no spoiled little creature, not that he'd expected her to be.

Darius tucked Meredith's free arm in his and led her inside the theater. Her eyes grew round as she took in the large stage, flanked by the gilded theater boxes on either side. Lush red curtains draped over the stage, illuminated by bright lamps. A decadent dimness hung about the rest of the theater, adding a hint of mystery to the milling crowds and the wealthy attendees that had begun to fill the seats. Darius had always enjoyed the theater, but had rarely attended plays in the last few years. It was Kit's marriage to Suzannah that had brought him back one of the great pleasures of his life, and he found himself eager to see the performance.

"This way," he said as he led Meredith up a staircase to the left and down to the private boxes closest to the stage. Kit and Suzannah would be joining them soon, while the boxes on the opposite side would be filled by Vincent, Felix, Warren and Lionel.

Kit met them as they entered the box. "Ahh, Darius." He then bowed to Meredith. "Miss Montague, may I introduce you to my wife, Suzannah?" He stepped back to reveal the petite figure of his wife. She was a lovely woman, with blonde hair and hazel eyes, much like Meredith's. Where Kit was large and as intimidating as a badger, his wife was a sweet little kitten who wielded an incredible talent with a paintbrush.

"Miss Montague, it is lovely to meet you," Suzannah

stepped forward and held out a hand. "I would like to have you over for tea tomorrow if that would suit you?"

Meredith gave Darius a hopeful look, and he nodded his approval.

"Thank you. I would like that very much, Lady Kentwell."

Suzannah brightened. "Wonderful. You must come and sit down at the front with me to have the best view." Suzannah gently took Meredith's hand and urged her toward the front of the box.

Kit lingered next to Darius in the doorway. "You did not have Miss Montague with you when you attended the unveiling of my portrait this evening. You said she arrived from Yorkshire?"

"She arrived just as I had retrieved my gloves," said Darius. "It was an unexpected encounter. I should have left her at home to recover from her journey, but my uncle's death seems to have robbed me of my sense."

"I'm sorry about your uncle, if I remember you were deuced close to him."

"I was," Darius admitted. That bleak hole in his chest seemed to be carved out wider and wider by grief and regret. "I didn't visit him in Yorkshire, and I should have. He came to London only occasionally. I feel as though I lost too much time with him."

Kit placed a hand on his shoulder and gave it a gentle squeeze.

"And what of the girl?"

"Hmm?" Darius pulled his thoughts away from his uncle.

"Who is she?" Kit prompted. "I thought you only had one cousin. That fellow Harry? I admit I'm damned curious where she fits into all this. Out with it." Kit's dark brown eyes sparkled with mischief. Darius was glad to see a hint of the old Kit in his friend, even if it did come at his own expense.

"Miss Montague was his ward, and she was sent to me upon his death. It seems I am charged with the task of finding her husband. A good one."

Brows rising, Kit glanced at his wife and Meredith. "Your uncle's ward?" The question was there, silent, but still Darius heard it. Was she Uncle Ben's child? That was what Kit wished to know.

"She is the daughter of a woman my uncle once loved very deeply. Enough that when the man she choose to be with instead of my uncle left them, my uncle stepped in to care for that woman and his child." He could see Kit putting the pieces together. Meredith wasn't even Uncle Ben's illegitimate child, but another man's.

"Ahh...Well, then my next question is, will you be respecting the rules of mourning?" Kit inquired.

Mourning...blast and damn. He hadn't even thought of that. What the devil was wrong with him? But to lose a whole year in mourning? That would not help with his task of finding her a husband. He glanced at Meredith, who seemed to be glowing with joy talking to Suzannah despite her exhaustion.

"No, my uncle wouldn't wish for that. He always despised the custom. And it will slow down my ability to introduce Meredith to society." Darius met Kit's gaze. "You do not mind that she and Suzannah might form a friendship, then?"

Kit gave him a baffled look. "Why would I mind?"

"Because of the circumstances surrounding her birth."

Kit chuckled as he understood. "I served seven years in Australia's penal colony. I'm hardly one to pass judgement on others.."

"You forgot to mention that you were wrongfully convicted," Darius added.

Kit flexed his arms slightly. "That doesn't change my past."

There was a flash of pain in his friend's eyes. If Darius could have some stopped Kit from being transported to Australia seven years ago, he would have. He had fought like the devil to free his friend, but the three men who had set Kit up to take the fall for stealing goods from his own shipping company had laid their trap perfectly. Not even Darius or his father had had enough influence to keep him from transportation.

Kit deftly changed the subject away from his past. "I'm sure Suzannah will be happy to help you find a companion for Miss Montague."

"Companion?" Darius was confused by what he meant.

"Yes. As she is not your wife or any direct relation, she will need a companion to live with you. Someone to act as a chaperone, will she not? It would leave you and Miss

Montague free of gossip and strengthen her chances of a good match."

Darius had not even given that a thought, either. Where had his thoughts been? Oh yes, on Meredith's lips, her spectacular bosom, her eyes.

"You're right. I will gladly accept Suzannah's help if she offers it."

By now, the crowd had taken their seats, and as the red curtains on the stage were pulled back, a hush settled over everyone. Darius and Kit took their seats behind the ladies.

Darius leaned forward and passed her the second orange.

"You may eat your orange now, and mine too," he whispered in her ear.

"Thank you, Your Grace." Her breathless reply was so sweet, so soft and husky, it hit him with a powerful bolt of lust. He was glad for the dim theater atmosphere to hide his face as he sat back in his chair.

Kit was grinning at Darius like a jackal, damn him. The bastard *knew* he was attracted to Meredith.

Darius turned his focus to the stage and away from the woman who had literally stumbled into his life an hour ago.

3

The oranges were an unexpected treat, and Meredith enjoyed the first one immensely. She'd only had them a few times while living in Yorkshire, being a rare delicacy in that part of England. She hesitated when it came to eating the second, which Darius had so thoughtfully given to her. It was his, after all, and she'd already had the one. She turned back to offer him the second orange.

"Please eat," Darius whispered as he leaned in again to speak to her from behind. "I bought it for you." His voice in her ear and his warm breath against her neck in the dark were intoxicating. *Thrilling.* It sent a shiver down her spine and filled her with a languid heat in her lower belly.

After a brief hesitation, she ate the second orange, delicately peeling it upon the handkerchief in her lap and enjoying the slices one by one.

The play went on, the audience laughing and cheering

in all the right places. Meredith had never been to a proper play before. She'd attended a house party in Burton Agnes once where the hosting family had performed a silly little comedy which had amused everyone immensely. But she'd never seen anything quite like *this*.

The lamps at the edge of the stage lit up the actors, who danced about the sets and played their parts. The heavy fall of the bright red curtains accented the marvelous sets. The rich colors, the vibrant and life-like rooms and outdoor scenery made it feel as though she was glimpsing a dozen new places each time the sets changed and the painted backdrops were pushed out onto stage. Meredith gasped and laughed along with the crowd as everyone reacted to the dialogue. And then there was the music, the swells of exquisite sound that filled Meredith with an unspeakable joy. She felt alive in a way she never had before. She had loved her quiet life in Yorkshire, with its rolling sea and the quiet beach, as well as Uncle Ben's beautiful gardens and fields, and his vast library. But this taste of London life was something else entirely.

When the play paused for intermission, Lord Kentwell placed a hand on his wife's shoulder.

"Your backdrops look marvelous, my darling," he said, causing her to blush.

"His Grace mentioned that you painted the back-grounds. Did you paint all of them?" Meredith inquired. The countess nodded, her face reddening further.

"Yes. I worked here before I married my Kit." She lifted her face up to accept a kiss upon her cheek from the intimidating Lord Kentwell. A flash of envy shot through Meredith. She wanted to have what Suzannah and her husband had.

"You worked here?" asked Meredith.

"I still do." Suzannah grinned at her.

Meredith was shocked and realized her expression might come across as rude, so she added, "I mean, you are very talented, Lady Kentwell. I'm simply surprised."

"Well, I enjoy it, and I see no reason to change who I am simply because of my marriage. Even if it isn't expected societal behavior."

"Not that we care one wit what others think," Lord Kentwell added with a scowl.

Meredith did not expect to hear such things in London and found it surprisingly comforting. "You are very talented, Lady Kentwell," said Meredith. "The paintings seem to come alive on the stage. It is truly the most beautiful thing I've ever seen."

Suzannah laughed. "I hope you are not embarrassed to be sitting with a clerk's daughter who paints sets for plays. I know my marriage to Kit caused quite a stir for many of London's elite."

Suzannah laughed at Lord Kentwell's deepening scowl and patted her husband's hand which rested on her shoulder. Lord Kentwell's face softened a little.

"I do not mind at all," said Meredith. "Actually, I think it's rather splendid. You have a beautiful talent, and it is being put to use. Besides, I do not have any social standing,"

Meredith added. "I come from...less than auspicious circumstances as well, Lady Kentwell."

Meredith hoped she hadn't spoken too honestly, too earnestly, but she wanted Suzannah to understand that she would never sit in judgment on anyone.

"Then I shall see we shall be fast friends." She reached out and squeezed Meredith's arm with a smile. "Please call me Suzannah."

"Pardon us, ladies. We shall be back in a moment," Lord Kentwell said before he and Darius left the box.

"Where do you suppose they are going?" Meredith asked.

"I wager they are bound for the box opposite us." Suzannah handed Meredith a pair of opera glasses and pointed directly across the way to the opposite side of the stage. She glimpsed four other men sitting there and she recognized them from earlier that evening when she briefly met Lord Kentwell for the first time.

"Those are your husband's friends?"

"Indeed." Suzannah chuckled. "Have you had a chance to meet them?"

"Not exactly," Meredith admitted. "I only just arrived at the duke's home a few moments before we left for the theater."

"And what brings you to London? You're from the north, aren't you?"

"Yes. I came all the way from Yorkshire. But I'm afraid it is not under the best of circumstances."

"How do you mean?"

"The duke's uncle passed away this week. It is why I am here."

Suzannah gasped. "Goodness, I didn't know about Darius's uncle. I am very sorry to hear about that. I take it you were close to him?"

Meredith was puzzled how Suzannah so freely used Darius's Christian name, which, given what she knew of high society, was quite unexpected. But she sensed there was much she would come to learn about her new guardian in the days to come.

Meredith felt a flare of guilt and sorrow as something new occurred to her. "I only just realized I should be in mourning. I don't even own a black gown. And I certainly shouldn't be *here*. It is my first night in London and I have made a terrible blunder." Tears of shame and sorrow burned her eyes. She wanted to blame it on her exhaustion, but everything had happened so quickly. Some part of her hadn't quite accepted the truth that Uncle Ben was gone, and her life had been turned upside down. Only now was the reality sinking in.

Suzannah touched her hand. "It will be all right, Miss Montague. When Darius returns, you can speak to him about it. Until then, tell me about yourself."

"You must call me Meredith."

"Of course, Meredith."

Soon, she found herself telling Suzannah everything about her life. About her mother and how she came to live with Uncle Ben. It was surely unwise to share so much about herself, but there was something so calming about

Suzannah that she felt she could trust her, even with the most embarrassing aspects of her upbringing.

"Now we are friends in earnest," Suzannah said, once she had finished. "Now, I should be honest about my own history. My father was a clerk for a shipping company. Seven years ago, he was blackmailed into accusing Kit of grand larceny of goods from one of Kit's own ships."

"Kit... Your husband, Kit?"

Suzannah nodded, a sly smile on her face. "The same, though we barely knew each of other then. Kit was sentenced to serve seven years in Australia. When he returned, he sought vengeance against the men who had ruined him, including my father. But father had died prior to Kit's return, so he sought vengeance against me, in his stead."

Meredith gasped. "What did he intend to do?"

The smile grew. "Oh, I think you can imagine."

"But... you both seem so happy!"

"And we are. Kit's plans were ruined by the one thing he never expected. *Love.* It is a much longer story than that, of course, but I've said all that I should for now. I mention all this to say that Kit has bad days, as have I. We both know what it feels like as we are outsiders in a place where we should be welcomed. You are *one* of us, Meredith. You will never be alone so long as you live in the Devil's Square." Suzannah nodded toward the men in the box across from them. Darius and Kit were standing at the back of the box talking to the other four men who'd stood up and turned to converse at their arrival.

"They *all* live on the same street as His Grace?"

"Yes. They grew up together as boys, and those bonds run very deep."

"Who are they, exactly?" Meredith asked as she studied the men through the opera glasses again.

Suzannah gave her a wicked grin. "I like to call them *The Rogues of Devil's Square.*"

"Rogues?" Meredith had never met any gentleman with reputations wicked enough to be dubbed rogues. Even Harry was more a rake, and he lacked the charm that Darius's friends seemed to possess.

Suzannah giggled. "It is a rather dramatic nickname to be sure, but do not be frightened by it. Be *intrigued*. Besides, I believe it fits. You must consider what these men have done with their lives these past seven years. Rather than leave Kit to his fate and move on with their lives, they turned their minds toward acquiring knowledge and power to help Kit find justice when he someday returned to England. When you realize that justice and legality are not always aligned, you understand why I call them rogues."

She pointed to the box across the way. "You see that man on the far left, closest to the stage? The one with brown hair and hazel eyes? That is Lionel Thistlewaite, Viscount Basildon. He is the son of the Duke of Summerstone. He is the most methodical and coolheaded of the group. He has a darling little sister I shall introduce to you soon, Octavia. She is close to us in age."

Suzannah then pointed out the gentleman leaning on the railing of the box, laughing at someone's joke. "That's

Viscount Wyndham. His charm is dangerous, but he will protect you with his life if he knows you are with Darius. I believe he might be courting a ballet dancer... or was it an opera girl? I can never remember." She laughed lightly.

"What do you mean if he knows I'm *with* Darius?" Meredith focused on the two words.

"If you are under his protection as his ward. Like a sister perhaps, but not related by blood. Vincent will do anything to protect you."

Sister? Meredith blushed. She certainly did not think of Darius as a brother. If anything, her mind and body seemed quite determined to see him as an attractive man and a true temptation, even though they were still strangers to one another. She returned her focus to Darius's friends.

"What of the blond gentleman next to Vincent?"

"Felix Hawkins, the Marquess of Grey," Suzannah said. "And that last man, the one who looks like he is frowning, that is Warren Burrville. He seems to find trouble far too easily, but for the best of reasons. You will like all of them, I assure you," Suzannah promised and chuckled. "They are intimidating at first, but I think you will come to adore them as I do."

Meredith sighed. "I feel like a newborn child. I know nothing of life in London or what it means to be the ward of the Duke. I don't even know about His Grace's family. Uncle Ben didn't tell me much."

"Well, Darius is an only child. His mother died when he was a boy. She suffered some terrible fever, or so I've heard.

His father passed away a few years ago. His only relative now is his cousin."

"Harry," Meredith said with a nod.

"Yes, the one you said who propositioned you." Suzannah frowned. "Meredith, you must be careful. You were sent here to find a match, but there are many men in London who think like Mr. St. John. They will attempt to take advantage of you simply because they do not believe a woman in your position has the right to refuse them. But you can say no. All women should be able to."

"What if they don't listen?" Meredith asked quietly. She'd been reliving that moment with Harry over and over on the last five days. She realized how lucky she'd been that he let her go. He'd been strong enough to overpower her, but he hadn't. Whether it was because he had some sliver of morals in him or because his father hadn't yet passed, she did not know.

"Then you fight," Suzannah said. "You should ask Darius to teach you. He is quite skilled at fighting. He even works with the Bow Street Runners from time to time."

"He does?" That shocked Meredith.

"He is not a Runner, of course, but he helps them on cases. You should ask about that."

A hush fell on the crowd as the intermission ended. The play resumed a few moments later. Darius and Kit returned the box just in time. Darius's presence put Meredith at ease. She'd only known the man a few hours, but already she felt safe around him. His presence also thrilled her in a way she never felt before. Silly little imaginings kept popping in her head. She imagined him leaning forward so he could whisper to her again, and feeling his warm breath across the nape of her neck.

By the end of the play, Meredith was quite tired. Her travels had finally caught up with her. After she bid Kit and Suzannah goodbye, Darius escorted her to his coach. She sat on one side and he sat facing her again.

"Well? What did you think of the play?"

"It was magnificent." She yawned, and Darius laughed.

"Oh dear. You must be dead on your feet. I'll take you home at once, put you to bed." He paused. "Tomorrow, I suppose it will be a day of shopping and whatever else is needed to prepare you for your London debut. I must meet with Suzannah to have her advice on hiring a companion for you."

She struggled to stay awake and focus. "A companion?"

"Yes. It was pointed out to me this evening that as we are not blood related, I must have a companion, a female, to escort you about and live with us at the house as a chaperone."

For some reason warmth curled in her belly at the way he said "with us."

"Rest now, Miss Montague. I shall wake you when we arrive home."

Home. It sounded so lovely when he said it with that deep, rich voice.

"Please call me Meredith," she got out between yawns.

"Only if you call me Darius. We are family, and I believe society will allow us that intimacy at least."

"I quite agree..." she yawned again, "Darius."

DARIUS KNEW THE EXACT MOMENT MEREDITH DRIFTED TO SLEEP. Her head, nestled in the corner of the coach, sank even deeper into the cushioned walls. A heavy sigh escaped her as though her body had at last surrendered to its great need to rest.

Five days in the stagecoach, only one night in a proper bed, and she had done it all on her own. She was a capable woman, he would give her that, but even capable women were in danger when they traveled alone. He wished he could have been there at Uncle Ben's passing, to say his goodbyes and see Meredith safely and comfortably brought to his home here in London.

What had kept his uncle from writing to them sooner? Pride, perhaps. Pride and a deep regret. The last time they had spoken had been painful. They both said things they regretted.

Two years ago, Uncle Ben had been in London to visit Darius. Darius had been trying to speak about Harry's exploits, and how his uncle needed to take Harry in hand. Uncle Ben had turned the arguing to Darius' own activities, namely those of his involvement with the Bow Street runners.

"You're a duke now. You cannot simply run off into the night, flying headlong into danger whenever you wish. It is time

you settle down, find a duchess and produce an heir and a spare, just as your father did."

To which Darius had replied. *"At least I spend my time in services to others, which is more than I can say for your son."*

Uncle Ben had stared him at coldly, his blue eyes just like Darius's, as he responded with the last words of their fight. *"And when you get yourself killed... Harry will have your home and title. Think of all that he could ruin because you want to play the hero."*

The worst of it was that Uncle Ben was right. Darius loved to play the hero, loved to throw himself into a fight when someone needed help. It had almost killed him recently when he'd tried to save Suzannah from being abducted and murdered.

His shoulder still ached where he'd been shot, and his stomach was knotted with scar tissue from a knife wound which sometimes made walking, hell, even breathing hard. He had to use a cane on occasion when the pain that shot down his leg became too much to bear.

But it had been worth it. Kit and Suzannah had been in danger, and he put himself between Suzannah and death. But it didn't change the fact that Uncle Benjamin was right. Before, he'd had no one who needed him to be safe, to be responsible... Until now. The only thing that was a balm to his wounded heart was knowing that in his final hours, Uncle Ben had still trusted Darius with the thing be believed to be most precious...Meredith.

He turned to Meredith's sleeping form, and his lips curled into a smile. For the first time in a very long time, he didn't feel quite so alone. Yes, he had his friends, and they were a huge part of his life, but there was still a part of himself he had keep in reserve, hidden from everyone. Something about Meredith made him want to open that part of himself up, share his secrets, thoughts and dreams with her. Was it because she was so like him in that way? Having to live a life that didn't seem to fully fit one's heart?

I'm certainly not alone. At least, not right now.

He would have to see her married off soon, but for now, he had a companion. She was a grown woman who did not need a guardian, but he would abide by his uncle's wishes. And for now, that made Meredith Montague *his.*

The coach stopped in front of his home, but he didn't have the heart to wake Meredith. The coach door opened, and he held a finger to his lips up at the footman, indicating the man should remain quiet. Darius scooped Meredith up in his arms and carried her from the coach. Despite the pain in his shoulder, he liked the weight and feel of Meredith in his arms.

Mr. Chelsea met them at the open door.

"Do you have the Seaside room ready for her?" Darius asked.

"Yes, Your Grace. Nell is waiting to put her to bed."

"Excellent. Send a note to Lady Kentwell. Ask her to meet me here for breakfast tomorrow so we can discuss hiring a lady's companion for Miss Montague."

"Yes, Your Grace." Chelsea, bless the man, didn't question the propriety of Darius carrying a sleeping woman upstairs.

Darius proceeded upstairs to the Seaside room. The blankets had been turned down in anticipation of Meredith's return. He settled his charge on the bed and she roused enough to blink at him slowly, her dark lashes fanning up and down over her lovely hazel eyes.

"I could kiss you," Meredith murmured dreamily.

"Could you?" He found himself teasing her with a grin. He guessed that she was half-asleep, possibly even dreaming given her expression and her barely open eyes.

"Hmm…" she almost purred. "But I've never kissed a man before… I fear I might be dreadful at it."

"I doubt that. Ladies tend to be natural kissers." He reached over her to fluff the pillow behind her head. Suddenly, she reached up and curled her fingers in his cravat, pulling him down to her. He nearly fell on top of her, but braced one of his arms on the pillows beside her in the nick of time. And then…

It all happened too fast, their lips brushing against each other and that sweet perfume of hers blended with the taste of oranges and innocence on her lips. His heart clenched as something within him filled with sunlight, pouring a quiet, exquisite joy through his body and into the depths of his very soul.

He couldn't resist the temptation of kissing her back. At that moment, he did not care that it crossed a line. She was in his care, but she was also a grown woman with a sound mind and no blood relation to him. And she had kissed *him* first.

Lord, the taste of her was intoxicating. When her soft

lips parted, a sigh broke away from her lips. He opened his eyes, and was startled to find she'd fallen asleep.

Well...that was a first for him. His kisses had never put a woman to sleep before. Darius frowned as he studied Meredith's sleeping face before he bent and pressed a kiss to her forehead. An unexpected wave of tenderness filled him. No wonder his uncle had cared for this woman. There was something about her, like the pull of gravity that drew him to her and made him desire to hold onto her forever.

"Your Grace?" the maid said softly as she entered the bedchamber, bearing a pitcher of water and a glass on a tray.

"Ahh, Nell, thank you." Darius hastily backed away from the bed. "Please let Miss Montague sleep late tomorrow. If you do not mind, I would like to elevate you to be her lady's maid. I can hire someone to see to your duties." He gingerly touched his cravat. Part of the once carefully folded cloth had come undone when Meredith grabbed him. Had the maid noticed?

Nell's gaze thankfully wasn't on him or his somewhat mussed wardrobe.

"Thank you, Your Grace. I would be honored to tend to Miss Montague."

"Excellent. Right, well... I'll be off then. You may undress her."

Darius fled the room, but the taste of Meredith's kiss was imprinted on his lips forever.

4

It was a little past midday when Meredith woke with a groan as she realized she had slept in. But her bed was so soft and warm, and she felt truly at peace for the first time since Uncle Ben had fallen ill. She rubbed her eyes and stared up at a ceiling painted to look like a windswept clouds. A solemn string of thoughts paraded through her mind as she simply lay there, the birds singing outside her window.

For the last two months of Uncle Ben's illness, she had worked tirelessly to care for him. She had gotten a stiff neck and aching back after a month of sleeping in a chair at his bedside each night and waking at the slightest sound he made.

Now Uncle Ben was gone forever. There would be no more quiet mornings reading the paper over breakfast, no ride through the fields or shared readings from novels by the fire. She was in a strange city, under a strange roof, in a strange bed. The life she'd come to love at Burton House was over.

A deep well of grief filled her chest. She hadn't known sorrow could carry such a terrible weight. When her mother had died, Meredith had grieved, but she hadn't mourned her passing like Uncle Ben's. Perhaps it was because she'd always believed her mother blamed her for so much that had gone wrong in her life.

She'd never said so openly, but a kept woman was easier to see to than a kept woman and a bastard child. Meredith had loved her mother, but the day Meredith had moved in with Uncle Ben it felt like she finally been allowed to breathe, to exist without apology.

And now she was a burden again. What role would she play in Darius's household? Would she be afraid to take up space, or would the darkly handsome Duke of Tiverton let her share his world and experience a different life, one that held perhaps just a bit of adventure?

Oh Lord... Darius...

She'd had the most wicked dream about him last night. He had been carrying her in his arms like some dashing knight, and she'd pulled his head down to kiss her. She'd been bold, eager, and he responded in kind, showing her that kisses were just what she hoped they would be. What a wonderful dream.

But it was only a dream, and thank goodness for that. If her new guardian knew she had fantasies about him, he might throw her out of his house...

Or, a little voice whispered wickedly, he *might* seduce her.

She was innocent in the ways of men, but she had seen the way he looked at her last evening. He'd desired her, or at the least, she'd inspired some passion within him. She'd never wanted to inspire that in a man like Harry, yet it was different with Darius because she desired him as well. What would it be like to be the object of Darius's desires? To taste the magic of love and passion with him?

But as quickly as the thought was born it was snuffed out. Darius couldn't marry a woman like her. It would be beyond scandalous. She would ruin his family's name and destroy every connection in society he possessed if he married her. A duke could not marry an illegitimately born woman with no family.

But she had to acknowledge in her heart of hearts, she would have loved to have been courted by him...to be loved by him and love him in return.

But it was a fantasy, a fool's dream, and she was not raised to be a fool.

Meredith pushed the covers of her bed back and slipped off the fourposter bed. She pushed the tall sash window up so the fresh air could pass through the room, then pulled up a chair to sit next to it and take in the scent of the blooming flowers below.

Her window overlooked Darius's back gardens, and she had a good view of the townhouse directly behind Darius's. She retrieved the pair of opera glasses Suzannah had given her the previous evening, undeniably curious about the lives of those that lived in those other grand houses. Their closest neighbors in Yorkshire had been over a mile away.

She lifted up the glasses and studied the house beyond Darius's, glimpsing a bedchamber that was visible through a pair of large bay windows. A woman sat up in the bed, speaking to someone she could not see. A moment later, a man of middling years came into view. She couldn't hear what the woman said to the man, but it seemed to infuriate him. He snarled something back at the woman and she gave a weak, coughing laugh in response as she slipped out of bed and sat down in a wheelchair and after a moment of adjusting her dressing robe, the woman rolled out of sight. The man vanished from view. The echo of a slamming door reached across Darius's back garden.

"Oh dear…" It seemed Darius's neighbors were quarreling. But how could anyone be unhappy while living in such a beautiful part of the city?

A polite cough disturbed her secret observations of the neighbors. Her heart stopped as she feared it might be Darius.

"Miss?"

Meredith turned around and breathed a sigh of relief. She'd been afraid for a moment that Darius had caught her spying on the neighbors but it was Nell.

"Oh, hello Nell." She greeted the maid with a smile.

"Are you ready to dress, miss? The footmen are laying out luncheon in the dining room, if you wish to join His Grace and Lady Kentwell."

"Lunch already," Meredith said to herself, then realized what else Nell had said. "Lady Kentwell is here?"

"Yes. She arrived for breakfast and has been here ever since."

Meredith rushed to remove her nightgown, then froze. She didn't remember going to bed last evening after the play. She only recalled part of the coach ride home with Darius.

"Oh heavens. Nell, did I change into my nightgown last night?"

"I changed you, miss. You fell asleep in the coach and His Grace carried you up to bed."

Meredith's hands, which had been jerking at the laces of the nightgown at her throat, halted in place. Memories from her delicious dream replayed in her mind.

She *had* been dreaming, hadn't she? She couldn't have kissed Darius. Surely not.

"You were fair worn out," Nell continued, "and he didn't have the heart to wake you." She pulled out one of Meredith's white muslin gowns from the armoire before she laid out a clean chemise, stays and stockings on the bed.

After dressing her, Nell combed Meredith's hair out, gently styling it in a loose knot.

"Do you know why Lady Kentwell is here? Did her husband come with her?"

"It is just Lady Kentwell. She and His Grace have been discussing candidates for a companion for you."

"Oh, yes. Of course." Meredith had almost forgotten that discussion last night. She stepped into her slippers and

Nell wrapped the ribbons around her ankles, tying them in place.

"Thank you ever so much, Nell."

Meredith hastened out of her chamber and followed the scent of food to the dining room. She hadn't had any opportunity for a tour of the house last evening when she'd arrived, but perhaps later today she could ask Nell to show her where all of the rooms were. The thought of asking Darius felt too...*intimate* right now.

A footman opened the door to the dining room for her. She stepped into a room with white paneling and yellow and green flower wallpaper that was wonderfully cheerful and warm. It instantly made her feel at home. Large, lush paintings of gardens covered most of the walls. The table could easily seat twenty people, but at the moment was only occupied at the far end.

Darius sat at a chair at the end and Lady Kentwell was perched on the seat directly to his right. Dozens of sheets of paper were spread out before them, and they spoke quietly as they examined them.

As they hadn't noticed her yet, and she hadn't eaten, Meredith turned her attention to the food. Her stomach grumbled at that moment, but thankfully Darius didn't hear. The food was set in chafing dishes on a walnut sideboard along one side of the room. Darius noticed her entrance into the room and immediately stood up.

"Ahh Meredith. I trust you slept well? I instructed Nell not to wake you. You've had a long journey."

"Yes, thank you. I slept very well," Meredith was

touched by Darius's thoughtfulness. Her gaze dropped to his mouth, and she remembered how boldly she'd grabbed him and pulled him down to kiss her. Assuming that had happened. Lord...she prayed that was a dream. If she'd really done that, she would expire right there.

Suzannah patted the chair beside her. "Please get something to eat and come sit with us. We would like your opinion on some candidates."

Meredith was famished, and hastily filled the plate with slices of beef, potatoes and then added some plums and a single current tart. Darius pulled out a chair for her. As she sat down and he pushed her in toward the table, his fingertips brushed her shoulders. Heat blossomed inside her in the wake of his innocent caress. All he'd done was help her sit and yet she was on fire with the thought of what it might feel like to have his hands on other places of her body. Forbidden places.

Was she no better than her mother? Shame washed away all desire from her for the moment. Her mother had been swept away by passion and she knew that it had ruined her future.

"We have narrowed down the potential candidates to three." Suzannah placed three advertisements in front of Meredith. She welcomed the distraction from her disquieting thoughts.

"We have ruled out anyone too young or old. I believe you need a middle aged woman of decent status, preferably widowed." Suzannah rested her chin in her hand as she waited for Meredith to look over the selections.

Meredith pointed to the last one.

"This one says she enjoys being active, taking rides in the park, walks and reading. But she's not afraid of a little excitement and adventure. I suppose that would frighten off most people who would want dour and serious chaperones," Meredith mused. "If I am to have a companion, I would greatly love a woman who would embrace life rather than try to deny me of it." Meredith snuck a glance at Darius, who watched her closely.

He noticed her look and smiled softly. "I rather agree, actually. I want you to have no silly peahens for a chaperone, nor fire breathing dragons. It would be nice to have a good woman to keep us both out of trouble, as it were, but not abridge our freedoms."

Suzannah laughed. "Abridge your freedoms? Darius, I doubt *any* woman would seek to check *your* behavior."

Meredith watched Suzannah and Darius's easy camaraderie with a pang of envy. How had she grown to be so close to a gentleman who was not her husband? The countess was lucky, very lucky indeed.

"Very well then. I will write to Mrs. Petersham and see if she will meet with us," Darius said. "That brings us to the next order of business, Meredith. Your wardrobe."

Meredith, her mouth now full of food, gulped painfully as she tried to swallow.

"Wardrobe? I'm afraid I do not possess the funds for—"

"Meredith, my uncle requested I take care of you, and that includes a roof over your head, food in your belly, connecting you to eligible men, and that certainly requires a new wardrobe."

Darius continued to watch her with those piercing eyes that she feared saw too much. There was no way this clever, smart man would have kissed her last night. She definitely had dreamed it. Darius was too refined, too in control ever to kiss her.

She suddenly felt ill with embarrassment. "Oh..."

As if sensing her distress, Suzannah reached out and patted her hand.

"Kit did the same with me. It is no use arguing with a gentleman who is determined to see that his lady is well turned out."

"Exactly," Darius leaned back in his chair and steepled his fingers. "Now please eat and we shall depart for Bond Street."

Meredith continued her meal in silence as she listened to Suzannah and Darius discuss people she didn't know and places she'd never been to.

When I marry someday, I want to belong. I want to have a shared history with my husband and know his world so well it becomes my own.

She wanted that so badly her chest ached.

Once she had finished, Darius went to summon his coach, leaving Suzannah and Meredith to wait in the entryway.

"You don't mind that I accompany you to the dressmaker?" Suzannah asked.

Meredith smiled at her new friend. "Of course not. I'm glad for your company."

"Good. Darius has impeccable taste, I assure you, but we ladies always need each other in times of wardrobe building."

Meredith laughed. "I quite agree on that. It would be good to have your insight as to what I should wear for London. I've only ever kept a simple wardrobe suited for the country."

Suzannah tightened the strings of her reticule. "Besides, someone must chaperone you until we hire someone. I want you to have the best of chances finding a husband, and while Darius is more than honorable, tongues have a way of wagging, especially when it comes to untruths."

Meredith was glad that Suzannah was so willing to help someone she'd only just met. "Thank you, truly."

"Of course. I promised you we would be friends."

Darius heard the last of the ladies' conversation as he joined them in the foyer. It gladdened his heart to see Suzannah so open and welcoming to Meredith. She already treated the young woman like family, just as he would wish his friends to. He retrieved his cane from Mr. Chelsea, wincing as he took a step that tugged the wrong way at the scar tissue on his stomach.

Chelsea offered a hand to steady him. "Your Grace?"

"I'm all right," Darius assured him. Then he noticed

Suzannah's suddenly teary eyes, and Meredith's confusion and concern.

"Blast it, Suzannah. Do not cry or I shall send you home."

Suzannah's eyes flashed. "You cannot expect me to forget that you were nearly killed because of me."

With a frustrated growl, he tapped his cane on the floor. "I *do* expect you to forget it, because I will not suffer your tears. If Kit sees you with red eyes, he will thrash me."

"Nonsense. He will embrace you for saving me."

Meredith was clearly confused, but he was in no mood to explain himself.

"Shall we go?" he said a little too curtly.

"Meredith, if you live with Darius, you shall have to accustom yourself to the fact that Darius does not like to make women cry, even if he did save their lives."

Meredith's face reddened at being caught in the middle of this argument. Darius glowered at Suzannah, then gestured for them to proceed ahead of him to the waiting coach.

"Will you tell me what happened?" Meredith whispered to Suzannah.

"I was shot and stabbed," Darius cut in, "neither of which affected my hearing. The bullet tore through my shoulder. The knife pierced my abdomen. I was protecting Suzannah from Kit's enemies. And I would do it again, so she should save her blasted tears," he said roughly.

"And he is simply *wonderful* for saving me," Suzannah

added to Meredith with a knowing look. "Even if he pretends to be a bit beastly about it."

"I am *not* pretending."

That was the end of the matter, thankfully. Suzannah dried her eyes and spoke to Meredith about wardrobe possibilities while Darius sat wondering how he felt like he lost a battle that he didn't even know he'd been fighting. By the time they arrived at the first stop on Bond Street, carriages crowded the street and the press of shoppers made Darius's head ache.

He held up a hand as he got out of the coach first. "Just a moment, ladies."

Several gentleman lounged idly by the doors of the shops, their eyes keenly searching for young ladies. But so long as Darius was there, they would not speak a word to Suzannah or Meredith. The sidewalk was full of fashionably attired ladies, smartly dressed gentleman, and footmen who rushed after their masters and ladies, laden with parcels and hatboxes.

"Suzannah, you shall go first." Darius assisted her out and one of his footmen followed Suzannah into the nearest linen-draper shop. Then Darius turned to help Meredith out of the coach. He grasped her by the waist, bringing her close to him so she avoided any dirt near the curb of the street. Her breath caught, and he was dazzled for a moment by the bloom of fresh color in her cheeks.

"Th—thank you," she whispered as she lifted her lashes. Her hazel eyes banished the world around them so that only she existed. "Please don't be cross with Suzannah.

You are a hero. You saved her. Any woman would feel deeply grateful to a man who did that."

Her words humbled him. He swallowed hard and nodded. "I do not wish to see a lady cry," he said quite honestly. "Any lady."

"She's right," Meredith added softly. "You *are* rather wonderful."

He nearly stumbled as he started to take Meredith's arm in his own. *She thinks I'm wonderful?* Damned if that didn't make him feel as though he could conquer the world.

Uncle Ben's words returned to him. He wanted to play the hero and had it had nearly killed him. There was no glory in such a foolish thing, seeking out trouble the way he did.

They stepped into the linen-draper shop, surrounded by bolts of brightly colored fabric. Silks, satins, muslin, and lace in dozens of color and patterns formed a vibrant display on the walls and racks. Several women were in the shop moving about excitedly, examining the colors and touching the fabrics.

Meredith joined Suzannah at the counter where bolts of bright colors like ripe peaches and brilliant summer blue skies were being paired together. Darius took in the silent stories on the faces of the customers around him. It was his habit to observe the people around him and that hadn't changed, even during an innocent shopping trip.

An older woman covered in fine silk ordered a harried shop worker to collect dozens of fabrics. She was clearly shopping out of boredom, no doubt nearly ready to buy everything that came before her simply to pass the time.

Another woman, dressed in the height of fashion, was looking over the wares with a sigh of disinterest, as though she came here often and never found anything that inspired her.

Next he turned his gaze to a pair of women, one a rich woman of middling years and the other seemed to be of debut age. The young woman addressed the elder as her aunt whenever she spoke to her. The young lady eyed the satin wistfully, and yet uttered not a word as her aunt waxed on about avoiding the frills and silly fashions which the aunt had seen fit to wear herself,.

The last woman had a bold colored, low-necked gown. She was playfully stroking her fingers over a roll of Belgian lace. A Cyprian, or a high-class lady of the night, if he had to guess. One desiring a gentleman to come and buy some lace for her or perhaps offer her even more. He flashed a polite but cool smile at her before he rejoined his two ladies.

Suzannah was explaining to the linen-draper about Meredith's wardrobe needs. It was going to be expensive, but Darius had over twenty-thousand pounds a year to his name and had no siblings with which to share his fortune, so he was free to spend his money as he pleased. And it pleased him well to see Meredith's excited little gasps each time a brightly colored bolt of fabric was added to the pile on the counter for the shopkeeper to measure and cut.

After the linen-drapers they moved on to the milliner's, where they acquired a ridiculous stack of hatboxes, and finally, the modiste. His beleaguered footman was clearly relieved to abandon the yards of fabric they'd purchased on the dressmaker's counter.

Darius lounged on a settee facing the dressing rooms and the trio of large mirrors where Meredith was standing to be fitted. The dressmaker, seeing Darius's coach had arrived, closed the shop for a private fitting session. It suited him well enough to have the place all to themselves. He chuckled as the modiste measured Meredith and prodded at her abundant bosom with a frown, as though wanting to find a way to squash her breasts down flat. If the woman dared to cover those magnificent breasts, she would never hear the end of it from him. Best to end this folly quickly. He waved the dressmaker over.

"Yes, Your Grace?" the woman asked as he rose from the settee.

"Miss Montague has a very lovely figure, does she not?" he asked.

"She...yes, she does." The woman clearly feared she would give him the wrong answer.

"Then let us be sure that we show her to her best advantage, and not try to *hide* anything overly much?" he said carefully.

"Yes, yes, of course." The dressmaker let out a breath of relief. "If you don't mind such fashions, I can certainly display her... assets in a way that won't cause any scandal."

"I leave her in your capable hands." He resumed his seat and let the dressmaker return to her task.

More than once, Meredith cast him a beseeching glance

as Suzannah and the modiste discussed various dresses. Unable to ignore her looks of dread for long, Darius stood and came over to her as she perched shyly on the little pedestal surrounded by the mirrors. The raised pedestal brought her level to his face, which pleased him more than it should because it put her lips in perfect alignment with his own.

He was reminded of the kiss she'd stolen from him last night. A kiss that continued to vex him in the sweetest and yet most wicked way. Did she remember that she'd kissed him? He couldn't ask, not here, at any rate.

"Darius," she whispered. "Surely this is all too much?"

"What?" he asked innocently, though he knew exactly what she was talking about.

"I need only a few gowns. Suzannah has already ordered *twenty*."

"Did my uncle not buy you gowns each year?" Darius asked.

"He tried," Meredith replied. "But I didn't let him. Though I wished I was his natural born child, I was not. I could not in good conscience accept anything that wasn't absolutely necessary."

Darius considered her words seriously, realizing then just how his pretty ward saw herself...as an unworthy burden upon others. She was so very wrong on that account and he was going to teach her.

"I must regrettably inform you that as *my* ward, as long as you are in a duke's household in London, all of this"—he waved a hand around the dressmaker's shop—"is absolutely necessary. I fear you must resign yourself to a wardrobe so exquisite that you would sparkle like a diamond at every engagement we attend. Such is the burden you must bear."

Meredith's eyes widened, then narrowed as she realized how he had trapped her into accepting the lavish new wardrobe.

"Drat," she murmured. Darius burst out laughing so hard that it Suzannah looked over to him in shock.

He recovered himself and returned to his seat. Maybe it wasn't so bad to escort Meredith about town and shower her with gifts. He'd always enjoyed the practice of spoiling his mistresses, but had to remember Meredith was not his mistress.

She was a young lady in need of an excellent match, not to share his bed, no matter how much she tempted him. And Meredith Montague tempted him *deeply*. With her soulful hazel eyes, her love for Uncle Ben, and her overdeveloped determination to never be a bother to anyone, it made him half-mad to do just about anything for her.

And that, he acknowledged as he paid the dressmaker's bill, was exactly the problem. Darius had always prided himself on his control over his desires, but Meredith frayed that control like no other woman ever had. He was going to have to be damned careful, or he would risk far more than just his control. He'd risk Meredith's ruination.

5

If there was one thing Meredith truly loved, it was an English garden at dusk. The Duke of Tiverton's town-house gardens were exceptionally beautiful. Rather than a perfectly curated series of hedgerows, he had gravel pathways that meandered in gentle curves around the space between his house and the garden wall that over-looked the townhouse behind them.

There was a wildness to the roses and creeping vines that fringed the back of the house. The garden shed shielded by ivy in the far corner made if feel as if the land had been forgotten under some fairy's spell. Yet the pots of flowers that sat atop pedestals were filled to the brim with a curated perfection of beautiful blooms that restored a semblance of order to the scene. The blend of colors caught her eyes, and everything attracted bees and butterflies which filled the garden with a teeming sense of life in gentle motion. With the sun setting just behind the horizon of the skyline, the world had turned the sky a lilac color and the clouds were striated with pink light as the final beams of light cut across the heavens.

I could spend my entire life in this garden, she realized with a contented sigh.

Meredith lifted the skirts of her white muslin gown and carefully stepped over a patch of peonies so that she could leave the gravel path and walk on the dew-covered grass. There was a small little heart-shaped hole in the back garden wall that had caught her attention, and she was determined to get a better look at it.

Whoever had built the wall had created a sort of window in a lovely pattern to let someone peer between Darius's garden and the garden of the house behind his. She couldn't deny she was a bit curious as she approached the wall. To see over the top, she'd need to stand upon a bench and then perhaps a box or a crate before she would be able to peer over the other side, but with the advantage of the little window, she could see part of the other garden.

When she reached the window within the stone wall, she peeked through, taking in the wild, clearly uncared for garden of the other house. She stared at the garden a moment longer before a movement caught her attention. A woman was rolling in an invalid chair down the path and it seemed she was headed toward where Meredith stood.

The woman was blond-haired and in her middling years. Meredith could tell the woman had once been exquisitely beautiful, but there seemed to be a cloak of illness around her now that had withered away the vigor and loveliness of the woman's features. The lady rolled to a stop and glanced around with a sigh. Her gaze flitted past Meredith and then she jerked back and gasped, her face paling.

"Good morning," Meredith called out shyly. "I didn't meant to startle you."

The woman smiled a little, the expression weary as she relaxed. "It's all right." She turned her chair toward Meredith to face her fully and wheeled closer.

"I'm Meredith Montague, the ward of the Duke of Tiverton," Meredith introduced herself, feeling rather silly talking through the window of a stone wall.

"I'm Minerva Crell," the woman said. She adjusted her blanket over her lap.

"It's lovely to meet you," Meredith replied.

Minerva's eyes held a hint of shadows as she nodded. "Yes...it is nice to meet you as well. It feels as though it's been ages since I've talked to anyone but my servants or husband."

"Would you like to come over for tea?" Meredith offered. She hoped Minerva would agree. The sadness that radiated off her was so strong that Meredith wanted to comfort the woman in any way she could.

"Not today, I am too tired, but soon perhaps. I would like that very much, if my husband allows it." Minerva sighed and she pulled her shawl tighter about her shoulders, wincing slightly as though she was in pain.

"Are you all right?" Meredith asked in concern.

"What? Oh...yes...I just am rather clumsy. Always

bruising myself..." She looked away and then cleared her throat as she met Meredith's gaze again. "I would very much like to visit with you over tea..." she seemed to be repeating herself as though she'd possibly said this to other people who wished to see her. It struck Meredith as odd, and it worried her a little but she didn't wish to pry into her neighbor's life.

"I understand. Please let me know whenever you feel up to it, I've only recently moved to London and would very much like to know my neighbors." She meant it too. If she could give this woman some companionship, she would be glad to do it.

Minerva's slender hands plucked at the blanket on her lap. "It is a pity that we will be moving to the country soon. My husband believes it will be good for my health. I admit, I love the country, but I fear I will feel even more isolated than I do now." Once again she winced as she moved and a frisson of concern shot through Meredith.

"When will you be leaving?" She didn't like the idea of this poor woman living out in the country when it was clear she was so lonely.

"We have not yet determined the date of our departure, but my husband has just found a house for us and is hiring staff this week."

"Please be sure to let me know before you depart, I would like to make sure you come over at least once for tea."

The other woman chuckled. "You won't have to

convince me, dear. I've see that handsome duke of yours, and it would be pleasant so share tea with him."

"Oh, he's not my duke..." Meredith blushed and glanced back at Darius's house.

"Oh?" Minerva's brows rose.

"He's my guardian...his uncle who recently passed asked him to help me come out in society and find a husband."

"I see. I wish I could help you there. I haven't been out in society for over fifteen years. I daresay no one would even remember me." Minerva's loneliness was so clear in her voice.

"All the more reason for you to join me for tea soon. I could introduce you to people as I meet them."

"That sounds wonderful."

"Miss Montague!" Nell's voice called across the gardens as the maid showed up on the terrace. "You must come in now!"

"I'm so sorry, I am being summoned," Meredith said.

"Not to worry, dear. It was lovely to have met you." Minerva waved a frail hand at her before Meredith left her small peek hole and walked back toward Darius's home.

AN HOUR LATER, MEREDITH CLIMBED OUT OF THE BATH IN HER dressing room and accepted the towel from Nell.

The maid grinned at her. "I have your new gown laid out, miss. You'll look splendid tonight."

"I'm glad you think so. I am too nervous to even think about it." Darius had mentioned that His Royal Highness, the Prince Regent, would be attending the ball this evening, and Darius had planned to introduce her to him. As she had missed her chance to debut in the spring when she would have been presented officially in court, she was now to receive the Prince's approval, something that they hoped would set her up for the rest of the season.

Meredith finished drying and Nell helped her into her chemise and stays. The ball gown was one that the dressmaker had rushed to prepare for this evening. It was a pale blue, the color of a frosted lake. Beneath the top skirt was a layer of cream petticoats with spring flowers embroidered on the hem, and when she lifted her skirts, the petticoats would peek through, revealing the secret garden along the bottom. Her short sleeves and bodice had creeping vines trailing along them, with budding blooms in soft blushes of pink and peach.

Unlike most ball gowns designed to be stunningly intricate in decoration, it was sedate in its embellishments, but it was light to wear and therefore perfect for dancing. Nell tied a cream-colored sash around Meredith's waist into a bow at the back, which accented her hips in a way that made Meredith feel very aware of herself as a woman.

Nell styled her hair in the latest fashion, letting loose curls bounce down against the back of Meredith's neck while the rest of her hair was pulled up with pink ribbons. It was far more fuss than she had ever been accustomed to.

Then the maid brought over a black velvet box and opened it for Meredith.

"His Grace brought this to your room while you were bathing."

A delicate necklace with brilliant clusters of diamonds sparkled against the black velvet. Matching girandole style earrings perched neatly above the necklace on the cushions of the jewel box.

Meredith gasped, her eyes widening. "Oh no, I couldn't possibly wear these."

"You must. They belonged to the late duchess. She was a fine lady, or so Mr. Chelsea says. It would be an insult to not wear them if the duke wishes you to."

Meredith sighed. "Yes, you're quite right." The last thing she wanted was to hurt Darius after he'd treated her so wonderfully. The jewels were the most lovely thing she'd ever seen. She simply didn't feel *worthy* of them.

"Shall I put them on, miss?"

"Thank you, Nell." She seated herself at the vanity table, facing the mirror.

A deep voice intruded from the doorway. "Allow me."

Meredith turned to see Darius leaning against the door-jamb, partially silhouetted by the lamps in the corridor. It was like staring at a darkly attractive god of the underworld as he waited to pull her into his sinful realm.

How was it that Darius could fill her head with such fanciful ideas?

"You may leave us, Nell," Darius said. Nell bobbed a curtsy and left.

"Darius," Meredith said his name both in warning and with longing.

"Meredith, you look almost perfect this evening."

"Almost? I—" She whirled back to face the mirror, searching for any imperfection, and that was when she saw Darius had come to stand directly behind her. His mouth slid into a teasing grin as he met her gaze in the mirror.

Darius came over and took the necklace from the box. He placed it around her neck and fastened the clasp.

"There...now you are perfection itself."

She reached up to caress the diamonds that lay against her collarbone. Her eyes met his through the mirror. She drew in a sharp breath as she saw the lust in those bright blue eyes of his. Her bedchamber was far too dark, as night had fallen and the muted lamplight only heightened her awareness of him and the fact that they were alone.

"Thank you for the jewels," she said. "Nell said they belonged to your mother?"

"Yes. She had a great many pieces which are sitting unworn and unloved in a safe in my study. I believe it is time they are brought out and shared with the world again." He handed her the earrings and watched as she clasped them onto her ears.

"Meredith," he said, his gaze dropping to her lips. "We must talk."

"About?" Her own voice grew faint. She couldn't help but look at his mouth as well. Lord, she wanted him to kiss her.

"About...that look you just gave me." His expression

turned almost hungry. "It makes me want to toss you on this bed and ravish you senseless."

Meredith made a soft sound as his words created a splendid flash of erotic visions in her mind.

"You must stop begging me with those beautiful eyes, or I fear I shall kiss you again."

"*Again*?" She clung to that word, her heart racing. Surely it had been a dream?

"You don't remember?" Darius asked in a low, seductive voice. "Because I do, love. The *taste* of you haunts me still. It has turned me mad with hunger for you."

He moved a step closer to her until her breasts rubbed against his chest. "Close your eyes," Darius warned, "or I'll do what you are begging me to do."

She tried. She tried to shut her eyes, but Darius St. John had such a power to bewitch her.

"Blast—" he snarled, and lowered his head toward hers, all control seemingly gone.

A sudden crash and a shriek in the distance had them both jerking apart.

Meredith gasped. "What on earth was that?"

"I believe it came from outside." Darius strode to the window that faced the back gardens. The window sash was up and he leaned over the sill. Meredith joined him, her shoulder touching his as they stared out at the house behind Darius's.

Through the distant windows of the other house, they could see a woman lying in bed as she screamed at someone that they could not see. When the woman had argued with her husband previously, Meredith could not make out the words. But now the woman shouted loud enough to carry in the still night air.

"You think to *replace* me?"

Another crash. A vase hit the wall by the woman's head and shattered.

Meredith sucked in a breath and drew closer to Darius who put an arm around her as though wishing to shield her from the ugliness of what they were witnessing.

The woman's husband came to view as he stopped past the window. "You'll regret this, Minerva!" Then he stormed out of the room.

Minerva got out of bed, wrapped herself in a shawl and hobbled over to an invalid chair, and once she was seated, she rolled after her husband, disappearing from sight.

"They fight quite a lot," Meredith told Darius quietly. "It's such a shame."

"That's Louis Crell and his wife, Minerva. I barely know them. I believe Minerva was a rich heiress, and she married Louis for love. But it seems that that love has soured."

"I met Mrs. Crell in the gardens today. We spoke through that small heart-shaped hole in the garden walls. She seemed very lonely. I hope you don't mind that I invited her to tea when she feels up to it."

"That's very kind of you. She is most welcome here. It has been a while since I have seen her."

"She seems to be ill. She was in an invalid chair," Meredith added.

"Yes, she is. I remember hearing she was unwell several years ago." He cleared his throat.

"Darius..." she hesitated a moment. "I am a little worried about her. She mentioned she was clumsy and that she had bruises...and now that I've seen them fighting...you don't believe he's hurt her, do you?"

Darius's eyes narrowed. "If he has...it is hard to convict a man of that crime unless she's terribly injured. It's a failing in our laws to be sure, but short of murder, a man can beat his wife for almost any reason." He scowled. "We will watch her, and if I see him touch her, I will intervene, regardless of the law."

At Darius's promise, she relaxed somewhat. At least they agreed on the right course of action, that someone like Darius who had power and influence, should intervene if abuse was indeed present in the Crell household.

"We should go or we'll be late to Lady Hazlitt's ball."

Meredith allowed him to put her shawl about her shoulders. Then she slid her gloves on before they went down to meet the coach. Once inside, the coach started to move when Darius put a hand to his thighs and cursed before he called for the driver to halt.

"I forgot my blasted cane. I believe I shall need it tonight." He leapt out of the coach, leaving her alone as he hastened back toward the house. "I will be back in a moment."

Meredith toyed with the tasseled ends of her silk shawl while she waited. Just then, sharp screams cut through the night, and Meredith lurched toward the carriage window, peering out to see what had happened. The alley next to the mews which stabled Darius's horses and carriage was lit by only a thin strip of moonlight.

She glimpsed a figure thrashing about in the shadows. No...it was two figures...and they were fighting. There was a flash of a blade in the moonlight before it vanished. Meredith flung the coach door open and scrambled down.

"Miss?" Leigh Johnson, one of Darius's footmen, hopped from his perch on the coach to assist her. She pushed him away as she peered into the alley again. The figures she glimpsed were *gone*.

"Leigh, would you run down into the alley and see if anyone is hurt? I thought I saw two people fighting."

"I heard the scream as well. I shall have a look, miss." The footman trotted down the alley, vanishing briefly before he emerged from the shadows and returned to her.

"I'm sorry, Miss Montague, but no one was there."

"That mew does belong to His Grace, doesn't it?" She was certain it was, but wanted confirmation.

"Yes, miss, but the Crells share it with him sometimes. I believe they pay a small fee to stable their horses there, but they don't own a coach."

"The Crells, you're sure?"

"Yes, miss," Leigh replied. "Are you well? You've turned quite pale, miss." The footman took her hand to steady her. She felt ill hearing that scream echo in her head.

"I swore I saw two people fighting." She closed her eyes, trying to recall what she'd seen. A tall figure grappling with a shorter figure. The taller one had a blade, most certainly.

And that scream, high-pitched, full of terror, and cut off so quickly.

"I didn't see anything, miss, but I did hear a scream." Leigh assured her. "Perhaps it was a trick of the light? It's easy to see things that aren't there in the dark. And these alleys can carry an echo in odd ways on cold nights. Might it have happened somewhere else?"

As if to prove that point, they heard a steady tap-tap-tap grow louder, only there was no one to be seen. Then the source of the sound shifted, back towards the house.

"Leigh? What's all this about?" Darius demanded, his cane tapping lightly on the ground as he appeared out of the night before them.

"I saw something in the mews, I'm sure of it," Meredith said. "Two people were fighting, and we both heard a scream. Oh Darius, please, will you go look with me just to be sure?"

Darius glanced at the footman.

"I already looked, Your Grace. I did not see anyone."

"Stay here," he ordered Meredith. "I shall go." He was in the mews for a good minute or two before he returned, a slight frown upon his lips.

"You say you heard a scream?" he asked.

She nodded.

"It was possible it was a horse. They can scream quite loud, especially if startled."

"It was human. A woman. I'm certain of it," Meredith insisted.

Darius's gaze softened. "Whatever it was, it must've

been nothing serious. Now, we really must go. The Prince Regent is allowed to be late, but not us, and I've called in all of my favors to ensure you will meet him this evening."

Meredith glanced toward the dark alley once more before she allowed Darius to help her back into his coach. She had seen something. Something terrible, she was certain. What had happened there?

Darius would think her mad if she continued to obsess with this matter, so she focused instead on what should frighten her, the fact that she was going to meet the Prince Regent tonight.

"Well, well," a voice chuckled. Darius's friend Warren Burville had joined him at the refreshment table. "You've created a stir tonight with the little gem you've brought to the ball."

Warren's jade green eyes fixed on Meredith as she spun in a circle while dancing with a young man. She was on her seventh dance already, and her card was completely full. If Darius hadn't claimed the final waltz before he had set her loose in the ballroom, he would have had no chance of dancing with her tonight.

"What are they saying about her?" He trusted Warren to be honest with him.

"That she is far too pretty to remain unchaperoned under your roof. There is much speculation about that. Some say that she must be someone special, an orphan with a gilded pedigree or some such thing. Why else would the illustrious Duke of Tiverton parade about such a treasure? More than a few of the matrons remember your mother and those diamonds your father gave her on their wedding day, and how those very diamonds now rest on Miss Montague's skin as if they belong there." He grinned devilishly at Darius over his glass of punch.

Darius frowned as Meredith and her current dance partner twirled past again. When the young fellow met Darius's black gaze, he stumbled the second step and hastily recovered.

Warren nudged Darius with an elbow. "Careful man, your green is showing."

"He was holding her too close," Darius muttered. "It's not a bloody waltz."

"You know, Darius, she would make a good wife, assuming you are interested in the lady, of course. She is beautiful, kind, and intelligent, according to Suzannah. She has been singing Miss Montague's praises this evening."

"Whether I'm interested or not does not matter," said Darius. "Any woman I choose must have impeccable breeding and unquestionably respected family lineage."

Warren narrowed his eyes in silent judgment at Darius's words.

"Oh, don't be like that," said Darius. "It's not snobbery. It is because my bride will be judged by everyone. If she is found wanting in the slightest way, rumors will grow, and her invitations will dwindle to nothing. She would be without friends, without a circle of support. I cannot watch a woman I care about whither from the loss of sunlight like that. You know how cruel society can be if they think they have an interloper in their midst."

Warren sipped his drink again. "So you hope to marry her off to a man who could offer *less* protection than you could from society's cold reach?"

"No, it wouldn't be like that," Darius argued. "With a lesser man, she would not be seen as a schemer. She would be more than suitable for wealthy tradesmen, or the wife of a doctor or barrister. But a man of title? That would be more of a curse than a boon to her."

Even as he said this, the words tasted like ash in his mouth. He didn't want Meredith to belong to anyone but him. But because he cared for her and for his uncle's memory, he could not turn her into his mistress. Meredith deserved marriage to a kind, respectable man who would honor and respect her. Darius would see she had that, even if it damn near killed him to keep his hands off her.

The dance came to a sudden halt and a wave of excited whispers announced that the Prince of Wales had finally arrived.

Darius grasped a champagne flute from a passing footman's tray and downed it before he gave the flabbergasted servant the glass back. It was time to see Meredith make an impression upon the gentlemen present tonight.

George, the Prince of Wales entered the ballroom, flanked by a few well-dressed gentlemen that Darius knew were his close friends.

Darius intercepted Meredith on her way to form a line

to meet the prince, threading her arm through his. She gazed up at him questioningly, her cheeks flushed in a way that made him think of peonies at sunset. He wished that he was instead whisking her away into the gardens to kiss her until she was flushed that shade of pink in other, more secret and delicious, places.

"Darius, I can't breathe." Meredith's gaze darted between him and the prince as he made his way along the line, greeting guests.

"Yes, you can. Remember, you're beautiful and you are brave. That is all you need to meet the Prince Regent."

Meredith's laugh held a hint of hysteria. "Is that all?"

He gave her arm a soothing rub. "Yes. All will be well."

Prince George spotted Darius as he moved down the line of guests waiting to greet him.

When he reached them, Darius bowed. "Your Royal Highness. May I present my ward, Miss Meredith Montague?"

George's gaze moved over Meredith as she dipped into a curtsy.

"Your Royal Highness," Meredith raised her lashes and returned the Prince Regent's gaze with a steady one of her own.

The prince's lips curved into a smile. "It is quite a pleasure to meet you, my dear, quite a pleasure indeed. May I presume you have a dance free?" At this question, Meredith's confidence faltered. She looked to Darius for rescue since her dance card was full.

"I'm afraid Miss Montague's card is full. However, I

hold the last waltz, Sir. I would gladly cede that honor to you if you would grant me to."

George's gaze showed he understood that Darius was helping Meredith save face.

"You may do me the honor then, Tiverton." He waited as Meredith erased Darius's name from the last dance and offered her card to the prince, who politely penciled his name in the now free space.

"We shall meet again for the last waltz, Miss Montague. Tiverton." George inclined his head before he moved on to the next group of guests.

Warren chuckled. "You best be careful. It would be considered treason to be jealous of the Prince of Wales."

Meredith looked away and blushed.

"Now, I believe it's high time you introduced me, old boy," Warren said, his green eyes now focused on Meredith.

"Of course. Meredith, this is Warren Burville. He lives next door to Kit and Suzannah. Warren, this is Miss Montague, my ward."

Warren bowed over Meredith's hand, pressing a faint kiss to her fingers.

"It's lovely to meet you. I believe we saw each other before at the play but—" Meredith began.

"But Darius bustled you away so his *wicked* friends could not seduce you," Warren finished.

"Yes." Meredith laughed as she and Warren looked at Darius to see his reaction.

The woman was *adorable*. When had she become so?

Darius frowned as Meredith turned her focus once more to Warren.

"I understand you have no free dances, Miss Montague. Pity that. I would have happily claimed several if only to scandalize Lady Hazlitt's guests and win a smile from you."

Meredith blushed. "I shall take that as a compliment, Mr. Burville."

"You should. And it's Warren, if you please. Only strangers and enemies call me Mr. Burville."

"Warren, then." Meredith's hazel eyes were full of mischief, but before she could say anything, she was claimed for her next dance. Darius could only watch, feeling bereft of her glowing presence and suffering Warren's teasing.

Lady Hazlitt's ball was everything Meredith hoped it would be, except she didn't get to dance with Darius. She was more than thankful that the evening had distracted her from most of her worries and that strange scream she'd heard. The sound still echoed in her mind, but she was able to push it away whenever she was escorted back onto the floor by a new dance partner.

The final waltz was announced, and she anxiously waited for the prince to claim her. She curtsied low when he approached and accepted his hand.

As the Prince of Walves escorted her onto the dance floor, he pulled her close.

"Shall I make your Tiverton wickedly jealous, Miss Montague?"

"What?" Meredith gasped and then hastily apologized. "I'm sorry, I don't understand what you mean, Sir."

George chuckled. "Oh come now. The man's mad for you. Never seen him like this before in all the years I've known him. He's always been the best sort of man. Good-natured, polite, but right now he's throwing daggers with his eyes at me. Which makes me wonder why. Just *who* are you to wield such power over a man like him?"

Meredith turned in the prince's arms, her tongue tied. "I..."

"Come now. You must keep no secrets from me, Miss Montague. But I can assure you, whatever you tell me will remain a secret. Tiverton called you his ward. How did this come to pass?"

"His uncle Benjamin St. John raised me as his ward and recently died. It was his last request that the duke take me in and assist me in finding a suitable match. It is why he brought me here tonight."

"You have my deepest condolences," George said. "Pardon the bluntness of my question, but were you St. John's by-blow?"

She winced at the crass phrasing. "Was I Mr. St. John's child? No, Sir, although I dearly wish I was. My mother had me out of wedlock, and I barely remember my real father. He is dead, too. My mother was once beloved by Mr. St. John, and he agreed to take us both in and care for us. So you see, I am simply... no one."

The prince's eyes narrowed. "*No one* is no one, my dear. We put much stock on birth here, but it wounds me to hear you say that about yourself. You are a beautiful woman, and you seem kind and humble. Does that sound like no one? I dare say that many decent men would throw themselves at you for husbands, regardless of your past. Tell me who you desire, and I will aid you in your conquest of him, my dear."

Meredith was stunned by the offer. "But why?"

"You feel doomed because of how you were born. I wish to assure you this is not the case. I know this because I *am* doomed because of how I was born. I have wealth and privilege, but you possess more freedom that I ever will. So I will use what power I have to aid you. Now, tell me, who do you desire?"

Meredith's gaze strayed to Darius, who prowled at the edge of the dance floor like a wolf, his eyes locked on her.

"Ahh, so the desire flows both ways, does it?" George mused. "Tricky... but not impossible. If you want him, we must be clever about it."

Meredith gasped at his words. "Sir, I cannot..."

The prince laughed. "My dear, do you, or do you not, want Tiverton for a husband?"

She did. Even though she and Darius were strangers in so many ways, she already felt safe with him. She felt such a strong desire for him too. She wished she could ignore it, but the truth was...she did want Darius for a husband. To belong to him, to call him hers in return, and be a part of his world, not because of wealth or status, but because she could be herself around him and his friends. That simple thing meant everything to her

"I see." The prince's voice softened even though she hadn't answered him. "You've chosen wisely, Miss Montague. Tiverton isn't simply noble of blood, but noble of heart. Damned rare to find these days in my court. However, the task ahead will not be easy. Tiverton has never courted anyone seriously, nor given any indication of a desire to wed. We must discern the reason for that. I give you leave to write to me at the palace, and I shall write to you in return. Between the two of us, we will find a way to trap this fellow for you."

"Oh, but I don't want to *trap* him."

"Nonsense. Men are the only creatures who prosper in the captivity of a good marriage to someone they love. He will be quite content once the marriage license is signed and you are the willing captor of his heart."

Meredith blushed at the prince's words.

The waltz ended. George inclined his head at Meredith and she curtsied as the room applauded the end of the ball.

But Meredith couldn't focus on that at the moment. Her mind was spinning. The Prince of Wales wanted to help her catch Darius as a husband!

6

A number of men swamped Meredith after the Prince of Wales escorted her off the dance floor. She was asked multiple times if she would be home for gentleman callers the next day. Flustered, she answered she would be, but she hoped that Darius would not be upset with her for saying that. She hadn't had a chance to speak with him since George had waltzed with her, and she was still stunned that the prince had offered to help her catch Darius as a husband.

A voice cut through the din of gentleman, all trying to speak to her at once. "I say, let the lady breathe, gentlemen."

At this new voice, several young men retreated away, allowing her to see who had spoken. A tall, dark blond man with startling gray eyes and a wicked smile parted the crowd without effort, his strides confident as he came towards her. He wore a red waistcoat that matched his daring attitude.

"That's right, pups, off you go." The man gave a shooing motion with one hand, chasing off the rest of the crowd that had threatened to overwhelm Meredith. When she and the man were alone, she realized she recognized him.

"I know you!" she exclaimed and then blushed at her girlish outburst.

He winked. "Felix Hawkins, the Marquess of Grey, at your service, Miss Montague."

"Lady Kentwell pointed you out to me at the theater," she added more softly. "You are one of Darius's friends."

Felix chuckled. "She is a dear creature, our Suzannah," Felix said with genuine honesty. Again, Meredith wished she knew how a woman like Suzannah had been so fortunate to be so adored by these men.

"But enough about Kit's fair lady. I want to know why Darius hasn't yet introduced you to us."

"Us?" Meredith asked.

Felix gestured with a nod to someone behind her, and she saw three other men ringing around her, the other men from the night Darius had taken her to the theater.

"It seems Darius has sought to keep you away from us scoundrels." Felix gestured toward something across the ballroom. "Therefore, we had to devise a way to distract him."

Meredith saw Darius arm-in-arm with Lady Hazlitt. The older woman was engaged in animated conversation, and it was clear from his surreptitious looks around the room that he was desperately looking for someone, anyone, to aid him in a polite escape.

"A bit unkind of us, I admit, but ultimately harmless," said Felix. "Now, for the proper introductions. Miss Montague, this is Mr. Vincent Windham."

A dark-haired man with soft, seductive brown eyes stepped forward and bowed to her.

"This is Lionel Thistlewaite, Viscount Basildon."

Lionel was also dark haired, and had captivating hazel eyes. His face, while not cruel, held a distant, analytical quality that gave Meredith the impression he was studying her for faults or charms, but which one she wasn't sure. This man would take his time in making his opinion of her.

"And lastly, this is Mr. Warren Burville."

"We've already had the pleasure," Warren said with a roguish grin. "I see you survived your dance with the Prince Regent. You created quite a stir. Well done." He raised the glass of punch he carried in a toast.

"Thank you." Meredith relaxed a little. Even though Darius's friends were intimidatingly attractive, she felt no fear, just a feminine shyness that she wasn't used to. But they were all wonderfully kind, and it was rather fun to have them all wanting to meet her. She'd never experienced such excitement in Yorkshire.

"Thank you, for chasing those men away, Lord Grey. I was becoming quite flustered."

"Anytime, my dear, anytime. Those pups will be lining up at your door tomorrow after your excellent showing with the Prince Regent. If Darius fails to chase them off, send a messenger and we will come to rescue you. We live on the same street, after all."

"You live on Knightley Street as well?" she asked Felix.

Felix chuckled. "Of course! We're the *reason* they call it Devil's Square, you see."

Rather than be frightened by that, or at the least, reasonably hesitant, she wanted to laugh as well. These men didn't strike her as devils, but simply charming men like Darius who seemed deeply interested in her, not just as a woman, but as a person. They were teasing, affectionate and without artifice, just like Darius. They peppered her with questions about her dances, what she thought of London, and if Darius was behaving himself, which made her blush.

A wonderful warmth filled Meredith's chest as she spoke to them. She believed them. They might be known as rogues to the general populace, but these friends of Darius were honorable men, and would protect those Darius would protect, even if that person was less conventional than the usual debutante.

Perhaps they would not even mind if Darius were to marry one such as her. Perhaps they would stand alongside Darius and the bride he chose, accepting her into their ranks with the same warmth they had for Suzannah.

But Suzannah was not tainted by the illegitimacy of her birth as she was. Meredith decided against telling them—even the possibility of being rejected by men and their golden touched lives, was too much for her to consider. She would enjoy these precious moments while she could—the truth of her birth would come out soon enough.

"Blast, he's escaped Lady Hazlitt," Vincent warned as Darius strode toward them, his expression thunderous.

"Felix, you—" Darius stopped whatever he'd been about to say when he saw Meredith hidden amongst his friends. "Ahh, Meredith, there you are." Darius' expression softened. "I see you've met my friends."

"*Are* we your friends?" Lionel asked with a wry grin. "Because the way you are acting makes us feel like you see us as some sort of Drury Lane villains."

Darius stared at her, searching her face with concern. Warmth blossomed in Meredith's cheeks at the intimacy that she felt from that simple look. She wanted to dive into those eyes, which were a sea of purest blue. What she wouldn't have given in that moment for him to steal her away to the dance floor, or the gardens, it didn't matter. She just had a desperate need to be alone with him.

"I'm quite fine, Darius. Lord Grey and the others rescued me from an overly eager group of men. I must warn you, I was pushed, and I said I would be receiving visitors tomorrow. I hope I have not spoken out of place. It is your home, after all. I have no right to accept callers without your permission."

"It is quite fine," Darius said, albeit a little stiffly. "It is, after all, what you are here for, to meet eligible young men. I shall be present, of course, since we don't yet have a suitable chaperone."

"*This* I must see," Warren replied. "Expect me to join

you." The other men began teasing Darius that they ought to come as well to ensure that the standards of propriety were met with. Darius soon silenced his friends with a glare.

Warren winked at Meredith while Darius was looking away. Meredith nearly choked as she stifled a giggle. Then Darius turned his focus on her still-red face. He offered her his arm with a warm smile that melted her entire body.

"I believe it is time to take you home, Meredith."

She glanced at the others and mouthed a silent *thank you* at Felix before letting Darius take her away. Felix gave a playful salute as though she were a general in the king's army. Was this how Suzannah felt? To be included in the secret circle of these men's lives? Meredith held a little tighter onto Darius, feeling for the first time, if only briefly, that she belonged here. Belonged with him.

"Do you think he knows?" Warren asked Felix as they watched Darius and Meredith leave, parting the crowds in their wake. Warren had never seen Darius so ruffled before, or so fixated on a woman. And the poor girl had only been in Darius's life less than a few days.

"That he's in danger of falling in love?" Felix chuckled. "No, the poor sod has no idea at all. I wager it will take three months before he figures it out."

"A hundred pounds says that it takes him two," Lionel countered.

Vincent grinned. "You know how Darius is...it doesn't take much for him to leap into action once his instincts are engaged. I wager a thousand that he won't last two *weeks*."

"What are you devils up to?" Kit demanded, but he said it teasingly as he joined them. Suzannah was on his arm, and she too eyed them with suspicion.

"Nothing, old boy," Warren said quickly.

Kit's darling wife arched a brow in challenge. "Nothing certainly looks an awful lot like *something*.".

Warren stifled his laugh with a cough. "We were merely discussing how... protective Darius seems to be over his new ward."

"She was important to his uncle, and now that his uncle has passed, he feels he must do all he can to assure Miss Montague's future is secured," Kit said as if the solution was simple enough.

"One does not throw daggers with one's eyes over a woman unless one is jealous," Vincent said. "And Darius is positively hurling weaponry at anyone daring to get too close to her."

"Which is hardly the best approach when his task is to find her a husband," Lionel agreed. "Darius is in trouble, and he simply doesn't know it yet." He crossed his arms, his brow lowered in thought.

"You believe Darius has *feelings* for Meredith?" Suzannah asked.

"Yes." They replied in unison. Suzannah's eyes widened.

"Then it is good they will be interviewing a chaperone

soon. Meredith will need protection from the rest of the world, and him as well."

Kit chuckled softly. "Darius is too noble to do anything he shouldn't."

"Temptation is a powerful thing," Suzannah warned. "Sometimes, the more something is forbidden, the more thrilling it is to acquire. I seem to remember you had sworn to destroy me, only to kiss me instead. And that kiss led to *far* more serious things."

Kit's lips parted, but he had no rebuttal. Warren saw the exact second his friend realized his wife was right.

"When are they interviewing a chaperone?" Kit asked her.

"Soon."

"They'd better make it tomorrow," Kit muttered.

The others laughed. Suzannah was right. The temptation of something forbidden, especially one as sweet-natured as Meredith, could be too much for even the saintly Duke of Tiverton.

Warren, for one, was happy to see the oh so perfect Darius finally falling in love.

MEREDITH SIGHED IN RELIEF AS SHE SLIPPED HER FEET INTO A PAIR of cozy mule slippers lined with fur. After dancing the entire night, she was exhausted, and her feet were surprisingly sore from her succession of vigorous dances.

"I brought some warm milk and biscuits," Nell said as

she put down a tray on the little table by Meredith's bed. "I hope it helps you settle down after all the excitement."

"Nell, you are an absolute angel."

"You must tell me all about the ball tomorrow," Nell bargained with a smile.

"Absolutely."

The maid slipped out of the bedchamber, leaving Meredith to nibble on a biscuit and sip her milk before she took up a chair by the window facing the gardens.

It was a quiet night with a lovely cool breeze drifting through the open window, carrying the scents of flowers. Meredith let out a sigh and allowed herself a moment to *be*. She did not think of the ball or the dance with the Prince Regent, however. Instead, her thoughts drifted to Uncle Ben, and how he'd been the one to teach her to enjoy a moment like this.

A soft glow of light in the distance caught Meredith's attention. It was in the Crell house, beyond the garden wall. The light moved into the bedchamber that faced the back of Darius's house. Meredith retrieved her opera glasses and lifted them up, spotting the lamp more clearly.

The person who carried it was Mr. Crell, the tall dark-haired man with silver at his temples. He moved past an empty bed that had been stripped of its sheets. Meredith frowned. Why had the bed been stripped? Where was his wife?

After meeting Mrs. Crell today, Meredith had asked her maid what she knew of the woman. Nell had mentioned that morning that Mrs. Crell usually remained in bed or in a chair most of the time, but could walk on better days with the help of a cane. The staff at Darius's house rarely saw her outside except on nice days.

A sliver of unease pricked at Meredith and she shuddered. It wasn't without an innocent explanation. He could have had his servants washing the linens, and he and his wife were sleeping in a different bedchamber. It was simply hard to believe that the task not been completed by the end of the day.

A hand clasped her shoulder, and Meredith shrieked, leaping to her feet.

"Hush!" The palm covered her mouth and she was pulled back against a hard body. "It's only me." Darius slowly lowered his hand from her mouth and released her.

Meredith whirled around. "Darius! You *frightened* me!" she whispered.

"I apologize. When I knocked, you didn't answer." His blue eyes glowed in the lamplight.

"Oh, I'm so sorry." She glanced back out the window. "I was just..." Her voice trailed off.

Darius joined her. "What were you watching?"

"The Crell house. You have a decent view of some of their rooms, you know." She handed him the opera glasses.

"Spying on the neighbors?" he asked with a laugh. "How scandalous."

"I'm not spying, I'm just curious. I noticed tonight that the sheets have been stripped off the bed in the master bedchamber. I haven't seen Mrs. Crell today either."

A sudden terrible thought struck her, and she clutched

Darius's sleeve as he peered through the glasses at the other house.

"Darius... You don't suppose...she's passed away?"

"It is possible, she was very ill."

"But she looked well enough when I met her today in the gardens."

Darius's gaze softened. "Death can steal upon even the most healthy-looking souls, Meredith. Would you like me for me to have Mr. Chelsea inquire about her health tomorrow?"

"Could you?" Meredith asked.

"I will speak to Chelsea about it tomorrow morning."

Meredith turned her gaze back to the gardens when a new... and far more sinister thought crossed her mind.

"What is it? You've gone very pale suddenly." Darius asked as he handed her back the opera glasses.

"That scream tonight... That perhaps..." Lord, she was being too melodramatic to even think it, let alone say it.

Darius's gaze sharpened. "Perhaps what?"

"That something happened to Mrs. Crell? Nell mentioned that she was an invalid and rarely left her bed or her wheelchair. Now her chamber is empty, and I saw two people struggling in the mews, and I know that scream I heard was no horse. It sounded female."

Please don't think I'm mad.

"You think that something befell Mrs. Crell?"

"Yes," Meredith replied, shivering.

Darius lifted the glasses up again and looked at the house.

"Given the argument we saw the other day, it's fair to say that Crell and his wife do not have the most amiable of relationships. What you saw tonight does give me some doubts," he said. "I shall make inquiries on the morrow. You should go to bed."

Meredith shook her head. "I couldn't possibly sleep," she confessed. "This has all rather upset me."

Darius set the opera glasses down on the chair next to the window. "Come with me. I'll pour you some brandy. That will calm your nerves."

Darius gently took her hand. A heat blossomed in the touch of their palms that made Meredith's chest burst with a matching warmth.

He led her across the hall to his own chamber. It was inappropriate for her to be in his rooms alone with him, but no servants were awake now to see what she was doing.

He went to a drink cabinet and opened it, pulling out a pair of glasses. Then he found a decanter of brandy and poured them each a glass.

"Please sit and drink it." He pointed to a pair of armchairs facing the fireplace which was lit. The soft pop and crackle of the logs was soothing as Meredith eased into the nearest chair, cupping the brandy glass in her hands. Darius sat down in the other chair across from her and they both drank in silence for several minutes. Darius's face grew solemn until he suddenly spoke.

"I wish I had been there... When Uncle Ben passed."

"As do I," she said. "Why did you fall out with him?" She

instantly regretted asking such a private question. But to her surprise, he answered her.

"I was trying to warn him about Harry, that his son was not behaving well in London. Ben grew upset with me, telling me that I was being reckless with my own life, which he was not completely wrong about. We quarreled, and after that, we only exchanged the briefest of letters on occasion. I regret it deeply." Darius's gaze moved from the fire to her. "He was the last of my family, and I wasn't even there. I didn't even know he was ill."

"He didn't want anyone to know, Darius," Meredith said. "He kept telling me and Mrs. Todd that it would be silly to write to anyone. He said would be well again before anyone could arrive." She swallowed the lump in her throat. "I so desperately wanted to believe that, it blinded me from the truth. It is my fault."

Darius threw back the rest of his brandy and scowled at her. "Why? Why do you do that?" he asked gruffly.

"Do what?"

He set his empty brandy glass on the little table by his chair. "Take the blame upon yourself? You do it for almost everything."

"What do you mean? I don't—"

"You do, by God, you do." He stared at her, those penetrating eyes peering deep into her soul. "Why do you believe *you* caused all these problems?"

"I—" Meredith's throat tightened. She didn't want to say it, didn't want to hear what the voice inside her head said when she tried not to listen.

Darius pointed to the floor in front of him. "Come here."

She obeyed, moving out of her chair and standing in front of him in nothing but her dressing gown and slippers.

He reached out, grasping her waist, and pulled her onto his lap so that she sat across his powerful thighs. She should have protested sitting so intimately on his lap, but she didn't. It felt too easy, too natural for her to be right where she was.

"Now, tell me, *why* you punish yourself so?" he demanded in a quiet but forceful tone.

"Because..." Her voice faltered as her hands pressed against his chest. She could feel his heartbeat through the fabric of his shirt. She stared at his face, his lips, and her entire body seemed to melt again. His thighs tightened beneath her as he stared back at her.

They were so close now, so wonderfully close, and her words would ruin this moment. But he deserved to know the truth.

"Because it *is* my fault. If my mother never had a child, she and my father would've been happy."

"Is that what your mother told you?" Darius asked, his voice soft his arms wrapped around her, almost cradling her. His body was so wonderfully warm, and his arms were firm and gentle. Safe, she was always safe with him. How could a man she barely know make her feel that way?

"No, but—"

"Did she ever *imply* that?"

"No, but—"

"You assumed," he guessed. "Your father never would

have left his wife. Men rarely do for their mistresses. The scandal of divorce is usually not worth it. What happened between your parents was never for one instant your fault."

"But Uncle Ben—"

"You cannot possibly take his death on your shoulders, either." Darius's voice deepened, turned rougher. "You are not a burden, Meredith. Not to Uncle Ben, not to me. If anyone ever makes you feel that way, remove them from your circle of acquaintances at once. The world will put every sin and fault upon your pretty shoulders if you let it, and you must resist. They are not your sins, not your faults, so cast them off."

Meredith was spellbound by Darius' words and the earnest gleam in his eyes. She wasn't a burden? Her lip trembled at the thought, and she felt torn between kissing him and weeping.

"You must stop looking at me like that, like I'm some bloody hero because—" he bit off the rest of his words.

She curled her hands in his waistcoat, the silk smooth and rich beneath her fingers. It occurred to her then just how little fabric was between their bodies... "Because?"

Darius's blue eyes darkened. "Because you make me want to be *everything* for you," Darius murmured softly and leaned in, his lips touching hers. The kiss was *almost* chaste.

"You make me want to be everything *for you."*

Darius's words filled her head, making her dizzy with delight while his enchanting kiss had been potent enough to steal her soul. His tongue parted her lips, flicking gently at her own, and she wrapped her arms around his shoulders, clutching him. He made her feel alive, yet safe so long as he held her.

How could she feel so much for this man? Perhaps it was because of all she had been through, and right now she would cling to any source of kindness? No, it had to be something more. Because when Darius touched her, her body burned in secret places, her breath quickened and her heart jolted as though lightning had struck her.

Darius's mouth moved over hers slowly, as if he had a thousand years to take his time kissing her and no other concerns to tear him away. Meredith slid one hand hesitantly into his hair, clutching the strands lightly.

"Meredith," he growled when their mouths finally parted.

She nibbled his bottom lip, wanting the kiss to resume. "Yes?"

"I shouldn't take advantage of you," he said with an adorable uncertainty for a man who was so often so sure of himself.

"You aren't," she assured him. "It's only a kiss." Where this brazen, confident side of her came from, she couldn't be sure. But she knew that this kiss was *everything*. They couldn't stop now, not when it felt so wonderful. If she had her way, she'd never leave his lap.

He leaned his forehead against hers, breathing harder as he closed his eyes. His hands dug into her hips as he held her and she felt a little thrill shoot through her at the thought that he wanted to hold her so desperately.

"Only a kiss..." he echoed. "Quite innocent, really..." His

gaze was a mixture of seductive and sweet. Then his lips were on hers again. Nothing else mattered but the taste of a duke's kiss.

It was some time later before Meredith returned to her bed, exhausted, but happy, her mouth swollen from Darius's attentions. It was only as she lay down, the candles and lamps having been extinguished, that the words of Shakespeare's Romeo and Juliet drifted through her mind.

"Thus with a kiss, I die."

It was *only* a kiss... But Meredith would gladly have died to know the feel of Darius's mouth again. To feel that sense of belonging to him, if only for a few forbidden moments.

7

Meredith and Darius took their lunch in the gardens the following morning, at a table Mr. Chelsea had arranged for them. When the household had heard how Meredith had dined with Darius's uncle in the gardens, they seemed charmed by the idea and took the opportunity to offer it to her.

Meredith had tried to stop the footmen from carrying out a table to the back terrace, something she had always done, but Mr. Chelsea had politely instructed the servants to ignore Meredith's orders and proceed as instructed.

"You are a valued member of this household, Miss Montague and we are pleased to serve you on such occasions," The butler had said with such sincerity that her heart had clenched with a rush of emotions.

Meredith could do nothing but stand there, blushing as she witnessed such a thoughtfulness from people who barely knew her. But it shouldn't have surprised her. They were Darius's staff, and just like him, they were wonderfully kind. She knew of course they were paid to serve Darius and his guests, but they didn't have to be kind or caring, yet they were. She credited that partially to the people themselves, but also because Darius was such a generous employer that he inspired such love and loyalty among his staff.

Darius came up beside her and gave her waist a gentle squeeze that sent butterflies through her belly. He led her out to the table and helped her into her seat, leaning in in to whisper in her ear.

"Never argue with our dear Mr. Chelsea, Meredith. The butler is always right." Darius gave a wink to Mr. Chelsea, who nodded in agreement, but Meredith was convinced she saw Mr. Chelsea's lips twitch with a smile beneath his stoic exterior.

Darius took a seat opposite her at the cozy little table, and they both accepted plates of food from the footmen. "You and Uncle Ben did this often?"

"Yes. It was our tradition when the weather suited." Meredith's face pinkened yet again as she tried to avoid Darius's gaze. She hadn't yet faced him after the endless kisses in his bedchamber last night, and she felt shier than ever. Somehow, being with Darius in the dark, she had been a different woman, a braver woman. He watched her steadily now, his eyes holding a gleam of mischief.

Is he truly not going to mention last night? Very well, she would not mention it either.

"Oh, that reminds me, Chelsea ran into Mr. Dobbs, the

Crell's butler. It seems that the Crells will be relocating to the countryside, somewhere just north of Surrey."

"Was Mrs. Crell well? Was he able to ascertain why the bedroom had been stripped of its sheets? I noticed the room was still empty this morning."

"Yes, as to that, Chelsea was able to learn that Mrs. Crell will be departing soon for the country, in advance of her husband. They've been packing up her things and she is eager to leave and settle in with the new staff."

"Eager? Are you quite sure? She sounded a little reluctant when I spoke to her. She didn't want to be alone in the countryside."

Darius frowned slightly. "That may be true, and it is possible that Dobbs wouldn't want to make his mistress appear unhappy about the move, but she is leaving. He said he was just seen to her breakfast when Mr. Chelsea had passed him on the street. As to the empty bedchamber, it seems that given the marital discord between Louis and Minerva, they have not been sharing a bedchamber in years. Louis sleeps on the opposite side of the house."

Darius did not have to point out to her how rational that explanation was for everything she'd seen, but she couldn't shake the sense that something was still...not right. Perhaps it was just that she knew Mrs. Crell was unhappy and was likely to be more unhappy in the country. There was little Meredith could do for the woman once she left London.

Turning to the butler, she met the man's gaze. "Thank

you so much for inquiring about Mrs. Crell and her health, Mr. Chelsea, I deeply appreciate it."

The butler's eyes softened on her. "Of course, Miss Montague."

She and Darius talked about their plans for the day and how he wanted to take her to Gunter's for a flavored ice soon. Delighted at the thought of spending time with Darius, she eagerly agreed to the plans. They were in the middle of a rather exciting discussion of gothic novels when a footman left the house and stepped out onto the terrace.

Mr. Chelsea received a silver tray from the approaching footman. "A letter has come for you, Miss Montague." He offered the tray to Meredith. She picked up the letter and gasped. It bore the Prince Regent's royal seal.

Darius leaned forward. "Is that what I think it is?"

"I believe it is." Her hands trembled as she broke the seal and read the letter.

Dear Miss Montague,

I hope last night's festivities have left you excited to see more of London. I have made some inquiries regarding the matter we discussed at Lady Hazlitt's ball. Once I have news, you will hear from me at once.

The prince had scrawled his name beneath his message.

"Heavens," said Meredith.

"Good heavens or bad heavens?" Darius asked with a

teasing glint in his blue eyes which were as clear as a summer sky today. She was coming to learn his moods through how the color changed.

"I... I believe *good* heavens." She paused, considering her next words carefully.

"Oh?" Darius sipped his tea, then picked up his newspaper where Mr. Chelsea had thoughtfully set it out for him.

"It seems the Prince of Wales wishes to aid me in my efforts to find a husband."

"What?" Darius, who had been about to peruse his paper, now cast it aside. "Truly?"

"Yes..." Perhaps it hadn't been wise to mention the prince's intentions.

Darius's eyes darkened a little. "While his aid is appreciated, I shall have the final say in who you marry."

The finality in his tone sparked a flare of anger in her. "Shouldn't *I* have the final say?" Meredith straightened her back, eyeing him stiffly. "Seeing as how I shall be trapped with the man, not *you*?"

Darius' eyes darkened, but he didn't appear upset. Rather, she thought she detected a faint appreciation of her defiance. His gaze turned thoughtful. "Do you see marriage as a trap?"

"No, I don't, not exactly, but..." *But marriage to anyone but you would feel like a trap*, she silently added. Out loud, she edited her thoughts. "Any marriage to the wrong person would feel like a trap."

She considered how she'd been sitting up on his lap last

night, kissing him. Now here they were, calmly discussing her marriage to another man. Did he not care at all? Then again, how could he? Men were driven by their desires, and their fates were not tied to marriage the way a woman's was. How could he understand that those kisses meant everything to her if they meant nothing to him?

"On that, we agree." He took another sip of his tea. "What do you seek in a man then?"

"Someone kind... Someone who enjoys learning, a man who would not mind sharing himself with me and letting me share myself with him. I would like to be on an equal footing in my marriage, but..." Her fingertips slid over the note from the prince as she suddenly frowned. "Given the circumstances of my birth, such a thing might not be possible." That simple truth was the source of her deepest misery.

"If it is not, then you shall not marry," Darius declared as if that settled the matter.

Meredith paused in her eating to stare at him. "But...I *must* marry."

"Why? You could accept my support for the remainder of your life."

It took her a moment to realize that he'd just offered her what his cousin Harry had, with possibly the same intentions since she'd been on his lap last night, kissing him. Yet, her heart told her that Darius would never be cruel, never hurt her or force her to do anything, not like Harry would have. Still, her heart sank even lower at realizing this. Even if he did treat her with the utmost respect, that would be all she could hope for. It wasn't as though she and Darius could ever marry, she was too far beneath him in status. It would be a disastrous match, and it could do immeasurable damage to his life.

"Your cousin already offered that to me, how could you even suggest that?" She knew she failed to hide the pain in her tone because he reached for her hand, catching it when she tried to pull away.

"No, sweetheart, not like that. You'd stay as my ward, my responsibility for the remainder of my life. I'd see that you had a trust put in place so that you'd be safe from people like Harry, just as my uncle did."

Even if she did agree to stay with Darius like that, it couldn't be forever. She had a terrible thought. He could not marry someone like her, but he would have to marry someone or else Harry would take his title and his estate. It was a future no one except harry wanted to come to pass.

"And when you marry? You cannot put off the expectations of your position forever. I would no doubt be considered some pitiful creature the future Duchess of Tiverton would despise." She pulled her hand free of his as a pit dropped out in her stomach.

The thought of being a charity case to Darius had become so upsetting that she got up from the table and rushed toward the back gardens, needing a moment to calm herself.

Marriage wasn't important to her. Belonging to someone who loved her was what mattered, but unfortunately that would not be an easy thing to secure, especially when her heart tugged her in the direction of Darius. She did not have the luxury of being a woman of independent means who could afford the consequences of being an unmarried woman who took a lover. She sat on a stone bench against the tall back wall of the gardens and caught her breath. She fisted her hands in her skirts, wrinkling the lovely green gown she wore.

"Meredith?" Darius came down the path to join her, looking far too handsome in his cream trousers and his blue waistcoat. Why did he have to be so tempting? She noticed how the noonday sun played with the strands of his dark hair, making them look almost purple. She knotted her fingers in her skirts, feeling suddenly very young and silly in a way she hadn't in years. And the way he looked at her...as though she was precious, as though he didn't want to let her out of his sight, made that ache in her heart deepen to the purest part of her very soul.

She wanted to run to him, bury her face against his chest and be held by him. But he wasn't hers to touch, wasn't hers to hold or kiss. What they'd shared last night was a dream, a life she had only a moment to taste before she had to wake up.

"Meredith," Darius sat down beside her on the bench, angling his body towards her, their knees brushing. He took one of her hands in his, his face solemn. Those blue eyes of his were troubled waters now, dark and churning.

"I never meant to imply that you would be cared for out of pity. Blast, I am making a mess of this." He bent his head so that their faces were almost touching, and his dark lashes fanned down briefly before he lifted his gaze again to hers. "You are not and never will be a burden or an object of pity to me. You are like family, though I've only known you for a few days. I wish to take care of you. Please let me do that."

It would be so easy to say yes, to let herself believe that she could belong here with him. That she could truly belong to him in the way that she wanted to from the moment she first met him. But that wasn't what he was offering her. He was offering her nothing more than what Uncle Ben had given her, a safe place to be stay, a roof over her head, clothes and food. He wasn't offering love, or that deeper sense of connection that came from the most secret parts of one's heart. And the longer she stayed with him, the more she would want that connection...that *love* from him. Because it was simply impossible not to fall in love with a man like Darius.

"Darius, I cannot—" she began in a whisper, but the sound of a voice nearby choked her into silence.

"Ahh, there you are, sir. I am ready to make the final preparations." A man spoke from the other side of the garden wall. It was clear from the sound of his voice, the man was closer to the Crell's house and was walking towards the direction of the garden wall where Darius and Meredith were standing on just the other side.

"You've seen to what I've asked?" Another male voice asked. "Just as I've set it out for you?"

"Yes sir...your things are ready to be taken to the hired coach when you are ready to depart," Dobbs replied.

"You've made sure to pack *everything*?" the second voice snapped.

"Yes...even those other items. It will be dealt with as you've requested." Dobbs sounded offended at who she guessed was Mr. Crell, when he challenged the butler's performance.

"Once I've settled there, I won't be back for a good long while. Close the house by the end of the week and I shall make plans to sell it. Once you've completed that, you may join me."

Darius held a finger up to his lips, indicating for them to remain silent. He crept carefully down the wall toward where the heart- shaped window had been left open in the stones. Darius positioned himself to peer through the window without being seen by the two men on the other side of the wall. Meredith moved to join him. She clutched his arm, curling her fingers around it as her heart jumped against her ribs.

"And the jewelry, sir?" Dobbs seemed to hesitate to say more.

"Bury them until it's safe to sell them."

The other man, Dobbs, mumbled some reply. The sound of boots on gravel grew distant as the men on the other side of the wall walked away.

Darius ducked away from the heart-shaped window in the wall, his lips curving down in a frown as he looked at her.

"That was Mr. Crell and his butler."

"Did you see Mrs. Crell?" Meredith stood close beside

him as he gently caught her by the waist, holding her still as he peered through the window again before ducking back.

"No, I see no sign of Mrs. Crell. She must be inside ready to leave with him."

"I truly hope that she is well. Why would he tell his butler to bury jewelry in the garden and then sell it?" That sounded sinister to her.

"I don't know," Darius replied. "Mr. Chelsea might be able to learn more. He and Dobbs have talked on occasion on matters regarding the shared stables. I'm sure he can devise some way to run into the man again."

"Darius, I can't forget that scream I heard," she confessed. "And now Mrs. Crell's jewelry is being buried in the garden..." She reached up to grasp his shoulders.

"It could be someone else's jewelry..." Darius suggested but by his tone she knew he didn't believe it either.

"There is no logical reason to bury jewelry in the garden," she pointed out. "Not unless you are desperate to hide something."

"I agree." With a tender hand, he brushed his knuckles over her cheek. "I know something doesn't feel right. We will continue to look into this. I promise."

His hands still lingered around her waist and she waited a moment too long to let go of his shoulders as they stared at one another, but neither of them said anything.

Darius cleared his throat. "Come and finish lunch. Then we must prepare for an afternoon of gentlemen callers." Darius didn't sound all that pleased by the notion.

That brought her out of her thoughts about the mystery at the Crell house and thinking again of her uncertain future and what she truly wanted. She felt something crinkle in the pocket of her dress and realized she still had the letter from the prince who was willing to help her win Darius as a husband. If the prince believed she could have him, then shouldn't she have more faith in herself?

"You could send them away," Meredith suggested in a quiet tone. It was entirely too bold, but she had to find a way to let him know what she wanted without making a fool of herself.

"Your callers? I wouldn't dare," Darius said. "You said you would be here this afternoon, and I shan't let you lose the opportunity to meet any man you might like." He choked a little bit on the word 'like.'

One she liked... not loved. She doubted that Darius had noted the distinction.

Meredith held her emotions in check this time as she allowed Darius to escort her back to the table to finish their meal. She wished he would have agreed to chase away her callers. She didn't want to entertain anyone today, though that was the entire reason she'd come to London.

The thought left a deep pit form in her stomach, and she dreaded entertaining those she might *like*, while under the heated gaze of the only one she truly wanted.

"MR. WARREN BURVILLE," MR. CHELSEA ANNOUNCED AS HE stepped into the drawing room. Darius and Meredith stood to greet their first guest. "To see Miss Montague," Chelsea added with an wry expression.

Darius blinked. Warren was here to see Meredith, not him? The man had to be teasing him, surely. He'd known Warren most of his life and the man had never shown the slightest interest in *courting*. Now he was here to see Meredith, a woman who only last night was on Daruis's lap, kissing him. He didn't know what to think of that, other than he had the sudden urge to throw a punch straight at the man's face.

"What the bloody hell are you doing here?" Darius asked as Warren walked past Mr. Chelsea. His friend held an enormous bouquet of flowers and wore a honey-colored waistcoat that perfectly matched Meredith's eyes. It was a waistcoat that Darius had rarely seen him wear.

"Come to see the show, old boy," Warren replied. A smirk flashed across his face before he politely bowed to Meredith and offered her the large bouquet. It was a blend of red and pink roses along with some daisies. Darius arched her brow at his friend as Meredith buried her face in the soft petals to take in their scent.

Darius, like any decent gentleman, had an understanding of the language of flowers and believed that sending a message of passion and love along with innocence was entirely inappropriate for a young woman that a man had no real interest in.

"Passionate love?" Darius gripped Warren's shoulder as

Meredith handed the flowers to Mr. Chelsea to put in a vase.

Warren's green eyes sparkled with mischief. "You think Miss Montague is not worth passionate love? Damn me, Darius, you must be blind." He watched Meredith speak to the butler, his eyes alight with sensual interest.

"Of course she is worthy of passionate love. That's not the point. You are not the type to court a woman."

"Who says I'm not?" Warren asked with a raised chin.

Darius glared at him, calling his bluff. "What the devil are you playing at?" He continued to speak in hushed tones so that Meredith would not hear them argue.

Warren shot him a look as if he were a half-wit. "You really don't know?"

Darius's hands fisted at his sides. "Clearly, I don't. Perhaps you ought to enlighten me, Warren." He drawled the last few words darkly, which had no effect on his friend whatsoever. If Warren didn't explain himself soon, he was going to be tossed out on his ear in two seconds.

With a dramatic sigh, Warren waved a hand at Meredith and the drawing room around them. "You are about to be descended upon by dozens of young bucks vying for Miss Montague's attention. Only the bravest will remain here if they see me and my vase of flowers. Only the boldest will dare face me in a battle of courtship."

"But you don't mean to...?"

Rather than reply to Darius's unfinished question, Warren spotted a tray of teacakes that the cook had prepared and marched over to the refreshment table as

Meredith returned. It left Darius standing there, muttering to himself, wondering why he couldn't understand what was happening in his own bloody house.

Warren wasn't going to court Meredith. Warren was the sort of man who had a lady in every village or city in England who was ready to take him to bed without any expectations whatsoever. He was not a man to fall in love, not in the way that would see him leg-shackled. Yet here he was, bringing flowers to Meredith like a lovestruck lad.

"Thank you so much for the flowers, Warren. They are lovely." Meredith poured him a cup of tea.

"*Warren*, is it?" Darius muttered in a mocking tone as Warren sat on the settee with Meredith. Darius was *not* going to let Warren sit that close to his ward. Darius came and wedged himself between the two. Warren let out an *oof* as Darius squished Warren and Meredith against the sides of the settee.

Warren shot a dark look at Darius. "Well... This is unexpectedly *cozy*."

"Darius, perhaps you could see how Mr. Chelsea is coming along with that vase?" Meredith asked in an equally strained voice.

"No," he said. "As your guardian, I must remain in his room with you while—"

"*Fine*. I will do it." Meredith tried to extricate herself from the settee. "Darius, you're sitting on my gown—oh!" She fell onto Darius's lap, then twisted when he half tried to stand, causing her to be tossed straight into Warren's waiting arms.

"Well, who knew I'd be lucky enough to have the lady throw herself at me? Perhaps I should take up courting? I seem to be bloody brilliant at it," Warren chuckled as he helped Meredith stand up. She gave Darius a furious glare, her face as pink as the roses Warren had brought and huffed so hard that a loose tendril of her hair flew skyward before falling back against her cheek. She nearly ran from the room without a backward glance.

"Just what do you think you are doing?" Darius demanded as Warren took another bite of his teacake seemingly unruffled. The bastard actually grinned at him.

"I am making my courtship look convincing. What else?" Warren said.

"That is entirely unnecessary," Darius informed them.

"Isn't it though?"

"There are no suitors here yet for you to impress," Darius pointed out, holding his arms out to encompass the now empty room.

"Well, I am new to this. Practice was required." Warren retrieved his plate and finished off his teacake before eyeing the refreshment table again. "I thought you wanted to marry the girl off? And since you won't marry her yourself, I thought you'd need help in the matter."

Darius got up from the settee, scowling. The idea of anyone marrying Meredith put him in the foulest of moods. He couldn't marry Meredith, but he did wish she could stay with him, and continue as they were now. Shared kisses in the dark, quiet drinks by the fire, morning breakfasts on the back terrace. Deep down he knew that continuing as they'd done so far wouldn't be enough. He wanted more when it came to her, and that was exactly the problem because he *couldn't* have more.

He wished like hell that she didn't need to get married. But her words from this morning still echoed in his mind. It was unlikely any future Duchess of Tiverton would understand his financial support of a young, beautiful woman who wasn't blood related.

The memory of last night's kisses was still present in his mind. He shouldn't have kissed her, but she had needed comfort and sometimes comfort came in the form of kisses. He hadn't taken advantage of her, hadn't done anything to ruin her, at least in his opinion. It was only a few kisses; she had said so herself last night. And those kisses had been like something out of his dreams. Her lips had been soft, supple, her weight upon his lap perfect. He'd wanted to hold her forever and explore the mysteries of her sweet mouth.

"Even you cannot have it both ways," Warren said, pulling Darius away from his thoughts. "She must marry, as must you at some point. You can't let that bounder Harry inherit your title or your fortune. Can you imagine him moving into Knightley Street? The rest of us would kill him."

Warren was right. He couldn't let Harry inherit everything, but the idea of marrying just anyone always seemed wrong. His parents had been a love match, and he had wanted that kind of love for himself, even if it meant searching the world for it.

When Meredith returned with the vase of flowers,

Darius rose from the settee to take it from her. Their fingers brushed on the porcelain basin, and her soft hazel eyes met his.

"Please be kind to Warren. He has been very sweet to me," she whispered. "Besides, what if no one comes today? I would be terribly embarrassed. But with Warren here, I won't be…"

He knew what she hadn't said. She wouldn't be so *ashamed*.

Darius held her gaze, gentling his voice. "If no one comes today, it will be because they fear *me*."

"And rightly so!" Warren added, then looked away before Darius could glare at him.

Mr. Chelsea entered the room and cleared his throat. "Miss Montague, you have three visitors. Mr. Evers, Mr. Toleman and Mr. Brandywine."

"Ah, our first victims," said Warren.

"*Hush*," snapped Darius.

A light of excitement mingled with relief filled Meredith's eyes. He was happy to see that crushed look gone from her, but the moment she looked away, he was scowling again. More men in his drawing room to see her…to talk to her, to make her laugh, to court her…in all the ways he couldn't.

Bloody hell…

Meredith turned away from Darius, as regal as a princess. "Please show them in."

He was left holding the vase as she went to greet the three men. They were close to Darius's age, and he recalled them having danced with Meredith last night. Something Darius hadn't been able to do because he'd given his one and only dance away to the prince.

He hastily set the vase on the table only to have Meredith hand him another batch of flowers from Mr. Evers. When Darius started to turn away, Meredith called him back, and proceeded to hand him two more bouquets from Mr. Brandywine and Mr. Toleman. These were thick with towering blooms that nearly blinded him as he tried to see over the tops of the flowers. He was supposed to be putting these gentleman callers through their paces and questioning them about their intentions. Instead, he was juggling what seemed to be every flower from the hothouses of London.

"Chelsea?" he called out. "Help!" His muffled cry barely escaped the towering roses.

Thankfully, his butler heard him and hastily arrived to collect the bouquets from him.

"Thank you." He tugged on the bottom of his waistcoat and finally went to join the three other men.

Warren resumed his strategic location on the settee, eating a cucumber sandwich and grinning at Darius. He raised his cup of tea in a little salute. Darius tried to erase his frown as he faced Meredith's callers.

"Gentlemen," Darius greeted them, shaking their hands.

He did his best not to interfere with Meredith as she poured everyone tea and saw to the refreshments. Warren had eaten his third helping of teacakes and had turned his attention to the cucumber sandwiches, clearly unbothered by the new arrivals. It was hard for Darius to force himself to smile and be congenial whenever he glimpsed Meredith smiling or laughing at something one of gentlemen said. It wasn't because he didn't want her to smile or laugh. On the contrary, her laughter always took his breath away, but *he* wanted to be the one causing her such moments of joy. Right now he felt like some fool that was merely hovering on the edges of her beautiful world, unable to touch her, to bask in her light.

Meredith's green and white gown trimmed with small gold tassels was bewitching in the way it displayed her exquisite curves. Every man in the room was focused raptly on the young lady. Determined to distract himself, Darius caught Warren's eye and indicated his friend should come over to him with a subtle jerk of his head. Once he and Warren were a ways off, Warren cast a glance back at the small crowd.

"You know, I believe Evers might be a fine chap."

"What?" Darius asked.

"Jordan Evers. Always liked the fellow," Warren explained. "Good taste in horses, reads a fair amount, and he possesses a decent townhouse and fortune. He's always been a solid man when it comes to the ladies. Meredith would do well with him."

"Oh, right," Darius shot Meredith's suitor a look before giving himself a shake to focus. "No, it's not that. I have something I could use your help with."

"Not suitor related?" Warren grinned.

"No. Something more worrisome."

"Something more worrisome than three chaps fawning over our Miss Montague right under your nose?" Warren teased.

Darius was at a loss as to how to respond because he certainly didn't want anyone man fawning over Meredith. But what he wanted to talk about would help Meredith, because he couldn't get that worried look in her eyes out of his mind.

"Please, Warren, it's a serious matter. One that has greatly distressed Meredith and I believe you can help put her mind at ease."

Warren sobered at Darius's tone. "What do you need help with?"

"Mr. Crell, my neighbor directly behind this house is bound for the country today. Could you follow him and see if his wife, Mrs. Crell, travels with him or whether he meets her at his country house?"

"I certainly can, but why?"

Darius bit his lip, his voice softening further. "Last night, before leaving for the ball, Meredith heard a scream while she waited for me in my coach. She believes she saw someone in the mews next to my stables struggling with another person. I was fetching my cane and didn't hear it. Then Meredith noticed that the master bedchamber had been completely emptied at the Crell house, even the linens had been stripped and the wardrobes emptied of every bit of clothing. Chelsea spoke with the Crells' butler and was told that Mrs. Crell and Mr. Crell are moving to the country and that she is feeling better, but the woman is a known invalid, and has been for years. Meredith fears that Crell has done something to his wife. I told her of course that it could be as simple as the husband and wife sleeping in different rooms, and they've already packed up Mrs. Crell for the move, but still...something about this entire situation leaves me unsettled."

"I'll be happy to investigate, old boy," Warren said without hesitation.

"You had better go now and see what you find out. Trail him as far as you are able without being noticed."

"Wait, you aren't only saying this to get rid of me, are you?"

"I assure you, that is simply a happy coincidence," said Darius with a straight face.

Warren nodded and excused himself from the room, but not before bowing over Meredith and making a show to the other three men around her as he kissed her hand, making her blush.

The girl blushed too often for Darius's liking. She was so damned innocent. And Warren was right. His attentiveness to Meredith had only made the three suitors even more enamored with Meredith. It was going to be a bloody long afternoon.

8

Meredith was exhausted by the time the last of her callers left, of which there had been seven by the time the morning calls were over. She slumped down on the settee in the drawing room, heaving a sigh. Even when Darius re-entered the drawing room, having just seen the last of the men out, she didn't move from her spot.

"I didn't realize these calls would be this exhausting," she confessed as he spotted her. "You don't often call on ladies like this?"

He laughed. "Christ no. But I've never pursued anyone with the intent of marriage. I thought they would never leave. Then again, you were terribly entertaining to be around." Darius came over to where she lay lengthwise on the settee. "Mind if I join you?"

"Not at all. I'm afraid I can't move...simply too tired," she stifled a yawn.

"Not to worry." Darius bent, gently moving Meredith's legs so he could sit next to her, then placed her legs across his lap, allowing her to continue her repose. His head fell back on the settee, and his hands rested lightly on her shins.

It was an entirely inappropriate position for them, but it was undeniably comfortable and Meredith had no desire to move. Darius stretched his legs out and crossed them at the ankles before he closed his eyes. Meredith wondered if perhaps he was already asleep, but then he spoke.

"Mrs. Petersham will be here in an hour for her interview. Suzannah won't be able to attend, she has a prior engagement."

Darius stroked her shins with his fingertips. Her skirts were pulled down, covering her body, but she could feel the little caress, sweet and soothing through her petticoats and the dress itself. She should pull away, but she couldn't muster the will or desire.

Meredith yawned. "Could I rest until she arrives? If I had but a short time, I'm sure I could recover myself."

"Yes, that's a splendid idea." Darius yawned as well. "We'll just rest... here..."

And that was how Mr. Chelsea found them an hour later, both fast asleep. Meredith came awake at a gentle touch on her shoulder, and she realized she and Darius were still on the couch, her legs in his lap. Her face flamed as she realized how it must look to the butler to see them sleeping like this. In any other situation, it would have ruined her completely to be discovered alone with him like this, their bodies partially entwined, but in the sanctuary of Darius's home, it was only embarrassing.

Darius stirred. "What time is it?" He groaned as he sat up.

"Half past four, Your Grace," said Mr. Chelsea. "Mrs. Petersham is waiting in the hall. I thought it wise to give you a few minutes to collect yourselves." The butler's head nodded toward Meredith's legs on Darius's lap.

"Oh... Oh yes!" Meredith pulled her legs away and stood, rushing to the gilded mirror hanging on one wall to fix her hair and smooth out the wrinkles in her dress. Darius, blast the man, had no need to fix anything about himself. He simply stood and nodded once they were ready.

"Send her in, Chelsea."

Meredith stood at Darius's side so they could face her potential chaperone together, a hoard of butterflies taking flight in her stomach. Mr. Chelsea opened the door and announced Mrs. Petersham.

A middle-aged woman with auburn hair and pale blue eyes swept into the room. Her promenade gown was a rich bishop's blue, covered with a dark gold military-style spencer. She didn't look at all like what Meredith expected. She looked friendly, even warm, and Meredith developed an instant liking for the woman. She hoped her instincts were true and that this woman would work well as her chaperone.

"Mrs. Petersham." Darius stepped forward and bowed. "I am Darius St. John, the Duke Tiverton. This is my ward, Miss Meredith Montague."

Mrs. Petersham gave Meredith a warm smile, and her gaze turned respectfully back to Darius. She did not look matronly, and for that, Meredith was glad.

"Thank you, Your Grace. You may call me Frances if you like."

"Would you like some tea, Frances?" Meredith asked.

"Yes, thank you."

Darius showed her to a seat by the tea table. "Thank you for responding to our inquiry." He waited for Meredith to finish pouring tea, and then sat down.

"Of course. I am most curious to hear about what brings you to need a chaperone."

Meredith exchanged a glance with Darius, and he nodded at her. So she told Frances the tale of her upbringing, all the way to the events after Uncle Ben's death.

Frances sipped her tea and listened politely until she had finished. "So marriage is the desire?"

"Yes," Meredith said.

"To a kind, good and decent man, of course," Daruis added. "We will be attending the theater, balls and dinners and other social engagements. Would you be willing to accompany us on these outings so that no one can raise concerns about Meredith's reputation?"

"Of course," Frances assured him.

"Wonderful. Now, about your salary..." Darius offered Frances an amount that made Meredith's eyes widen.

"Oh no, that much won't be necessary. I will insist on taking twenty percent less than that. My husband, Mr. Petersham, left me well off. I don't wish to waste away of boredom in my widow's weeds or lose myself in grief. My husband, Daniel, would not have wanted that." Frances's gaze softened as she spoke about her late husband.

"I understand," Darius said. "Would you be able to move in this evening? We shall be dining here with a few of my friends, if you would like to join us."

"If you could send a coach for my things, I could be back in time for dinner."

"Mr. Chelsea will arrange that for you," Darius said. "I shall speak to him now."

When Darius left them alone, Frances reached out and patted Meredith's hand.

"You need not be shy, dear," Frances said with a twinkle in her eye. "I came from circumstances much like yours. I was the natural daughter of no one knows who and worked as a seamstress for nearly ten years. Then Daniel Petersham found me working in a shop in Cornwall and swept me off my feet. The next thing I know we'd married and moved to London."

"Thank you, Frances." Meredith relaxed. "London has been quite a change for me. I fear I'm still adjusting to it."

"I felt much the same when I first moved here. But do not worry, you are young and the city has so much to offer."

"Well, you should have nothing to fear. The duke is a fine guardian to have. I asked about him when I received his reply to my advertisement. Only good things were spoken in regard to him."

"Oh yes, Darius is a fine man, a *wonderful* man," she agreed.

"Then do not worry. We shall find you the perfect husband. Now, tell me, what are you reading lately? I was thinking we could visit a few circulating libraries this week if that would suit you? That way we could see a bit of the city, which would allow you to feel more at home here."

"Oh, that would be more than lovely." As she and Frances spoke of their mutual love of books over tea, Meredith knew she had found a new friend in her chaperone.

WARREN CHECKED THE TIME ON HIS POCKET WATCH AS HE lingered just inside the doorway of a coaching inn an hour outside of London. The taproom of the inn was filled with travelers, and the courtyard was crowded with coaches. Warren had trailed Mr. Crell from his townhouse that afternoon to this inn on horseback. So far, the man had been alone, and had spoken to no one other than the innkeeper. There was no sign of traveling with his wife which meant Warren was in for a wait and possibly another day of tailing Crell to his country house to see if his wife arrived there or was perhaps even already there waiting on Crell.

The fellow, Crell, now sat in a chair finishing his supper. Warren was bored. Why the devil had Darius sent him on such a mission? The man wasn't doing anything the least bit interesting. Wouldn't a man who might have possibly harmed his wife be looking more...guilty or at the least furtive?

Suddenly, Crell checked the time on the clock by the fireplace at the far end of the taproom and stood up. A new crowd of people flowed into the taproom as several coaches stopped outside. Crell searched the newcomers with clear interest. Warren straightened slightly, his vision sharpening on the latest arrivals to the inn.

A woman in a dark blue carriage dress and a large poke bonnet that somewhat shielded her face was amongst the latest passengers to enter with a servant on her heels. The moment Crell spotted her, Crell came toward the woman and held out his arms. He embraced the woman and led her upstairs after he spoke with the footman that had been traveling with her.

Warren cocked his head, watching the two climb the rickety set of stairs. Wasn't Mrs. Crell supposed to be an invalid? She certainly wasn't having any difficulty with the stairs. If anything, that woman had a spring to her steps.

The servant went back outside. Warren casually followed him, as though he was in need of a bit of fresh air.

Warren smiled politely at the footman. "Long day ahead for you?"

"Oh yes. Another two hours by coach tomorrow," the man said as he retrieved a trunk from the back of the coach. "And this bloody trunk hasn't made the job easy

"Let me help you." Warren grabbed the other handle of the trunk and helped the footman carry it to a storage area for the night. It did weigh rather heavy.

"Your master packing stones in this?" Warren teased.

"I have no idea. I do not know the man well. I've only

been hired for this journey and then I'm to return to London."

"Ahh," Warren replied, trying to keep his tone nonchalant.

"What about you?" the man asked as they headed back to the taproom.

"Oh, I'll be headed back to London in an hour," Warren said with a grin. He had what he'd come to find. A source of information. "Care for a drink? My treat, old boy."

The young man nodded eagerly and Warren guided him to a table inside before he waved down a bar wench.

"Shall we drink to the end of a long journey?" he asked as they knocked their pints of ale together in a toast.

The footman grinned, eager to enjoy his free ale. "To the end of long journeys."

Warren sat back in his chair, sipping his ale, waiting for the right moment to ask the man a few questions. He would get his chance soon enough.

Mrs. Petersham was perfect. Darius couldn't be more pleased with her as a chaperone. Rather than some fire-breathing dowager dragon, she was an amusing breath of companionable fresh air. Most importantly, she seemed to put Meredith at ease. At dinner, Mrs. Petersham had drawn out Meredith's smiles and conversation, making the young woman sparkle in front of his friends.

The only problem was that his friends, who had joined

them for dinner, were all now quite drawn to Meredith, providing Mrs. Petersham with her first true challenge.

Felix sat beside Meredith and seemed to be captivated by every little thing she said. Darius sat at the head of the table and could not miss the attention his friends were paying to his ward. He wasn't happy with that, even though he should be... Was it because Meredith wasn't his to claim in front of his friends? And that meant any of them had a chance to win her away? The thought made his stomach clench.

"Darius," Suzannah murmured next to him. He managed to tear his gaze away from Meredith.

"Yes?"

"Do you think Felix may be taken with Meredith?" They leaned closer to talk, staring at the pair in conversation. Darius didn't answer but merely grunted.

"I think she could be a rather lovely wife for a marquess," Suzannah said thoughtfully, as if his grunt had been a sufficient answer to continue the conversation.

"I did not have you set as a matchmaker, my little artist," Kit teased his wife, having eavesdropped on their whispered conversation.

Darius took a long draw from his wineglass. He did not want to imagine Meredith and Felix together, not like that. Felix was always ready to run off on any adventure. He was not the sort of man to settle down and enjoy quiet breakfasts on the back terrace or sip brandy in the evenings by the fire and read in companionable silence. No, Felix and Meredith simply wouldn't suit each other.

"Felix is too wild for her," Darius said to Suzannah. "And Kit is right, you do not strike me as a matchmaker."

"No," Suzannah agreed with a solemn look. "But Meredith needs a good match, and as her new friend, I want to see this accomplished."

Darius did adore Suzannah's fierce loyalty, but the thought of Meredith marrying and leaving soon left him restless. She didn't have to marry so quickly, did she? Surely she could take a year before she had to decide.

It was a myth that women needed to marry so young, after all. Many ladies of his acquaintance waited until they were twenty-three or twenty-four before choosing a husband. Silly fears of becoming spinsters aside, most women smartly gave themselves a few years to experience life before tying themselves to a husband. Meredith deserved the same. *He* certainly wouldn't force her to choose quickly... or at all if fate would allow it.

It's not as though I have a claim to her...he admitted to himself silently.

A few stolen kisses, a few moments of joy ... That was all he could have, and he shouldn't even have had that.

"Promise you will not rush her in making a decision," Darius said to Suzannah. "She's bound to match poorly if she chooses in haste."

"I won't. Of course I won't," Suzannah assured him. Tactfully changing the subject, she said, "Mrs. Petersham seems quite lovely. I think we did rather well."

"I agree. Meredith seems to blossom around her."

Kit chuckled as he cut into his roast duck. "Blossom?"

Heat suffused Darius's face. "You know what I mean. The woman seems to put Meredith at ease, and she's come out of her shyness a bit as a result."

From further down the table, Lionel asked, "I say, Darius, where's Warren?"

"He is seeing to a personal matter for me."

Lionel arched a brow. "What sort of personal matter?" Clearly, the word private did not apply to his friends. But he trusted them with most everything.

"Well, he—"

He was interrupted as Mr. Chelsea stepped into the dining room. "Mr. Burville has arrived, Your Grace."

Vincent chuckled. "Speak of the devil, and he shall appear."

"Does he wish to join us for dinner?" Darius asked.

"I believe so." Chelsea replied.

"Show him in when he's ready," Darius replied.

"Well, this is all very mysterious," Vincent mused as he and the others waited for Warren to join them.

A minute or so later, Warren entered the dining room. He made a hasty apology for his attire. It was clear that he had been riding and hadn't had time to change. Warren glanced around at everyone before he took a seat at the table.

"Well? What did you find out?" Darius prompted.

Warren took a long drink of wine before he spoke, and Darius stared at him growing a little impatient.

Finally, Warren spoke. "Crell traveled alone to a coaching inn about an hour outside of London. He met a woman there, I thought was Mrs. Crell. I thought you said the woman was an invalid?"

"She is. She can walk, but prefers to use an invalid chair," said Darius.

A dinner plate was placed in front of Warren. "Well, this woman did not look the least bit unwell and used no chair, nor did she seem to travel with one. She climbed the stairs without difficulty. I discreetly questioned a footman who traveled with this woman. She also came from London, but obviously not with Mr. Crell. They did plan to travel on together to a little house in the country about two hours away tomorrow."

"Who is this Crell fellow?" Vincent asked. "Name sounds familiar."

Darius could feel Meredith's gaze on him. "He is the neighbor directly behind me."

"And why are we having Warren follow your neighbor?" Lionel asked.

It amused Darius to hear Lionel say *we* as though what one man in their circle of friends was doing they were all involved in. And that was certainly true. They were often tangled up in one another's lives.

"There is a concern that something is amiss in my neighbor's household," Darius said diplomatically. "There is some concern for the welfare of his wife, Mrs. Crell."

"Wouldn't you want to address this matter with the Bow Street Runners?" Vincent asked. "Aren't they supposed to look into such matters?"

Darius nodded. "And I have every intention of

contacting Mr. Doyle of the Runners, once I have more information and possibly some proof that something has in fact happened in that house."

"Ahh, because once you set Doyle on it, Crell will likely be questioned, and he'll know someone that lives close to him suspects him of something."

"Yes, that's it exactly," Darius said. "We are the only house that has a good view into his back gardens and a few rooms of his house."

"I believe you'd better tell us the whole story then," said Lionel.

Seeing as how they were all people he trusted, and with a barely perceptible nod from Meredith, he recounted what Meredith had seen and heard in the mews, how they both witnessed the empty bedchamber, and heard Crell's orders to close the house, and bury some jewelry.

"It sounds as though the man truly has done something to his wife," Mrs. Petersham replied. "No woman would part with her jewelry, ill or not." Her bluntness quieted the table.

"Yes," said Meredith. "That is what I fear as well."

"The problem is, so far everything seems to have a possibly reasonable explanation. I don't want to bother the authorities with this until I have proof something terrible has in fact happened in that house." He also didn't want to prove his uncle right and do something foolish. He had more to lose now that Meredith was his ward. If he died, Harry would move into this house and Meredith would be utterly at his cousin's mercy again. He could not allow such a thing to happen.

"I see," said Felix. "Is there anything we can do to assist you?"

"Not at this moment," Darius said. "But if that changes, I shall tell you, of course."

Meredith spoke up. "Warren, might I ask what the woman that Mr. Crell met with looked like?" Her shyness had vanished now that she was fixated on the mystery.

Warren played with the stem of his wineglass. "I'm afraid she wore one of those ridiculous poke bonnets. Couldn't get a decent look at her face, but I glimpsed dark hair when she passed by me."

"Dark hair? You're sure?" Meredith pressed.

"Yes. I saw her face only briefly, but I do know that her hair was quite dark."

"And her figure? Was she slender or fuller?"

"Slender? No, she was quite gifted with curves. Why do you ask?"

"Because Mr. Crell's wife possessed pale blonde hair, and her figure was very slender."

"Oh dear," Mrs. Petersham said.

A chill trespassed along Darius's spine. He deeply hoped that Warren's research into the matter would be the end of this. But it seemed to only raise more questions.

"So it seems at the very least, Crell is involved with a mistress," Warren concluded. "But that doesn't necessarily mean he's done away with his wife. Dash it, I wish I'd stayed at the fellow's house longer to see if I saw a second woman, but I thought that the woman I'd seen was the one you were looking for."

"I see why you want to get to the bottom of this," said Lionel. He drummed his fingertips lightly on the table as if thinking everything through.

"Never a dull moment at Darius's house," Vincent chuckled.

Warren, unbothered by the fact that he had just trailed a possible murderer for most of the evening, tucked into his dinner. Darius met Meredith's concerned gaze. Was she right? Had her fears for Mrs. Crell's safety been justified? It seemed Darius was going to have to find proof of something to take his friend Doyle at the Bow Street Runners.

"Well, it certainly won't be dull with those gentlemen around," Frances told Meredith as they climbed the stairs after dinner. Suzannah and Kit had gone home for the night, but Darius and his remaining friends were in the billiard room, smoking cigars and drinking brandy. The sound of warm, masculine laughter coming from below blended with the sweet scent of their cigars. It was strangely comforting.

"I suppose it won't. I do like them all immensely," Meredith confessed.

Frances chuckled. "I can understand that, my dear. They are very handsome and intelligent, and they seem like the *right* sort of trouble."

"The right sort of trouble?" Meredith stifled a giggle, which made Frances laugh. It was a wonderful sound, as though Frances was used to laughing often. Meredith liked that about her. Frances wasn't afraid to live and take up space in the world. It was the way Meredith wanted to live someday.

"Oh yes, certainly trouble. But *splendid* trouble, the sort that brings out parts of us we might otherwise keep hidden. Mr. Petersham was very much like Mr. Wyndham, quiet but undeniably charming. It's hard for a woman to resist a man like that. Seeing Mr. Wyndham brings back memories of my husband."

"Do you miss him?"

Frances paused at the top of the stairs, her gaze growing distant. "With all my soul. But that's the strange thing about grief. Our hearts keep healing and growing even after the reason for living has gone. Human hearts are quite stubborn things, you see."

Meredith gently squeezed Frances's hand. The woman patted her fingertips.

"Someday you will feel that you have grown around the grief you feel from losing your uncle. That pain will feel less because you've added more new joy to your life. But you must work at it every day in order for that moment to come."

Meredith thought of Darius and the joy that he gave her, the quiet rush of excitement she felt when she first saw him in the morning, the flashes of exquisite heat whenever his hands touched her. And then there was his kisses...those created infinite feelings of joy that defied measurement.

Frances hesitated. "Which reminds me... I believe we should speak privately." She led Meredith into her bedchamber and made sure no servants were lingering before she closed the door. She grasped Meredith's hands in hers. "I've noticed that you seem drawn to Lord Tiverton. Are you in love with him?"

"I barely know him," Meredith said perhaps a bit too quickly. "We are strangers—"

"Lightning can strike between strangers," Frances said in a knowing, but gentle voice. "Tell me truthfully, child. If you could have anyone as your husband, would you choose him?"

Meredith didn't answer right away. There was something in the way Frances had mentioned lightning striking between strangers. It wasn't that she'd loved Darius at first sight, no, but she'd sensed that he could become the greatest love of her life, if she dared to let it happen. And the more time she spent with him, the more certain she was of that future. It was strange. She had lived a life not knowing she could ever find someone like him, yet she had. She knew too well that she would never get to truly have him.

She searched her heart for a long moment before she answered with a nod.

Frances's face softened. "Very well. Then we will work to make that happen for you."

"But what if he doesn't feel the same about me? If he married me, society would punish him dearly for it. The nature of my birth is too much of a scandal for a duke." It was terrifying to admit these fears aloud, but Frances needed to understand where she was coming from.

Someone like her could only hope to be a mistress to him, and she had come to believe she deserved more than that.

"You are young, Meredith. Even with all you've experienced in your life, you are still innocent in the ways of men and love. Out of all of the men flirting with you tonight, only one looked at you in the way that mattered. As if you were the only person in the room. That was Lord Tiverton." She gently touched Meredith's cheek in a motherly way, and Meredith's eyes prickled with tears. Frances chuckled. "*And* he seemed rather jealous of the way the others acted with you."

"But that doesn't change the nature of my birth," Meredith pressed. "It will forever be an obstacle."

"Has he said that to you?"

"No..."

"Then consider that it may not matter to him at all. Give the duke a chance before you throw your own happiness out of the window, because Lord Tiverton seems to look at you as if *you* are his entire world."

Meredith's heart wildly leapt with hope at Frances's words. Maybe...maybe she did have a chance, however small, to capture happiness. If that was the case, she desperately needed Frances's advice and therefore needed to trust her with what had happened with Darius, at least a little.

"Frances, if a man kisses you, does that signify a promise?"

Her new chaperone eyed her thoughtfully. "It depends

upon the man. If you have been kissed by Tiverton, then I would think it might well mean a promise. But you still need to hear the words from him. Be careful. Some men will take whatever a woman is willing to give them and do not always understand that what you give them is precious and cannot be given a second time." Frances gave her a hug. "Now, be safe, my young friend. Remember, never give a man what you aren't willing to lose. That includes your heart."

"Thank you."

Having someone to talk to, someone who would not judge her, was such a comfort to Meredith. She'd realized how alone she'd been until now. Mrs. Todd in Yorkshire had been sweet but had kept the barrier up, because she saw Meredith as part of Uncle Ben's family and not staff.

"Goodnight." Frances gave a smile that showed she was ready to retire for the evening and left Meredith alone in her bedchamber.

Nell came in a short while later and helped her change into her new dark blue velvet dressing gown. She blew out the candles and was asleep within minutes.

Sometime after midnight, Meredith woke, needing a glass of water. As she sat back on the bed, drinking, she saw a flash from the corner of her eye. Meredith looked to the window facing the gardens.

It was near pitch black outside with only a sliver of the moon hanging in the night sky. A swaying, glowing orb moved slowly in the Crells' gardens. Meredith frantically searched the room for her opera glasses. Once she found them, she sat down in the chair by the window, lifting them to her eyes to spy more clearly on the light.

It was a lantern that dimly illuminated the man who carried it. She did not think it was Mr. Crell at this distance, it was impossible to tell who she was seeing. The man stopped walking and set the lantern upon the ground.

What was he doing? The figure began to move about around the lantern, just visible past the garden wall that separated Darius's garden from the Crells'.

Meredith rushed to the door and stepped into the corridor, listening for servants, but no one was in the hall and the lamps were doused. She had to wake Darius. She crossed the distance between their doors. She knocked softly, but he didn't answer. She turned the knob, and eased the door open. She could only just make out the shape of a man sleeping in the vast fourposter bed in front of her.

"Darius," she whispered again. Still no response.

Meredith crept closer. When her legs touched the side of Darius's bed, she patted around until she found his body. She lightly shook Darius's shoulder.

He made a low, disgruntled rumble. She shook him again.

"Let me sleep, love..." he muttered and then he grasped her by the waist, pulling her onto the bed as he rolled her over in his sleep, taking her with him and pinning her beneath him in the bed.

"Hmmm." This time the noise he made was entirely more agreeable, and his lips feathered along her throat as he sleepily kissed her, eyes still closed. One of his hands moved from her waist up to cup her breast through her nightgown.

"Oh!" She hissed at the almost sharp pleasure his palm created as he kneaded her breast gently with those long elegant fingers. "Darius…" she whispered, only half-hoping to wake him.

"Yes, my darling," he murmured sleepily. "Do you like that?" He lightly pinched her nipple through the cloth.

Meredith arched beneath him. She did like it so very much, and a large part of her wished she hadn't woken up.

"Be a good girl and let me *touch* you," he whispered as his lips nipped her throat. Then the hand on her breast slid lower, past her waist, setting her body on fire. His fingers bunched up her nightgown and soon that wicked hand was parting her legs, his fingers exploring her feminine folds. She should protest, stop this immediately, especially after what Frances had said tonight. But she also desperately wanted him to touch her.

When Darius's fingers slid inside her, reaching a place that had never known a touch like this, the last thing she wanted was for him to stop. Yet a part of her was still rational enough to try to wake him again.

"Darius, wake up!" She pushed his shoulders, but the excitement of his touch, that simple exploration of her body, overwhelmed her. She dug her fingertips into his skin, holding onto him as he continued to kiss her neck, her collarbone, and then her lips. The sweet taste of brandy still coated his lips. His eyes were still closed, and the lethargic way he moved made her realize he was still mostly asleep.

But oh, she couldn't find it in her to care, not when the sweetest ache was building in her womb like an unquenchable fire. And then it hit her, lights bursting across her vision, like a keg of gunpowder exploding. Unimaginable pleasure obliterated the last of her rational thoughts.

"Oh, Darius." She whimpered in joy, still on a cloud. "Darius…"

Suddenly he stiffened above her. Darius's head jerked up. In the dark, his usually bright blue eyes were a sliver of midnight sea, but she could still see the shock upon his face.

"Meredith?" He jerked away from her as if she'd turned into a snake lying in his bed. "What… What the devil are you doing in my bed?"

Shame and anger brought her crashing back to earth.

"I … I was just trying to wake you, but you pulled me into the bed." She hastily jerked at her nightgown and nearly fell out of bed trying to put space between herself and a very naked Darius.

He stared at her as if she were the mad one. "I did *what*?"

"You pulled me into your bed," Meredith said. Her shame deepened. It was clear from his reaction he'd been dreaming about some other woman. She was a fool. An absolute and utter fool.

"I should go—" She started for the bedchamber door, but he leapt out of bed, bedsheet pulled up around his hips, barely covering his backside as he caught her arm with his other hand. His grip was firm but gentle.

"Wait... Why did you want to wake me?"

Oh lord! She'd completely forgotten the reason she'd come here.

"There's someone in the Crells' garden. I saw a light. I wanted you to come with me and investigate."

"What sort of light?"

"A lantern, I believe. But I can go alone if you do not wish to accompany me."

"You absolutely will *not* go alone. Wait for me in the corridor. Put on your house slippers and a dressing gown. It will be cold."

Meredith hastily returned to her bedchamber to fetch her dressing gown and slippers. It was a relief to have a reason to forget what had just happened in Darius's bedchamber.

He joined her a few minutes later, wearing trousers, a shirt, and boots.

"Let's move quickly. We may have already wasted too much time as it is."

She flinched. That moment of exquisite passion in his arms...in his bed... had been a waste of time? But then he grasped her hand, lacing his fingers through hers, and the pain in her chest eased.

He led the way, his long legs taking the distance so quickly that she had to run to keep up with him. They exited the house and moved quietly toward the back garden wall. They stopped by the heart-shaped hole in the wall.

"I can't see anything from here..." Darius's voice was

barely audible as he pulled her close to him. "I need to look over the wall."

They climbed up onto the bench, with Darius grasping Meredith's waist and helping her up. Darius peered over the top of the wall. Meredith held her breath, waiting for him to speak. He was still for a long time. He lowered himself back down so that they were face-to-face.

"As far as I can tell, it's not Crell. I believe it is Dobbs, his butler. He's either just dug something up or finished burying something."

Meredith leaned closer to Darius, placing a hand on his arm as he stood up again and peered over the wall. "Is he still there?"

"No, he walked off just now. Wait here." Darius leapt off the bench and headed for the distant garden shed. When he returned, he held a shovel. He climbed back up onto the bench and gave her the shovel.

"Hold this."

She took hold of the shovel's shaft and Darius half jumped, levering his body over the wall and then dropped down to the ground on the other side.

"Pass me the shovel!" His whisper came over the wall. Meredith stood up on her tiptoes and handed the shovel down to him as best she could.

"Got it." Darius replied, and she let go of the shovel on her side.

While she waited, she searched Darius's garden shed and found a wooden crate. She put it on top of the bench before she climbed up onto it. It put her at a height to see over the stone wall herself. It was so dark that she could just make out Darius's form beneath the light of the silver sliver of the moon above. He dug, turning over the dirt. Then he knelt by the soil, digging with his hands before he froze. Meredith's heart hammered so hard that her blood was roaring in her ears. He'd found something.

He very slowly stood up again and began putting the soil back on the spot where he been digging. She wanted to speak, but the night was so quiet she didn't dare risk being heard by anyone that might be nearby.

"Take this." Darius said when he came close to the wall and spotted her. He held up the shovel's handle for her.

She grasped it and lifted it back over. "How will you get back over the wall? There's no bench and the window in the bricks isn't big enough for you to pass through."

Darius studied the wall, then backed up quite a few feet. Then suddenly he sprinted toward the wall and leapt up, his hands scrabbling on the stone. Meredith acted on instinct, leaning over to grasp his nearest arm and she braced her body, pulling hard as she helped him climb upward. He reached the top of the wall and hauled himself over it. He then dropped onto the bench, breathing hard. Darius covered his stomach with his hand as he hissed out a painful breath.

"Are you all right?" Meredith urged him to lean on her shoulder.

"It's that bloody knife wound. My flesh is scarred there. The doctor warned me it would have a terrible time healing. The flesh underneath is hard and can tear if I move a certain way."

"Tear?" Meredith's voice pitched in alarm.

"He said it wasn't necessarily a bad thing, just that scar tissue would be stretched out and it would feel awful when it happens. Give me a moment and I shall be well."

Meredith stroked his arm, hoping to soothe his pain even for a little while. He closed his eyes, breathing deeply for a few seconds.

"What did you see over there?" she dared to ask.

Darius's eyes open again. "A bloody sheet, rolled up, and inside it was a leather pouch containing a small handful of jewels, a few rings, and some necklaces."

Meredith let out a breath, her body tensing. "You're sure?"

"Unfortunately, I'm quite sure. Blood, when it is still fresh has a terrible smell. I am unfortunately quite familiar with that scent." He covered her hand on his arm with his own palm as he met her worried gaze. "Tell me again what you saw in the mews that night and what you heard. *Every* detail."

IT WAS A FEW HOURS PAST MIDNIGHT WHEN THEY RETURNED TO the house. Darius's body was on edge as he grappled with the truth. Crell had possibly *killed* someone that night, and Meredith had witnessed it from his coach.

"I shall go to the Bow Street Runners first thing tomorrow morning and tell them what we found."

Though that seemed to reassure Meredith, she was still trembling, and he knew it wasn't from the cold. When they stopped in front of her room, he caught her chin in his.

"Will you be all right tonight?" he asked.

She nodded, but those beautiful hazel eyes warned him that wasn't true.

"Meredith." He breathed her name and pulled her into his arms. She buried her face against his chest, her body shaking with silent sobs that tore at his heart.

He had forgotten how one could be so innocent of the wickedness of the world. He had grown used to murderers, blackmailers, and thieves in every dark corner of the city. But Meredith had never known any of this darkness. He now realized why his uncle had sent her to him. It wasn't just to find her a husband. Darius would know how to protect her from the evil in the world.

"There now." Darius stroked the loose hair around her shoulders, which was soft and silky beneath his hands. Comforting her comforted him in return.

When she finally stopped quaking, he lifted her chin. "Dry your eyes." He offered her a handkerchief from his trouser pocket. She wiped her tear-streamed face before handing it back.

"You've had such a terrible scare tonight, darling. You need to rest."

"I ca—can't. Too afraid." Meredith's confession was muffled against his chest.

"Then I will stay with you until you fall asleep." They reached her bedchamber and he ushered her inside. She was so like a child at that moment, trusting him as he tucked her into bed.

"How can you be so calm?" she asked, her hands clutching the sheets as she gazed up at him.

"I have trained myself to focus on the matter most important in the moment. Right now, that is keeping you safe. That sense of purpose and focus keeps me calm."

"Oh...maybe you could teach me how to do that someday," she replied.

"I'd be glad to."

He waited for her to get comfortable before he blew out the lamp, then settled in the chair facing Crell's house.

He kept his gaze on Meredith until she drifted to sleep. In the dark, with only a sliver of moonlight to see, his mind drifted back to the dream that he had been with Meredith in his bed—a dream that had become the sweetest reality when he'd woken up to her climaxing beneath him.

He'd wanted nothing more in that moment than to take her again, this time with something other than his fingers, and see her face in the glow of the lamps as she experienced that exquisite pleasure in his arms.

But he couldn't take advantage of her like that, not when she was destined to marry someone else. He'd taken enough from her as it was. He couldn't steal that final moment of intimacy from her, no matter how desperately he wanted to be the man she shared it with.

He forced himself to turn away from Meredith and look

at the Crell house beyond the garden wall. What he'd seen there tonight proved that Meredith's fears were no longer fanciful, but likely a terrifying reality. Crell had done something to his wife...but they needed to prove it to the authorities. Tomorrow at first light, he would send a message to Doyle at the Bow Street offices.

Sliding down a little in the chair to get comfortable, Darius crossed his arms over his chest and sighed. It was going to be a long night, and there was much that weighed upon his mind, as well as his heart.

10

Mr. Chelsea interrupted the breakfast that Darius had been enjoying with Meredith and Frances Petersham, though he did so in his practiced, unintrusive manner.

"There is a Mr. Henry Doyle from the Bow Street Runners to see you, Your Grace."

"Show him into the drawing room. We shall be there shortly." Darius rose and looked to Meredith. "I believe it would be wise for you to accompany me. Doyle will wish to question you about what you saw. I sent him a message early this morning detailing the incident in the garden."

Mrs. Petersham shared a look with Meredith before saying, "May I come as well, Your Grace?"

Darius assented. They had just shared the story with Mrs. Petersham not five minutes before Mr. Chelsea had come in, and she was eager to help in any way she could.

They met with Howard Doyle in the drawing room, and

Darius made the proper introductions. Doyle was a man in his early thirties, the son of a banking clerk who had developed a knack for reading people, which made him quite useful in the Bow Street ranks. Doyle had come to respect Darius as well in the last five years as Darius had assisted him with Bow Street matters.

Doyle wrote in a small notepad as he interviewed Meredith. Darius was proud of how calmly she conducted herself as she gave Doyle a thorough account of last night's events. When she had finished, Doyle turned to Darius, asking him what he had seen on the other side of the garden wall.

"I cannot be certain but I believe it was Dobbs, the Crells' butler."

Doyle brooded for a long moment as he stared at his notes, then let out a sigh.

"Very well. You and I shall pay a visit next door." Doyle stood and motioned for Darius to join him.

"Please stay here." Darius told Meredith and Mrs. Petersham. "We do not know what we will encounter there. If it is dangerous, I do not want either of you in harm's way."

What he actually feared was a body or something equally horrendous being discovered. He did not want Meredith to have such a vision in her memories.

He and Doyle walked around the street corner to the street behind Knightley. Doyle knocked on the door of the Crell house. It took several minutes before someone answered. Darius recognized the man as the butler, Dobbs.

"May I help you?" Dobbs asked. His gaze then slid to

Darius and his brows lowered. Darius didn't miss the man's reaction to him.

"My name is Howard Doyle. I am an investigator with the Bow Street Runners. This is the Duke of Tiverton. I have been informed by him that a crime has been committed on this property."

"What? No crime has been committed here." Dobbs lifted his chin and frowned.

"Nevertheless, I have a duty and a right to investigate such matters. I believe there is evidence of a crime buried in your gardens. Kindly move aside."

Dobbs was forced to let them into the house. Darius had only been inside the Crell house once before, many years ago, but it seemed most of the furniture had been sold off, and that which remained had been covered with white dust cloths. Darius's skin crawled as he felt that distinctive empty feeling of an abandoned dwelling.

"Show us to the gardens," Doyle commanded. The butler led them to the back door. No one else seemed to be inside the house except the curmudgeonly butler, confirming his suspicion that the servants were either in the country with Crell or they'd been let go, leaving Dobbs to finish whatever tasks Crell had set to him.

"Where did you see it?" Doyle asked Darius. He kept his tone quiet as they walked toward the back garden wall.

"It was here." Darius pointed to a spot of soil that was freshly turned over. He glanced up at own home over the garden wall, seeing Meredith's window.

Doyle looked to the butler. "Where do you keep your

gardening tools?" The man pointed to a garden shed in the corner of the garden.

Once armed with shovels, Darius and Doyle removed their coats and rolled up their sleeves to dig.

After several fruitless minutes, Doyle plunged his shovel into the soil and leaned on the handle, eyeing Darius with worry.

"We're nearly twice as deep as you said you dug last night, and we still haven't found anything." Doyle wiped his brow with his forearm, his face solemn.

Darius dragged a handkerchief over his own face to clear it of the sheen of sweat. The cloth and the bag of jewels he discovered last night were gone.

"I swear on my soul they were there, Doyle." He couldn't have dreamed that he'd climbed the wall last night or dug up that cloth. The smell of blood and death had been so fresh in his mind, even this morning. His stomach still ached from leaping to get back over the wall from last night. And, of course, Meredith had been there. Then how…?

"Mr. Dobbs, where are your master and mistress?" Doyle asked the butler.

Dobb straightened, his face a mask of austere pride.

"They retired to the country. I've been instructed to close the house down and sell the remaining furniture."

"Are there any plans for them to return to London?" Doyle asked.

"I do not believe so," Dobb said with an arrogant sniff. "The master mentioned the house would soon be sold."

Doyle watched the man carefully as he continued his questions. "What of Mrs. Crell? I understand she was an invalid."

"She is much improved and is the one who wished to move to the country." Dobbs explained.

"Was your mistress blonde or dark-haired?" Darius asked as he remembered what Meredith had asked Warren the day before.

Without hesitation, Dobbs replied that she was dark-haired.

Darius thought for just a moment he saw a flash of something in the butler's eyes as Doyle turned back to face him.

"I'm sorry, Your Grace. We must leave." Doyle took hold of the shovels and returned them to the shed. Darius retrieved their coats from the ground and met the butler's gaze once they were alone.

"Did your master pay you to lie for him?" Darius asked.

Dobbs scowled. "How dare you accuse me of lying! I do not care if you are a duke. You will leave this house at once!"

"Gladly." Darius growled. He met Doyle at the entrance to the house and they left without another word to that foul butler.

Once he and Doyle were on the outside doorstep with the door shut behind them, they put their coats back on and returned to Darius's home.

"For what it's worth, I believe you saw something, Tiverton. But without proof or something more than a young girl hearing screams and seeing something in the shadows through a coach window, I cannot make an arrest."

"Meredith is not some silly young girl," Darius said with more force than he'd intended.

Doyle shot Darius an amused grin. "She's Meredith now? Not *Miss* Montague? I thought this woman was your ward? Have you taken to other nightly activities with her other than digging up your neighbor's gardens?"

"Careful, Doyle," Darius warned. "She's a *lady*."

Doyle lifted his hands with a devilish grin. "If you'll recall, I'm happily married, and you'll end up that way too if you aren't careful."

"We are trying to prove a possible murder, Doyle."

"All I know is that if anyone discovers you're digging around in gardens at night with an unwed woman, you'll *end up* married. Heed my warning, Your Grace." Doyle touched the tip of his hat and parted ways with Darius at the turn leading back to Knightley Street.

The investigator was right, of course. He and Meredith shouldn't be skulking around at night together. There were *many* things they shouldn't be doing together, such as private kisses and what had happened last night. He'd...

Christ, he'd had his hand *between her legs* in his bed. That was enough to drive them to the altar if anyone should learn what had happened. But no one knew, and Darius would have to keep it that way.

He'd done a fine job this morning of briefly forgetting what he and Meredith had shared in his bed a few hours before, but now it had come back to him and it was the only thing he could think about.

The truth was, he'd been dreaming about her in his arms when she'd arrived, which is perhaps why he had not woken when she entered. That and the brandy he had shared with his friends before turning in. Then he had stroked her to climax. Somewhere in all that he had woken, and when she cried out, he'd realized it hadn't been a dream at all. She really had been beneath him, her lovely eyes dark as the night as she'd gazed up at him with such emotions that made his throat tighten even now just to think about them.

He would give anything to have her. To call her his darling wife and give her the world. But he couldn't.

When he forced himself to re-enter his home, Meredith and Mrs. Petersham were waiting for him in the entryway.

"What happened? We watched you and Mr. Doyle dig from the window in my room. It didn't seem like you found anything..." Meredith confessed, her cheeks rosy with excitement. Lord, she was so damn beautiful. It sometimes hurt to look at her, because it reminded him he couldn't have her.

He let out a slow breath, steeling himself. "Unfortunately, what I found last night was gone." Darius removed his coat and gave it to Chelsea, who would have his valet clean it of dirt.

Meredith gasped. "How could it be gone? I watched you re-bury it last night."

"Wait," Mrs. Petersham said. "You dug the cloth and

jewels up and you returned it to the ground back just after midnight, correct?"

"Yes," Darius said warily.

Meredith's chaperone tapped her chin thoughtfully. "That wretched butler Dobbs must have seen you climb over the wall and dig the cloth up. He could have waited for you and Meredith to leave, he dug it back up, and probably destroyed it. Did you check the townhouse? He might have tried to burn the cloth in a fireplace in one of the rooms or perhaps the kitchen...He wouldn't burn the jewels, they're too hard to destroy and too valuable."

"We didn't have a chance to look through the house," Darius admitted. "I convinced Doyle to go to the Crell house on very little evidence, and it was already questionable to barge into the home on just my word."

"Doyle doesn't think you are lying, does he?" Meredith asked. "I thought you worked with him. He should know you would never lie about something like this."

"He believes I saw what I saw last night, but without proof he cannot arrest anyone."

"Then Crell will get away with his crime." Mrs. Petersham's brows knitted together. "There must be something we can do."

"At the moment, there is nothing. For now, we must go about our day as we had intended. Meredith, I believe you are supposed to ride in the park this afternoon with Mr. Evers. Please ready yourself, as we must leave soon. Mrs. Petersham and I shall wait for you." Since they were planning a ride, he wasn't concerned that he was a bit sweaty. He took his riding coat when Chelsea gave it to him and put it on.

Meredith's face, which was already crestfallen, now turned bleak.

"Do you not like Mr. Evers?" Darius asked. "We can make an excuse if you wish to cancel your ride."

"What? Oh no, he is a fine man. I just can't imagine being out in the park enjoying myself while Crell gets away whatever he's done to Mrs. Crell."

"Sometimes the world is most unfair. However, we will not give up," Darius promised her. "Sometimes, time is required for an opportunity to present itself. In the meantime, you have a husband to find."

Meredith's shoulders slumped as she turned to go upstairs, resigned to their scheduled afternoon plans.

Mrs. Petersham was already wearing her riding habit and thus had no need to change. "Your Grace. I wonder if we might have a word in your study." Mrs. Petersham asked once Meredith was out of sight.

"Of course." He escorted Mrs. Petersham to his study and closed the door. When they were seated, he waited, more than a little curious about what she wished to say.

"I may be overstepping my bounds, but you are young and unmarried. Have you considered marriage?"

Darius chuckled. "Meredith is the one in need of a spouse, Frances, not me."

"You are opposed to marriage then?"

"Opposed?" He leaned back in his chair. "Not at all. Rather, I hold it in high esteem. It is something quite sacred to me. My parents were a love match, you see."

"And you want a love match for yourself?"

"Yes," he answered honestly.

"Then forgive my continued overstepping, but... have you considered marrying Meredith?"

Darius his chest tightened. "I won't lie and say that there haven't been moments where I've imagined that as a possible future. But I cannot."

"Oh? Why not?"

"Because she is not suitable."

Mrs. Petersham's brows rose. "How so?"

"Her family history. You must understand that there are expectations at my station, and not everyone in my position is lucky enough to be allowed a love match. If the burden lay only on my shoulders, that would be one thing. As much as she would make a perfectly suitable wife...a titled lady...a duchess, is another matter entirely. My duchess must have an impeccable family history, or she will not survive the scrutiny of society otherwise."

Mrs. Petersham frowned as she stared at him. "She would face criticism for being an illegitimate child with no parents of consequence, is that what you mean?"

"Yes exactly. The *haute ton* can be cruel. More than cruel. I've seen women cut down to size in the middle of a ballroom and were never invited to attend social functions again. I've seen men lose their honor on a turn of a card and found dead the next morning by their own hand because the disgrace was too much to bear. There will be those ready to destroy her simply because I chose her. I have no power to protect the woman I love from that fate. There would be too many times she would be away from me. And if she is hurt because she married me? I couldn't live with myself, Frances. That's the truth of it."

Frances was quiet a moment, her expression now pensive, rather than accusatory.

"As I recall, Lady Kentwell was a clerk's daughter, and she has been received quite well as a countess. Do you think it's possible Meredith could be welcomed in as easily as Lady Kentwell was?"

"Lady Kentwell is not illegitimate." He winced at his own words, but they were true. "And Kit is far more intimidating than I am. No one dares to breathe a word against his wife for fear that he will resort to his barbaric ways from when he was a convict in Australia."

"Forgive me, Your Grace, but you have more weapons at your disposal than your good looks and a rapier wit," she replied smoothly. "You have just as much influence as Lord Kentwell, and you can be just as dangerous. You are also a favorite of the Prince Regent, are you not? Does none of that help your cause?"

"A royal's favor can vanish in an instant. I could not risk a marriage simply because a prince decided to favor me for a time."

Mrs. Petersham stood up. "Well, I confess I am disappointed. I believed you were made of sterner stuff. If that is your answer, then I believe that either Mr. Evers or even Mr. Burville would make a good match for her. Both gentleman have shown an interest in Meredith which is a good indication of their intentions, and I will encourage her to consider one of them. You may not have the resolve to love the girl and marry her, but I believe one of them would." With that parting thought, Mrs. Petersham left the study. Darius sat there, knowing she was quite right.

But damn, the thought of Meredith marrying *anyone* felt like spikes being driven through his body. Mrs. Petersham would have him throw Meredith to the wolves, and he knew he was right in what he'd said. Meredith as a duchess would suffer. As a wife to a gentleman such as Warren, she would have no title but vast wealth. She would draw less ire from the aristocrats for marrying above her station.

He had sudden visions of Meredith in Warren's arms, riding across the grounds of Warren's country estate, Snowshill Manor, with Warren at her side.

Meredith holding a child with jade green eyes, just like Warren's. A child that he wanted to be *his*. To have his blue eyes and Meredith's stunning face and her gentle laugh…

Darius slammed his fist on his desk so hard it felt like he'd crushed every bone in his hand.

"Christ." Pain radiated up his arm as he stood. He was still rubbing his fingers when he met Meredith and Mrs. Petersham in the entryway.

"Did something fall in the study?" asked Mrs. Petersham.

"No."

Meredith's head tilted. "Oh? I swore I heard a loud—"

"Shall we get this over with?" he asked with a growl as he escorted them to the door.

He was once again in a foul mood. He couldn't have Meredith and he would spend the next couple of hours watching Mr. Evers court her. The Inquisition could not devise a more devious torture.

Mrs. Petersham gave him a sphinxlike look that he could not read as she passed him out the door. Darius gritted his teeth. What was it his father used to say?

He must grin and bear it even if it bloody well killed him.

"How are you finding London, Miss Montague?" Jordan Evers asked Meredith. The gentleman accompanying her on a ride was one of her first suitors and one she liked quite well. He was a second son to a baron and quite wealthy from successful investments, but what Meredith cared about was his kindness and his genuine interest in her. It also didn't hurt that he was quite handsome.

Their horses walked side-by-side in Hyde Park. Meredith didn't have to strain too much to look up at the gentleman beside her because she sat atop a tall, impressive mare rather than one of the smaller mounts most ladies rode. Darius didn't possess any dainty geldings or mares. When she'd seen his groom bring around this roan-colored mare, it had dwarfed its handler. She had needed a bit of help to mount the horse, but at the moment she was glad for its height.

Meredith turned her focus back to Mr. Evers's question. "London? Oh yes, I like it very much. It is busier than I'm used to, but I feel as though I'm settling in." That wasn't entirely a lie. She was enjoying the bustling pace a bit more now that she didn't feel so lost and hopeless.

"That's good to hear." Mr. Evers offered her a warm smile and briefly glanced behind them. Darius and Mrs. Petersham were a short distance away riding their own horses, providing a discreet escort for her and Mr. Evers.

"Pardon me for saying so, but Tiverton looks ready to *murder* me," Mr. Evers mused.

Meredith's face heated. Darius was being overprotective. Her first instinct was to blame herself, but for the first time in her life she stopped herself. Why should she feel responsible for what Darius did and how he acted? No...if there was guilt at play here, it fell upon his shoulders alone.

"He is overprotective. I think perhaps because he's never had a sister or other female relation to usher into society. I believe he is a bit...baffled as to how to act." This was true enough. He would have had more practice if he'd had a sister or even a cousin to chaperone before now.

"I could understand that, but I swear, the way he looks at you at times..." Mr. Evers seemed to realize what he was implying and cleared his throat. "Forgive me, I mean no offense, but is there an *understanding* between you and Tiverton?" Evers kept his voice low so as not to be overheard.

"An understanding? No..." Meredith wished with all her heart there was but there wasn't. There never could be.

She had heard part of the discussion between Frances and Darius about her unsuitability to be his duchess. She hadn't meant to eavesdrop, but she had come down the stairs, ready to ride and couldn't find either of them. She'd gone to his study, assuming they might be there. As she'd been about to open the door to see if Darius was inside, she'd overhead his conversation with Mrs. Petersham.

"She is not suitable... As much as she would make a perfectly suitable wife...a titled lady...a duchess, is another matter entirely..." Darius's words had embedded in her chest like knives. But she understood his concerns. That was the worst part of all. What hurt her the most though... was that he hadn't even given her a chance to prove his fears unfounded. He had assumed she couldn't survive his world. He hadn't even asked her what she thought about it. He had instantly dismissed her as a marriage option.

"I'm sorry. I should not have asked," Mr. Evers apologized. "I can tell it has upset you."

"Please, do not apologize." She looked around at the beautiful park spread out before them. It was such a lovely place to feel so crushed and without hope. "You are not the only one who believes he is interested in me. The situation is... complicated."

"It wouldn't be complicated for me. A man either loves

you or he does not. If he loves you, he should claim you without hesitation." Mr. Evers spoke as if that was the easiest thing to do.

Meredith turned to Mr. Evers. He was the epitome of a gentleman. Well-dressed, well-behaved, sincere in his intentions and honest. He was handsome, easily everything she should want in a husband. Yet she did not feel that inescapable pull toward him the way she had to Darius from the moment she met him.

"Mr. Evers, do you believe in lightning?"

He chuckled. "I suspect you are not asking me about the weather phenomenon but something else entirely?"

She smiled a little sadly. "You're right. I speak of another type of lightning."

Mr. Evers's eyes softened. "Ah, that elusive type of lightning that blinds you to all others. I take it you have been struck, but not by me?" When she didn't answer right away, he seemed to accept that as his answer. "Ah, well. I had suspected as much. But I cannot understand what keeps him from claiming you. The way he's been looking at me all afternoon, I feel confident in saying he wants you."

"It has to do with the matter of my birth, Mr. Evers. I have not yet been honest with you about that part of my life." She swallowed hard and hoped that in confessing her truths to him, he would not turn away. She desperately needed a friend.

"Then tell me, my dear lady. You seem to be on the verge of tears, and such a thing would be my undoing."

His kindness, not her history, were what brought tears to her eyes then.

"I come from no great family and have no money to my name. I'm illegitimate, and my parents have no special lineage to offset that stain. I am not the bastard child of a duke or an earl, just a gentleman who convinced my mother he was worth ruining her life over. He was not."

"Ahh...I see." Mr. Evers's tone was solemn. "While that may matter to some, a real man would not care. What matters is whether he loves the woman, whether his world is empty without her. I thought Tiverton was that sort of man, like me. But he has proved me wrong today, and it saddens me to admit it." A cloud of disapproval shadowed Mr. Evers's kind eyes as he glanced back at Darius.

"Please do not think ill of him. It is out of concern for me that he cannot act on his feelings. He fears that I cannot survive in his world because I will not be accepted by the *ton*. I know he isn't wrong about them, I just...I had hoped he would have asked me if I was brave enough to try."

Mr. Evers was quiet a long moment. Meredith tilted her head back, letting the dappled sunlight caress her face as they passed through a tunnel of towering trees. She wished she could banish her dark thoughts with the beauty of her surroundings. She had the sudden silly wish that she could transform into a tree, like a dryad from the old myths, and just *be* without fear, without shame.

"Society can be cruel, it is true. But Tiverton should have spoken to you about it. Your feelings deserve to be acknowledged. He should not have simply made an assumption as to the strength of your character."

Meredith quite agreed, but deep down she also feared that perhaps Darius liked her, but did not believe love between them was possible. Surely if he had loved her, he would have moved heaven and earth to be with her. Perhaps she did not matter enough to him for him to fight for her. He had only agreed that she would have been a suitable wife...not a wife he *wanted*. And that hurt her more than anything else ever had in her life.

"Someday you will find a man who will fight for you, Miss Montague. Lightning can strike twice, I assure you." Mr. Evers smiled at her, the warm expression so undeniably pleasant that despite her sorrows Meredith found herself smiling in return. "Let us enjoy our ride then, and not think of marriage or other such concerns. Tell me, have you read Mary Shelley's *Frankenstein?*"

"Oh yes." Meredith fell easily into an engrossing discussion on the shocking and captivating novel with Mr. Evers and was still animatedly discussing it with him when Darius rode up alongside them.

"It is late. We should go home now, Meredith." Darius gave Evers a nod and a smile, though his expression was a bit cold.

"I would like to call upon you tomorrow, Miss Montague." Mr. Evers said to her. His eyes said to her, *you have a friend in me if nothing else.*

"Thank you, Mr. Evers. I will be available for your call tomorrow."

"Excellent." He tipped his hat. "Then I shall take my leave. Mrs. Petersham. Your Grace." He rode off down the path deeper in Hyde Park, his horse kicking up the dirt on the path to create a small cloud behind him.

"What a lovely gentleman," Frances said. "Simply lovely."

Darius made a low, disgruntled sound, but Meredith didn't comment on it.

"Do we have a ball this evening?" Meredith asked.

"Yes, it is hosted by Lord and Lady Cavendish. They have a son, Gregory. Charming man." Frances said. Now that she'd settled into Meredith's life, she'd taken control of her social calendar with ease.

"Gregory is too young for you," Darius interrupted abruptly. "He's barely twenty-one, not much older than you are."

"Oh?" Meredith challenged. "Must I marry an *old* man?"

Darius shot her a look of surprise. "What? No, that's not what I said."

"Then why can't I marry someone close to my own age?"

Darius didn't immediately answer. "It's... it's just that you deserve someone more established. Cavendish is still young and wild, running about London dallying in vices."

"*Is* he?" Frances interjected with a tone of doubt. "I heard that he is pushing to create a Royal Astronomical Society, although I imagine that effort will take years to see to fruition. It seems to me that a man bold enough to study the stars is not likely running about spending his time exploring vices. When a man has the heavens to look at, why would he spend his time in a gambling hell?"

Darius's brows lowered, but he said nothing. Meredith turned her thoughts to tonight's ball. Perhaps she should listen to Mr. Evers and search for a second lightning strike. As much as her heart yearned for Darius, she had to be sensible. If Darius would not allow himself to love her, then she would find love elsewhere.

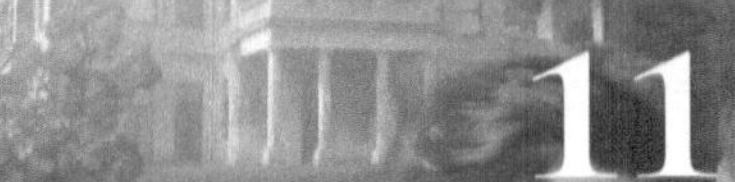

11

Meredith hadn't been able to get the mystery out of her mind. It seemed on the quiet nights, just when she was drifting asleep, she imagined she saw Minerva standing by Meredith's bedchamber window, looking out upon the gardens. Minerva had turned, the moonlight touching upon her face, a face that seemed troubled.

"I feel so very far away," the dream Minerva had whispered. *"I miss my gardens..."*

Meredith had shoved her bedsheets back and wiped at her eyes. When she'd opened them again, the strange vision was gone and Meredith was more than certain then that what she'd feared was indeed true. Minerva was no longer alive. She'd resolved that night that no matter what she would find out what happened to her neighbor.

It was a full two weeks later when Meredith was struck by an idea. Not one about finding a husband, but rather the mystery of the Crell house and how to solve the mystery of Minvera Crell's disappearance.

It came to her as she stood in the middle of a ballroom, facing Warren for a dance at one of the half-dozen balls she had attended in the last two weeks. Her mind had been wandering back to that hole in the garden wall and the void it represented. She could not let what had happened to Mrs. Crell go unanswered.

"I have it!" she whispered as Warren came toward her, their hands clasped as he spun her around.

"Have what?" Warren asked. She grinned at him. He had become such a close friend, always dancing with her and sitting with her at dinner, much to Darius's annoyance.

"I believe I know what to do to get Mr. Crell's attention."

"You *want* a possible murderer to pay attention to you?" Warren frowned slightly.

"Not when you put like *that*." Meredith hastily ducked her head when she realized that someone might overhear so she lowered her voice. Warren clasped one of her hands with his over their heads, drawing them close to each other. "But after Mr. Doyle made it clear we needed evidence, I've been pondering how to find some. I think I have the answer."

They danced away from each other and then came toward each other again. Then it was their turn to dance down the aisle of the other couples. She remained quiet until they were close once again, dancing in their own small circles where she felt confident no one would overhear what they were saying.

"You followed Mr. Crell to his house in the country, correct?"

Warren nodded.

"Could find your way back there?"

"Easily," he assured her. "Why?"

"I wish for you to deliver a letter to Mr. Crell from me. I will not sign it, nor will it have any identifying information on it. I want you to leave it at his house without any idea who has left it for him. It cannot be traced back to Darius or his home."

Warren's brows lifted. "Crell already suspects Darius is involved because he went with Doyle to Crell's house. That butler will surely have reported the event to his master."

"You're right. Why don't one of you take Darius hunting in the country for a few days? Chelsea could make sure Dobbs would hear that Darius is gone from the city, then it wouldn't look as though he had sent the note, or at the least there would be a witness that Darius was nowhere near Crell's country estate and Felix will be able to testify that Darius didn't hire a messenger to send it either.."

"Dare I ask what will be in this note?"

"An accusation," Meredith replied. "I will tell him that I have proof of what he did to Mrs. Crell and I want to be paid for my silence."

Warren's eyes widened. "You want to *blackmail* Crell?"

"Not at all. I only wish for him to think so. I will ask him to meet me during the day when Darius is off in the country. Then I can have Doyle listen in on my conversation with Mr. Crell and have him taken into custody if he confesses."

"And how exactly do you plan to make Crell confess in front of Doyle?"

Meredith grinned at her own cleverness. "He won't know Doyle will be there. I will have Doyle listen on the other side of the garden wall. He will be invisible to Mr. Crell."

Warren's eyes brightened. "You know, that's not a half bad plan."

"So you will agree to deliver the letter to him?"

Warren considered the matter. "Perhaps Felix can convince Darius to leave. His country house has fine grounds for shooting. I will speak with him about it tonight."

"Thank you, Warren." Meredith felt positively giddy when she and Warren finished their dance.

He escorted her back to Mrs. Petersham and Darius, but she slipped away for a quick visit to the refreshment tables. She wove her way through the crush of bodies and smiled when she saw Suzannah and Kit twirling out on the dance floor. Her heart twinged with longing. To have what they did, that easy love, that sense of rightness and belonging to one another... She would give anything to have that.

Her smile faltered. She had managed to forget only briefly that she might never have that, not unless she resolved to find someone who would love her the way she deserved to be loved. She paused behind the table laden with treats, but her appetite was now gone. A group of young women had their backs to Meredith as they watched the dancers. It was clear they had seen her approach because they started speaking, and Meredith was meant to overhear their whispered conversation.

"She's illegitimate, you know. Yes, that's what I heard." One young woman said to her companion.

"What is she even *doing* here? Why would Tiverton bring her out into society?"

"They say his uncle made Tiverton agree to take her in as his deathbed wish. He must have agreed out of honor and pity. Tiverton is quite gracious after all. He would not wish to turn her out, even if she is no better than a beggar."

"You don't think he..." one whispered, but the rest of what the woman said went unheard as a swell of music drowned out her words.

"Choose her over you? No, you are the daughter of an *earl*, he would never pass you over for some street born creature."

Street born? A flash of rage and pain gripped her. She wasn't *street born*, she was... she was...

She was no one. No one worth caring about, worth saving, worth...loving, especially not by someone like Darius. He had admitted as much to Mrs. Petersham.

She gasped in horror as Darius and Warren came toward the refreshment table. Meredith ducked behind a tall potted plant a few feet away before they spotted her, but she was close enough to continue to hear what the young women were saying when the two gentlemen approached the refreshments.

"Would you settle a point for us, Your Grace?" one asked.

"Yes?" Darius asked.

"That woman... your *ward* ... will you soon be rid of her so that you might hunt for a wife soon?"

"I beg your pardon?" Darius's voice deepened. "I have no desire to be rid of Miss Montague. She is a lovely young woman. Even the prince approves of her. Soon she will marry—"

Another woman laughed. "You must be teasing, Your Grace. But truthfully, you must see that woman is damaging your hunt for a wife. Can't you pay her and simply send her away?"

The silence that came from Darius was a knife to Meredith's heart. He wasn't going to defend her. He was going to let those women insult her as if she didn't matter.

Because I don't matter, not to the one person who matters to me.

She smothered a balled fist against her mouth to silence herself. Warren started to speak., but Meredith couldn't bear to stay and hear what else was said. Without a backward glance, Meredith bolted for a set of balcony doors that she prayed led to a terrace outside.

Air, she needed air...

"Can't you pay her and simply send her away?" Lady Mary Raikes asked Darius.

She was, objectively, a lovely brunette who possessed a pedigree dating back to the days of the Norman invasion. By the standards of the *ton*, she was the sort of woman who would be perfect as his duchess.

But all Darius could do was stare at her with a rage beyond words.

Send Meredith away? *Pay* her? Raikes's blunt rudeness took him completely off guard. So much so that he just stared at her in terrible, thunderous silence.

"Ah, Lady Mary, I see you are as detestable as always," Warren said with a cool smile.

Lady Mary arched a brow at him. "Who are *you* again? Oh yes, an untitled gentleman. You'll forgive me if I have no care to what your ilk thinks."

At this, Warren laughed harshly. "To forgive you, I would first have to have the misfortune of caring about your opinion...which I don't. Miss Montague is worth a thousand of you, Lady Mary. Perhaps that's what has your petticoats all twisted up? The thought that if Tiverton were to marry her over you, you'd know you aren't worth *anything* to him."

"Are you going to let him speak to me like that, Your Grace?"

Darius, finally able to see past the seething anger, opened his mouth to speak, but someone jumped out from behind a potted plant. It was Meredith. *His Meredith*...running from the ballroom, running from him. Because she'd overheard their conversation? She must have.

That black rage swelled within his head again as he met Lady Mary's gaze.

"Actually, I *will* let Mr. Burville speak to you like that, because if I dare stay in your presence one moment longer, *I* will say something that you will wish I hadn't." Without even excusing himself, Darius skirted around the refreshment table and headed for the balcony doors. He had to find her, tell her that he didn't agree with Lady Mary. That he'd never send her away. That she was worth far more than a thousand Lady Marys. She was worth *everything*.

The night was cold and smelled of rain and roses as Darius stepped into the gardens. He squinted in the direction of the garden path and caught a glimpse of Meredith's sky-blue ballgown vanishing around a towering hedgerow. He didn't call her name. If anyone else was in the garden, he didn't want to be overheard shouting for her because it could ruin Meredith's reputation if people assumed he was out here alone with her. He needed to get her back inside the ballroom at once.

He took off down the garden path, moving as fast as he could without running until he saw her once again. She sat on a marble bench, half in shadow. Darius stopped about fifteen feet away to take in the sight of her before she realized he was there. She was so impossibly lovely, even crying in the dark. And each of those tears shattered his heart.

In that moment, Darius admitted the truth. He'd fallen in love with this woman. The woman he could not have because tonight she had experienced the very thing he'd hoped to keep her safe from. His boots crunched on the gravel as he took a step forward. Her head jerked up at the sound.

"D—Darius?"

"Meredith," he breathed as he came toward her.

She stood up, backing away from him.

"We must go back inside before—" He stopped, instantly regretting his words.

Her face paled. "Why? Because if we are caught out here together, you might be forced to marry me? And you wouldn't want that, would you? To be saddled with me as your *unsuitable* bride?"

Unsuitable. His own distasteful words came back to him. How had she known about that? Had she overheard him speaking to Frances two weeks ago? If she had, it would certainly explain the distance she had put between them recently.

She had retreated to her bedchamber each night after dinner and had taken to sleeping in later in order to miss their breakfasts on the terrace. He had been so busy dealing with estate matters and considering what to do about Crell that he had not realized the change in her behavior until a couple of days ago. She had more callers each day, more rides in the park. Mrs. Petersham had insisted he should not attend those outings or else Meredith would not be comfortable with her suitors, though he suspected it had more to do with those suitors being uncomfortable around *him*.

Now he was seeing his life clearly for the first time in two weeks, and it wasn't a happy one...because he'd driven Meredith away from him. All because of his fears.

Meredith knew what he thought of her marriage prospects and Frances was desperately trying to help the girl find a husband quickly to escape him.

Words failed him. He stared at her, pain driving a wedge between them.

"Please go back inside, Your Grace," she said quietly. "I will return on my own soon. I simply need a moment to collect myself."

"No." He shouldn't have said it, but his refusal slipped out before he could stop himself.

She stared at him, her lips parted in shock.

"If you stay out here, I shall remain with you," he said. "For as long as is required."

"But you can't. And I need to be alone. I..." She wiped the tears that had begun streaming down her face.

"Meredith, the last thing you need is to be alone. What you heard in the ballroom was..." He took another few steps toward her.

"It was what you feared would happen. What you *knew* would happen." She sniffled and wiped at her cheeks with one gloved hand.

He could only nod. His throat had tightened so that he couldn't speak for a moment.

"You were right," she said quietly. "I thought I could prepare myself for such cruel words, but..." She sniffled again. Darius took a chance to move closer still. He was now within arm's reach of her.

"Please, just go," Meredith begged him, her voice breaking on the words.

"No," he said again, stronger this time.

She swiped the backs of her hands across her eyes. "I must look dreadful. I can't go in looking like this."

"On that we agree." He reached for her but she pulled away. "You heard me speaking to Frances about this, didn't you?" he asked.

Meredith nodded, and the misery on her face cut him deep. Deep enough that he found it hard to breathe.

"I never meant to hurt you. You will make someone a wonderful wife."

She dropped her head. "But not you." Darius had never hated himself more than he did at that moment. Before he could respond, she turned and ran deeper into the gardens.

"Meredith!" he called out, still trying to keep his voice down as he chased her. She took half a dozen turns before she ran into a dead end, and he blocked her escape by holding his arms out.

"Move!" she demanded.

"*No.*"

"Stop saying that!" She stomped her foot. It was so angry and yet so feminine that Darius would have smiled, only he felt too wretched inside to feel any joy. The heavy clouds above began to break, and the stone path was soon sprinkled with rain droplets.

"We must go back inside now, or we will *both* be drenched," she said.

"Not until I've said a few things," Darius replied, his voice as rough as the gravel beneath her dancing slippers. He towered over her, but she didn't shrink away this time. It gave him hope to continue.

"Meredith. You are beautiful, clever, and kind." His eyes held her in place, and the rain drops were icy cold against his slowly heating skin as he continued to say the words he'd been holding in for so long. "You fascinate and inspire me. If I could freely choose my wife, it would be *you*, without doubt or hesitation."

"But a duke has no choice?" Her tone was bitter.

"Tonight you witnessed how society would treat you. I cannot watch you endure that."

"You never asked me what *I* wanted. What if I were willing to endure that for you?" she asked, her face pale again as the rain grew heavier.

"Are you?" he asked. "Because you ran away tonight."

She drew back as though he'd slapped her, but she had to understand why he couldn't have her, why they couldn't live the dream they both so desperately wanted.

"I did not flee because of *their* words," she said at last. "I fled because *you* said nothing. I could endure anything if you only wanted me, if only I were yours. But tonight it has been made it abundantly clear I don't belong here... I don't belong *anywhere*. Perhaps I should've stayed in Yorkshire and become Harry's mistress."

He grabbed her by the shoulders. "Do not say such things. You *do* belong here. You belong with me."

Thunder rumbled above them, charged with an energy that passed from the clouds directly into Darius's soul.

She lifted her chin, her lovely hazel eyes darkened. "Prove it," Meredith challenged. That fire in her eyes he had come to adore had momentarily returned. *She* was brave. *He* was the coward. She'd drawn a line between them, and only he could cross it now.

If he did, there would be no going back. No more denying anything anymore, not his heart or his body.

The rain began to drench them and right then he felt anything was possible, even his own happiness.

He slid his hands to her waist, jerking her against him before he captured her mouth. He tasted the rain with her tears, and she sobbed once against his lips before kissing him back.

Lord, let me have this moment of heaven with her.

Darius didn't care that he was soaked, but he did care that she was. He pulled away to bend and scoop her up in his arms. She curled her arms around his neck and gazed at him.

"We're going back inside?" she asked in a quiet voice.

"No."

"Is 'no' your favorite word this evening, Your Grace?" Meredith said peevishly.

Darius laughed. "*No.* We are going somewhere private so I can do wicked things to you and so you will start calling me Darius again."

"Do wicked things to me?" Her voice was so sweet, so innocent, which was the exact opposite of his thoughts.

"*Yes.*"

"Finally a yes," she said and cuddled closer to him as he carried her off.

Darius smiled. "*That* is my favorite word."

12

Meredith held onto Darius's neck, more aware of his heat than the cold rain that soaked through her wool gown. She gazed up at his face as he carried her in his arms like a damsel from some gothic novel. His wet, dark hair curled at the ends, dripping onto his soaked shoulders. Everything from his straight nose and full lips to his square jaw were perfection, but right now she didn't see that. She saw *him*, the very real man with dark eyelashes heavy with glistening raindrops and a faint scar just under his chin. She wanted to kiss that scar, ask him how he had gotten it, press her lips to that bit of pale pink skin and ease his pains, even those that had begun to fade with time.

She did not ask him where they were going, nor did she try to argue that she was more than capable of walking. If he wished to carry her, she wasn't about to object.

A gazebo emerged at the long line of hedgerows in the distance, and Meredith wondered how Darius knew about it. They were, after all, in someone else's gardens. Had he taken another woman here at some other past ball? She shrugged that thought away. If he had, she didn't want to know.

The gazebo was dry inside, with two chairs and a settee made of wicker. Darius sat down upon the settee and settled her on his lap.

"Are we going to talk?" Meredith asked, disturbing the pleasant sound of the rain on the roof. She'd always liked the rain, the feel, smell, and sound of it. It was soothing.

Darius tightened his arms around her. "*No.*"

"There's that word again." Meredith reached up to trail her fingertips over his jaw, tracing his beautiful lips. "I thought your favorite word was yes?" He kissed her gloved fingertips, causing a wave of languid heat to roll through her, far stronger than the chill of her wet clothes. He tenderly slid her gloves off her arms and laid them aside.

"It is…and it will be yours as well once I am done with you," Darius nipped the pad of her fingertips and leaned over, nuzzling her neck. She hugged him tight, relishing the feel of his lips against her throat.

His hands moved to the back of her gown, slowly it unlacing , letting the bright blue silk drape down from her shoulders.

She slid free of the capped short sleeves and Darius's gaze lowered from her face to her breasts, which swelled against the stays she wore. She waited, her heart racing as he unlaced the stays next. She removed them slowly, letting them drop to the floor.

"Show them to me," Darius commanded, his dark tone full of hunger.

Meredith knew what he meant. Feeling a mixture of shyness and excitement, she unfastened the ties of her chemise. The thin fabric gaped open, hinting at her breasts more.

"*Show me.*" His growl sent her hands flying to her chemise, both desperate to obey and wanting the same thing just as much.

She pulled the neck of her chemise open further, exposing her breasts to his view.

"They are magnificent," he rasped before he dipped his neck to nuzzle the swells. Meredith gasped. Her breasts grew achy and heavy from Darius's attentions. He kissed his way to one nipple, tasting the pink peak between his lips and sucking. She dug her hands into his hair, holding his head to her breasts as a wild pulsing started between her thighs. She began to murmur the word *yes* over and over again, just as he predicted.

He chuckled against her skin, the rich sound of his sensual delight healing her lonely soul in a way she'd never imagined.

"Never hide these from me, my darling." Darius breathed before he gave her other breast his undivided attention.

She vowed she never would. Not from him. The feel of his mouth, the pressure of that sucking sensation was so wicked and oh so wonderful. She knew little of lovemaking, other than what the maids had mentioned in passing over the years at Uncle Ben's house, but she trusted Darius to be a masterful lover. One who would teach her what she was supposed to do. He gently bit one nipple before licking away the sting, then raised his head to look at her.

"I wish you could see yourself the way I do, Meredith. You upon my lap, breasts rosy from my mouth, cheeks flushed and your hair a wild, colorful tumble down your shoulders. You are an erotic dream like no other." His words shot straight to her heart. How could *she* be a dream for this man? He was *her* dream.

"I want to touch you." She bit her bottom lip, hoping he would not deny her. She couldn't forget the feeling of him lying atop her in his bed. She wanted to know that gentle weight of his body once more, to have the freedom to feel him and touch him.

"Then undress me," Darius said, his smile encouraging.

She tried not to hesitate, fearing he might come to his senses and change his mind. She worked her hands in the fold of his coat and pushed it off his shoulders. He shrugged the garment off, then settled her firmly over his lap so that she straddled him. Her skirt spooled around her waist as she reached for his waistcoat. Her excitement at seeing him without his clothes only heightened the clumsiness of her fingers. She threaded the buttons through their slits with trembling fingers, all the while feeling his heavy gaze upon her.

Meredith lifted her eyes as she pushed his waistcoat open and he slid his arms out of it. Her hands moved down his chest to his breeches. She curled her fingers in the white lawn fabric of his shirt and tugged it free from his pants. Then she lifted it over his head.

There. He was bare skinned and so was she, at least above the waist. She leaned against him, her soft breasts brushing against the hard planes of his chest. She touched her lips lightly to his, making him chuckle.

"Open your mouth and I shall show you how a wicked man kisses," he said, his tone low and husky.

She parted her lips, and he slid his tongue inside, thrusting in and out. She could feel her body respond to that rhythm on a purely instinctual level. As wicked as he was, there was infinite tenderness in all of his actions toward her. This was what she had been waiting for since she had first met him. *This connection, this passion.* She had just never imagined it would feel so overwhelming. Kissing Darius slowed her world to a stop. Even the rain seemed to hang suspended in the air. For a moment, she and Darius existed in a sacred realm *between* worlds.

"As much as I could kiss you like this all night ... I made a vow to do wicked things to you." Darius feathered his lips over hers once more, then placed his hands on her waist and lifted her up. He set her down on the settee and knelt on the ground at her feet, his hands on her knees.

"Wha...what are you doing, Your Grace?" Meredith asked, more than a little nervous as he pushed her skirts up to bare her thighs and nudged her legs apart.

"Hush and lie back, darling." He spread her legs even further and placed one of her calves over his shoulder. His hands were gentle, but his palms were slightly rough. She wondered how it was that a duke acquired calluses? Lord, those palms felt good on her sensitive skin. He moved closer, his warm breath coasting along her inner thighs. She realized he could see her *there*, that part of her body that he shouldn't see.

"Hush," he soothed. "I'm going to kiss you again, right here."

Darius placed a soft, tender kiss on her inner thigh, which felt wonderful. For a moment, she forgot that he could see the most secret part of her. But then his mouth moved and his tongue swirled around the sensitive bud of her arousal. She jerked and moaned as he tasted her with his tongue.

"Oh ... *oh my* ..." Meredith panted, trying to process the rush of sensations that Darius's mouth had given her. She wanted more, she—

Stars burst across her eyes as an unexpected burst of pleasure exploded inside her. She slumped against the back of the settee, relaxed, and utterly pleased in the most silly, scandalized way she could imagine. She stared at the roof of the gazebo above her, lost for words.

"That's it, my gorgeous girl," he said as he kissed her thigh again, then lightly sank his teeth into the flesh there in a playful bite that made her gasp. Aftershocks rippled through her, and Darius, damn him, only laughed, knowing full well what that playful bite had done to her.

"You, sir, are most wicked," Meredith protested.

Darius spread her legs wider as he moved up her body so that he now rested on the settee between her legs. He reached down to unfasten his breeches and slid them down just past his hips before he settled into the cradle of her thighs. She didn't have a chance to say anything before he stole her mouth in a raw, ruthless kiss that drove all other thoughts from her mind.

"It is London's mistake for thinking me a gentleman, when I am anything but." He bit her bottom lip, tugging on it lightly, then released it. She could only look at him in wonder and arduous longing.

"Are we ... finished?" she asked, uncertain of what should happen next.

"Far from it, my dear." He slanted his mouth over hers again, with another mind-numbing kiss that left the rest of the world behind them. Her legs spread wider, her skirts bunching beneath her breasts. Darius broke their kiss, and he pressed his forehead to hers as he shifted closer to her. Something hard began to nudge at her sex.

"I'm sorry, love," he murmured.

"Why—"

Pain sparked deep within her as she was suddenly, completely *filled*, by *him*. He'd entered her body, leaving her in agony!

"Breathe, sweetheart, breathe." Darius kissed her cheek

and held her still, pinning her against the settee with his body. Meredith clutched his bare shoulders, trying to get used to the unexpected pressure and that pinching sensation inside her.

Meredith bit her lip. "It hurts, Darius…"

"I know, sweetheart. You need to *breathe*." He kissed her forehead and held himself very still within her.

Breathe? How on earth could she breathe? But after a moment, with him gently encouraging her, she did manage to breathe and slowly the pressure eased away.

"It feels better," she confessed after a minute.

"Thank God," he whispered. A second later he moved, pulling his hips back and then gently slid inside her once more. The pressure was still there, but the more he moved, the more it faded.

"How do you feel?" he asked as he began a slow, easy rhythm of thrusts.

"Good." It was true. An excited pulse was now building in her womb, and she tightened her thighs around his hips.

Meredith lifted her gaze from his chest to his eyes. "Could you kiss me again?"

"Gladly." Darius leaned in, his mouth meeting hers as his body continued to move over hers, penetrating her deeply.

His hips moved faster now, pressing tight against her in hard thrusts, and she took it all, each second of his possession, knowing at last what it was that tempted people to sneak away and risk ruining themselves. And as she came apart beneath Darius she knew she was, in fact, ruined for all others. He cried out her name as his body shuddered above hers.

She held him tenderly as his movements slowed, speaking soft words to him. He gazed down at her, his blue eyes full of storms, with a look of awe that matched what she felt inside.

It was a long while before Darius withdrew from her, retrieving his clothes and hers from the ground. He used a handkerchief to clean her and himself and while she was a little embarrassed she was touched at his tenderness towards her. They dressed quickly in the dark, but the rain was still coming down hard. He told her to stay there and wait for his return.

"I will have my coach brought around. There is a way through the garden gates that will allow us to bypass the house. I shall return for you." He pulled her once more into his arms, kissing her before he vanished into the night.

Meredith sank back down onto the settee, wincing as her body, newly used, protested with a flash of soreness between her thighs. She rubbed her arms and stared into the darkness, wondering what tomorrow would bring now that she knew with a frightening certainty she could never love anyone but Darius.

He had made a mess of things tonight. Now he had to face the consequences. He had taken Meredith's virginity. He'd also forgotten to spill his seed elsewhere. Instead, he had stayed buried inside her, completely under her spell. There was a chance she could have a child from tonight's actions. It was entirely his fault. He was the one that should have known better. There was no other choice for either of them now but to get married.

He would have to find a way to protect her, to save her from all the gossip, but it would be difficult, if not impossible. Lady Mary Raikes had already chosen Meredith as a target, and Lady Mary had many friends and a vast amount of influence.

This ... *this* was what his fear had always been, but at least Meredith would be his and he would no longer feel mad for wanting her and not being able to have her. But the personal cost to her, what she might suffer just so he could satisfy his desires... that would keep him awake at night.

He exited the gardens and spied Mrs. Petersham at the edge of the balcony doors, standing just out of the reach of the rain. She spotted him just as quickly.

"Your Grace? Where's Meredith?" Frances asked as he joined her.

"She's waiting for me We need to bring the coach around to the garden gate and escort her home at once."

"What? Is she all right? Mr. Burville told me that Meredith overheard some gossip and ran to the gardens, but he said that you went after her." Frances met his gaze. "That wretched Lady Mary Raikes has been spewing rumors about Meredith and her unsuitability. I refuse to repeat what I've heard, but you should know it is being said."

"This is exactly what I wanted to avoid. Now... it seems I have no choice."

"What do you mean, no choice?" Meredith's chaperone asked. "No choice for what exactly?"

"I mean that we will have to marry, and soon."

Frances looked confused, then momentarily excited, but that expression soon faded beneath worry. "What has changed since last we spoke about your intentions?"

Darius didn't want to tell her, but Frances had a right to know enough of the change in his and Meredith's circumstances.

"I have compromised her."

"You don't mean here?"

"Yes."

"In the garden?"

"Yes."

She seemed to consider something. "That certainly didn't take long."

Darius raised a brow wondering exactly what kind of comment that was supposed to be, but Frances quickly changed the subject.

"I shall speak to someone about having the coach brought round at once."

"Thank you. I shall go and collect Meredith."

Darius retraced his steps to the garden gazebo where Meredith waited. She was leaning against one of the white pillars, watching him through the rain. Something gripped his heart as he stared back at the beautiful vision she presented, more real than anything he'd ever seen in his life. He came up the steps to her and wrapped his arms around her.

She was *his* now. He no longer had to fight the urge to touch her, to keep her at a distance.

She sighed against his lips as he kissed her. Meredith was cold and wet. Her shiver passed through to him, and he gently rubbed her arms before he retrieved her wet evening gloves from where they lay on the arm of the settee.

"Let's go home and warm you up," he said, kissing the crown of her damp hair.

He took her by the hand and they ran through the gardens toward the side gate that led up to the front drive-way, where his coach was waiting. Once inside, Frances wrapped her cloak around Meredith shoulders, and Darius told his driver to take them home.

No one spoke the entire way back, and for that Darius was grateful. He needed time to think, or perhaps not to think. It was hard to be sure.

Once they were home, Frances escorted Meredith upstairs where Nell would prepare her a hot bath. Darius went to his study to write his solicitor a letter about his upcoming marriage. He had just finished the letter when Chelsea politely rapped on his door.

"Come in."

The butler peered inside. "Mr. Burville has just arrived. I assume you wish to see him?"

Warren politely nudged the butler side so he could enter Darius's study. "Of *course* he wishes to see me, old boy." He was also drenched from the rain, which meant he'd ridden straight here following them home from the ball.

"What is it, Warren?" Darius asked.

"You left the ball like the devil himself was on your heels. When I didn't see Meredith return to the ballroom, I wanted to make sure the young lady was all right."

"Honestly, I don't know if she is," Darius admitted. "She overheard Lady Mary's unkind words about her and I know she is upset about that."

Warren tossed his hat on Darius's desk and sat down in a chair facing him.

"Lady Mary will not let your slight of her tonight go unpunished. Something must be done."

Darius met Warren's uncharacteristically worried gaze. "Something *will* be done, Warren. I can promise you that. In fact, I wish for you to accompany me tomorrow morning to procure a special license."

Warren laid his palms on his thighs and let out a soft whistle. "You don't mean..."

"Meredith and I will be married as soon as it can be arranged, hopefully at the end of next week."

"Well damn, there's a thousand pounds I won't be seeing again," Warren muttered.

"What?"

"Nothing. Meredith must be overjoyed," Warren said with a grin.

But Darius's stomach clenched with nerves. "She does not know as of yet. I will inform her in the morning."

"Isn't it fashionable these days for a woman to agree to marriage first?" Warren asked, half-teasing.

"She will agree, I'm certain of it."

Warren studied him closely, far too astute for Darius's liking because he knew whatever Warren was thinking was likely not going to be something he'd want to hear.

"Darius, not to draw rain clouds over your pending nuptials, but is this what *you* desire?"

That certainly wasn't what he'd expected his friend to say, and it was hard for words to express how much it meant to him right now. The bonds that had forged when they were young boys had only strengthened over time, and he was glad that his desire to marry Meredith hadn't threatened his friendship with Warren.

"I have wanted Meredith since the moment I saw her standing at my front door, so brave and yet so lost. But that wanting has softened ... *deepened* into something else. Something I dare not name lest I find myself becoming a fool for it."

"Then let me say it for you," Warren replied. "You *love* her."

Darius did, but tonight he must face the fact that he was forcing marriage on her because he'd lost his control. He'd taken her virginity and her future, all for his own selfish need to claim her forever as his. He was a fool for letting it happen, but he wasn't going to let her go now.

"She will not marry you if you force her to," said Warren. "Even if she returns your love, she won't allow you to make this match out of necessity for her honor."

Darius refused to heed his friend's warning. "She will marry me. She will have no choice. I compromised her tonight, which means there is a possibility of a child."

"You're a fool if you tell her that is why you must marry her. Trust me, Darius. Tell her how you truly feel, or you will lose her."

Darius knew Warren was speaking honestly, but Darius convinced himself that Meredith would be reasonable, that she'd see things from his perspective. If he started speaking of love and all the softer things she made him feel, she'd wonder why he hadn't asked her to marry him sooner, and it would circle back to his own bloody fears about her place in his world and whether she could survive. He didn't want to have that fight again.

"I hope you know what you're doing," Warren said, collecting his hat. "I shall meet you at nine o'clock to accompany you to the Doctor's Commons for the license." He gave Darius a nod and took his leave.

Darius leaned back in his chair, listening to the rain tap softly on the windows. He wondered how on earth he could find a way to speak of love. What he felt surpassed any description so simple as the word *love*. Kit should have bloody warned him what *this* felt like. This gravity and weightlessness, this storm and sunlight, this breath and breathlessness, all happening in one vast infinite beating of his heart.

It was a long while before he decided to go to bed. As he paused by Meredith's door, his hand touched the wood, and he imagined her sleeping against the backdrop of soothing rain sounds and dreaming.

Please let her dream of me ... because I have done nothing but dream of her since she entered my life.

With a sigh that quivered deep within his chest, he returned to his chamber across the hall to sleep and perhaps to dream of all the tomorrows he and Meredith would soon have together.

13

"No!" Meredith jerked her hand from Darius's grip and stepped away from him. The lovely morning light that had lulled her into warm thoughts of being in Darius's arms was now too bright, making her face hot and her body tense.

She was alone with Darius in his study, a scenario which she'd been hopeful for before he had stridently—*thoughtlessly*—told her that they would have to marry. It hadn't been a declaration of love, or a romantic sweeping into his arms as he professed he would die with her. No, he'd stated their upcoming marriage as a matter of fact, and it was simply a matter of choosing a date for the ceremony. Now he stood between her and the door she had hoped to escape through.

"No?" He arched a dark brow. "Is that *your* favorite word now?" His voice soft, seductive. She realized then that he didn't understand what he thought was teasing, would instead exasperate and wound her.

His words reminded her of last night, how they'd been so teasing and intimate with each other. Now it felt as though a knife had plunged into her heart, and she couldn't feel anything but pain...and anger. Oh yes, she was so *very* angry at him for turning her affection for him against her.

Last night had been such a wonderful gift. After the ball, she had fallen asleep dreaming of him, of his lips on her skin, his hands cupping and caressing her body and that powerful sense of connection when their bodies had joined together. It was everything she'd ever imagined and more. It was more than she'd ever hoped to share with a man. Then he'd ruined the memory by telling her ... no, by *informing* her they would marry.

There had been no romantic prelude, no words spoken from his heart. Only a statement of fact as dry as the reading of a bill in Parliament. She had barely finished her breakfast before he'd pulled her into the study and told her they would be married within a few weeks.

"Darius, I *cannot* marry you." *Not like this. Not forced.*

His blue eyes narrowed. "Why not?"

"Because you are only doing this out of a sense of duty and obligation." She twisted her hands in her skirts, unable to meet his gaze now that the words were out.

"My life is built upon my sense of duty and obligation. That is what it means to bear the title of Tiverton." That black bit of anguish in Meredith's stomach only grew deeper. He didn't seem to understand what she'd said. Or perhaps he did, but his response made it clear he didn't understand why it mattered to her.

"Do not force me, Darius."

He moved toward her, grasping her by the arms before she could dodge around the chair behind her.

"Meredith, you desire me," he whispered. "I know you do. I also know that you care for me..." He leaned down, his face nuzzling hers. The nearness of him, the heat of him, sent her senses spinning just as it had last night. She could feel that quickening in her blood as her body wound tight with the excited promise of what he could make her feel.

She hated that he was right. She cared so very much about him. She *loved* him. But that love was killing her because it wasn't returned.

"I do care ..." she admitted. "But that alone is not enough to tie us together." She pushed against his chest, desperate to put space between them, but he would not budge. She could not think clearly when he touched her. "You would be trapped with me, the wife you never wanted, the wife that shamed you in the eyes of society."

She could tell he still did not understand that marrying her would cost him his influence in society, or that a loveless marriage would destroy her. It did not matter that he had some affection for her. Affection was not the same as love.

"Send me away, Darius. Let me be a stranger to you once more. Then you will be free." Her shoulders slumped, her body suddenly heavy with misery. She did not know where the words had come from, but she had nearly died inside saying them.

His eyes darkened as he curled his fingers around the back of her neck and rubbed the tight knot of muscles there. He lifted her chin with his other hand, forcing her eyes to meet his.

"You would have me abandon you?" The flash of fury upon his face was like a storm sweeping over the Yorkshire dales. She braced for his fury, but he simply waited for her to speak instead.

"I..." She didn't know what to say. "Would it not it be better if you did?"

"Better for whom?" he growled. "Because it would not be better for me."

"Darius, please. Lady Mary made it abundantly clear what society thinks of me, and she is far from alone in that opinion. You cannot fight the *ton*. Not for me."

"But I thought that's what you wanted of me. To defend you and fight the world for you?"

She did. Lord, she did. But she didn't want him to come to her defense out of duty. She wanted him to come to her defense out of love. No one could truly love someone who forced them into such a situation.

"You shouldn't have to defend me." She tried to pull away again. "If I should marry, it should be to someone like Mr. Jordan Evers. He would—"

Darius captured her mouth with his, assaulting her senses with his masterful lips. He trapped her wrists behind her back with one of his hands while he fisted the other in the loose curls of her hair and held her still for his sensual exploration. She became vaguely aware of him backing her up against his desk, then the sounds of papers being pushed off it in a flurry of chaos before he lifted her up and set her down on its edge.

She murmured a question against his lips as his hands pushed her skirt up to her waist.

"Hush, woman," he said with a darkly commanding voice. She gasped as his fingers found their way between the folds of her sex, penetrating her.

"Oh!" She arched into him as he stroked her and teased her mercilessly. His mouth came down over hers again as he pleasured her.

"No one will touch this beautiful body but me, do you understand? You're *mine*, Meredith. Mine to kiss, mine to pleasure..."

He nipped her lips, and the sting made her womb clench in excitement. She grasped his shoulders and then dug her fingers into his hair, desperate to hold on to him as his wicked fingers did magical, wonderful, *sinful* things to her. He rocked against her, mirroring the thrusting of his fingers as he continued to kiss her. His lips parted hers, his tongue playing with hers. An erotic warmth spread throughout her body.

"That's it, sweetheart. Let me play with you."

Her face flushed at Darius's wicked words. He spoke as though she was only a plaything for his pleasure. But rather than feeling offended, it only made her wetter wherever his fingers touched her. She whimpered when he brushed his thumb over the sensitive pearl of her clit.

"Yes!" she panted. "More!" She wanted him to keep going, even as she twisted and writhed to escape the overly sensitive caresses. It was the most exquisite torture she ever could have imagined.

His low, rough chuckle against her kiss-swollen lips was like entering a dark heaven, tasting hedonistic pleasures in a way she never imagined possible. She couldn't imagine feeling safe enough with any other man to allow him to touch her like that. No one but Darius.

They moved together, his hand on her hips, chasing that bright pinnacle of pleasure. It was as though she was racing uphill in the bright morning sunlight on a summer day. Her skin burned sweetly beneath the light and her breath came faster, harder, as her body reached toward the peak and then she was falling, rolling, spinning madly as her body turned into a splash of colorful pleasure that had stars shooting across her closed eyelids.

Soft, warm lips gently caressed her as she drifted down to earth, and when her lashes fluttered open, she saw only Darius's handsome face.

The pure blue orbs of his eyes were like a summer spring sky gazing back at her with a possessive hunger tempered with tenderness. He stroked the pad of his thumb over her bottom lip, and she realized his other hand was still between her legs, gently stroking her tender flesh, drawing out trembling little aftershocks.

Meredith clutched his shoulders, feeling the hard

muscles of his body as they breathed together in the silence of the room. Then he withdrew his hand and wiped his fingers with a handkerchief.

"We shall be married, and soon. That is the end of this discussion," he said. "I must meet with Warren to arrange things. I shall return this afternoon."

Meredith was too sated from his touch to argue. Darius stole one last kiss from her before he left the study. She remained on his desk, still bewildered, her body limp and head muddled.

When she was able to collect herself, she fixed her skirts and walked on shaky legs to the study door. She had just a moment to see Darius putting on his coat and meeting Warren at the entryway before they departed. She approached the butler as he closed the door behind them.

"Chelsea, where has Darius gone?"

"To the Doctors' Commons."

"The Doctors' Commons?" she echoed. "Why is he bound there?"

"To apply for a special marriage license from the ecclesiastical courts. I believe he seeks an audience with the Archbishop of Canterbury to approve the application for the license."

Meredith swallowed hard. He had left to get a marriage license, which meant he hadn't listened to a word she said. No, he had seduced her into compliance.

"Thank you, Mr. Chelsea," she murmured and walked with dragging steps up to the bedchamber with a fresh sense of dread weighing her down.

Mrs. Petersham was coming down the corridor, adjusting a dark gold shawl over her dark brown silk gown that made her glow with warmth. She smiled at Meredith, but when Meredith didn't return it, the smile slipped away.

"Whatever is the matter, my dear?" She put an arm around Meredith's shoulders as they entered her bedchamber.

Meredith sank onto the chair facing her elegant vanity table and buried her face in her hands. "Darius is seeking a special license to marry me."

"I thought that's what you hoped for?" Mrs. Petersham placed her hands on Meredith's shoulders as she stood behind her chair, trying to soothe her.

"Yes, but not like this. He is only doing it because he feels it is his duty after we—" she halted, not wanting to admit what happened last night.

"If he has a reason to marry you, then it must be a good one."

Meredith lowered her hands from her face and met Mrs. Petersham's gaze in the mirror.

"Last night...at the ball...We were alone in the gardens... and..." She swallowed hard, mortified to admit what she'd done. "I allowed him to compromise me...fully."

Her chaperone did not seem as surprised as Meredith expected her to be.

"Unfortunately, I believed that was bound to happen, even with me watching you closely. You two are drawn to each other like a pair of cabbage butterflies. I knew it from the first moment I saw you together. The way you both dance around one another, drawing ever closer in a way neither of you even realized was a courtship. You are made for one another. What does it matter how you come together?"

Meredith thought of the beautiful pairs of white butterflies she often saw in Darius's gardens around dusk, swirling in circles around each other. It made her want to smile, but nothing erased the ache in her chest.

"What if a marriage is built upon duty alone and never flowers into love? That is what I fear. I will be a burden to him, a thing he was forced to deal with, not the woman his heart chose."

Mrs. Petersham gave her shoulders a gentle squeeze. "If there is anything that I have learned about love, it is this ... the most wonderful journeys are sometimes the hardest ones. Love, once achieved, may be easy, but the path toward it sometimes is not. Give yourself a chance to trust Darius. I know of few men on this earth who would let duty make them do something they truly did not wish to do, and Darius is not among them. You need to put this out of your mind for the time being. If you worry about it, you'll only find yourself turning in circles."

Mrs. Petersham was right. She should not worry about the situation with Darius, or she'd make herself even more anxious. Meredith's gaze drifted toward the window as she let out a heavy sigh. Her focus fell upon the Crell house. Mrs. Petersham joined her at the window.

"Have you given any more thought about how to catch that dreaded Mr. Crell? I've been pondering over it myself."

Meredith sat up a little straighter as she remembered something else from last evening she wished to share with her chaperone.

"I never had the chance to tell you what I came up with last night about how to catch Mr. Crell."

"Oh?" Mrs. Petersham drew up a chair to sit beside her.

"I think I should write Mr. Crell a letter. I will tell him to meet me at his home in the gardens at a certain day and time. Then, I will have Mr. Doyle come to listen to my conversation with Crell. He should be able to overhear what we say if he stands by the heart-shaped window in the garden wall. I will trick Mr. Crell into confessing his crimes."

Mrs. Petersham's eyes glowed. "Oh yes, that could work. But it will be dangerous. If what you fear is true about what this man has done to his wife, he may try to harm you."

"That is why I plan to have Warren ready to come to my defense, and Mr. Doyle will also be there to render aid if I need it. He will hide in the gardens and watch us in case I fall into some sort of trouble."

"Not Darius?"

"Lord, no. He must never find out. He wouldn't let me do this. Felix is going to tempt him away to the countryside for a shooting expedition for a few days. It will give me time to meet with Mr. Crell and catch him."

"I will agree to help you, so long as we take measures to ensure your safety."

"We have to catch him, Mrs. Petersham. We *have* to.

Mrs. Crell was a lonely woman, lonely and ill, and she did not deserve whatever fate befell her."

Mrs. Petersham nodded. "I agree. Men believe this is their world, and that we women simply must exist in it. I do not agree with that. Women have a right to be here, to exist the same as any man. It is cruel to let whatever happened to this woman never be discovered. We owe it to Mrs. Crell to fight for the truth of what has happened."

"I agree. Shall we collaborate on the wording for the letter?"

"Yes. Darius is out for a few hours, so we have a bit of time to craft the letter without fear of being disturbed."

Meredith was glad for the opportunity to focus on something other than Darius. She pulled out a sheet of paper and retrieved her inkpot and prepared her quill. She and Mr. Petersham made several drafts of the letter until they agreed upon the final wording.

CRELL,

I know what you did. I have proof of your crime. Your careless butler left something behind in the garden. Meet me in two days at seven o'clock in the evening. Bring a thousand pounds as payment for my silence, or I will take the evidence to the Bow Street Runners.

SHE DID NOT SIGN THE NOTE AND WAS CAREFUL TO WRITE IT WITH her left hand. She folded the note once, sealed it with no identifying mark and wrote only the name "Crell." Once that was done, she hid the letter in the pocket of her skirts to keep it safe until she had a chance to get it to Warren without Darius knowing.

"There is not much more we can do until I can entrust this letter to Warren."

"I see no reason to stay here and fret. Perhaps we should go to Gunter's for ices?" Mrs. Petersham volunteered.

Meredith agreed. If she stayed, she would only think about Darius and how he was acquiring their marriage license.

License or no, she intended to refuse him until he proved he wanted her not out of duty but out of love. Since coming to London, she had begun to see herself in a new light. She now believed that she deserved love and respect, and she would not marry without both, no matter how much Darius spoke about duty.

DARIUS STORMED OUT OF THE DOCTORS' COMMONS, WISHING HE could slam a thousand doors.

"Well, that did *not* go as I expected," Warren said as he followed on Darius's heels.

"It certainly didn't." Darius growled. He jerked his gloves on and set his hat on his head a bit too hard. The Archbishop had denied his application for a special license and without any reasonable grounds. It wasn't because the match was unsuitable or inappropriate. No, the Archbishop had informed Darius that any application for Miss Meredith Montague must be approved by the Prince of Wales himself. Such things happened from time to time. The crown could intervene to prevent licenses if it wished to, in rare situations. And it seemed this was one of them.

"Does this mean we are bound for Carlton House?" Warren asked.

"Yes." Even Prince George would not prevent Darius from doing right by Meredith.

Darius hailed his waiting coach, and the pair climbed inside once Darius informed his driver they were bound for Carlton House, the preferred residence of the Prince of Wales. It faced the south side of Pall Mall with its gardens abutting St. James Park, which is where the coach stopped.

At the moment, a fair number of people lingered near the gardens, hoping to catch a glimpse of the prince, but Darius didn't spare the onlookers a glance. He was all too aware of his rude behavior as he pushed past the onlookers and strode to the entrance to Carlton House, but at the moment he could not be made to care.

Darius was still fuming when he and Warren were granted entrance to the royal residence on the main floor. They entered a two-story, top-lit entrance hall decorated with Ionic columns of yellow marble scagliola. A servant had them wait there while he went to inform the prince.

Warren clasped his hands behind his back and admired the decorations around them as though he were in a museum. "You know, I've never been in Carlton House before."

As a favorite of the Crown, Darius had attended many dinners and meetings here over the last few years , but never a private audience with the prince. A small part of him warned caution, but he ignored that sensibility in favor of the side of him that raged at being denied his license.

After a wretched stretch of time, the servant returned and waved for them to follow him.

"His Royal Highness will see you now. Please, follow me."

The white-wigged servant dressed in royal livery led them down an octagon shaped hall, which was flanked by the grand staircase on the right and the courtyard on the left. They were taken down to the Circular Room. The room was adorned with a vast, glittering chandelier that hung from the wide, cloud-covered painted ceiling.

George, the Prince of Wales was seated in a chair by the fireplace, a newspaper spread open in front of him. He was the very picture of tranquility which only irritated Darius more. A footman stood close by, guarding a tea tray that was ready for whenever the prince wanted some refreshment.

The servant who had escorted Darius and Warren cleared his throat before speaking. "His Grace, the Duke of Tiverton and Mr. Warren Burville."

They approached and bowed...then waited for the prince to acknowledge them. The prince turned another page, ignoring them as he continued to read. He had to know why they were here. Darius stared directly at the prince while Warren politely examined the room as though he could wait all day.

They waited for what felt like an eternity before the prince lowered his paper. He passed the paper to the footman, who folded it and placed it upon a nearby table. Only then did the prince stand and walk toward them.

"Tiverton, let me hazard a guess as to why you are here. You sought out a license from the Archbishop for your ward to marry someone and were denied your application." The prince's voice held a note of disapproval, and Darius could not understand why.

Darius reigned in his temper. The last thing he wanted was to infuriate the future King of England. "That is correct."

Prince George nodded to himself. "Tea, gentlemen?" He waved for the footman to pour tea.

"No, thank you, Your Royal Highness." Darius waved off the offer of tea. "I've come to seek your approval. The Archbishop said he was under strict orders to reject any application for Miss Montague without your express permission, and he did not explain why."

"Nor would he, since I didn't provide him with an explanation. Who is the gentleman she will be marrying?" The prince sipped his tea with an amused light in his eyes. "Rumor has it there is quite a line of interested men. Some say Mr. Evers is the current contender for the young lady's heart."

Darius was not at all surprised by this knowledge of Meredith's marriage prospects. Ever since the prince had sent Meredith that letter following their meeting, Darius knew he'd taken an interest in her future.

"It is..." Darius straightened his shoulders, preparing for the prince's judgment. "Me, Sir. The license is for me."

"You?" George's brows rose. "Come now, Tiverton, do not jest with me."

"I am not, Sir."

"But you've never shown an interest in marriage before. Most of the eligible ladies have given up hope of catching you. You can't expect me to believe that a woman with Miss Montague's scandalous history is suitable to be the future Duchess of Tiverton. No, I simply do not believe it." The prince's tone was almost dismissive. "Timmons, poor the tea, please. Mr. Burville, would you like some tea?"

"Yes, thank you, Your Royal Highness," Warren replied as the Prince waved them over to sit down.

Darius refused to sit and began to pace around the room. Warren and the Prince George drank their tea and watched Darius prowl about.

"Well, are you going to tell me the truth of this matter?" George finally asked Darius. "And please stop that pacing. I find it distressing."

Darius halted near the chairs and waited for his stomach to stop twisting itself in knots. There was no other way around it. He would have to be honest with the prince.

"The truth is, I have a duty to marry Miss Montague."

"Oh dear, *duty* is it?" The prince attempted and failed to hide a little smile behind his teacup and Warren outright grinned.

"Oh yes," Warren interrupted. "As you must be aware, Sir, Tiverton's very soul is comprised of duty."

"Indeed, I do," George replied. "And that is why I'm not going to allow his marriage license to be approved."

"What?" Darius sputtered.

Prince George frowned at him, causing Darius to mutter a mortified apology.

"*Please*, Sir. It is of the utmost importance that I marry Miss Montague at once."

"What could be so important to drive you to the altar, Tiverton?" The prince's voice dropped slightly as he arched a brow, with a hint of mischief in his eyes. "Are you madly in love with the young lady?"

He was in lust, certainly, and obviously he cared for her. He even suspected he *was* falling in love with her, but he wasn't about to admit that to the prince.

"I find her company to be pleasing and I believe we shall do well together."

There was a heavy silence and Darius realized he'd made some terrible error in his choice of words, only what it was he hadn't the foggiest.

George set his cup down on its saucer with a sharp clatter. "Then I'm afraid the answer is still no, Tiverton."

Warren choked on his tea.

"But Sir, I—" It would only make matters worse if he admitted what he had done last night, but there seemed to be no other way forward. "Sir, the lady has been compromised," Darius said, his tone quiet, his cheeks on fire.

"By whom?" The prince asked.

He felt like a schoolboy called upon the carpets by his governess for spilling the pot on his father's favorite white rug. That had been an awful day, and it felt just the same as now...only far more than his father's disappointment was at stake.

"By *me*."

"I see." George leaned back in his chair. "And have you received Miss Montague's acceptance? We both agree that her feelings on the matter must be acknowledged and respected."

"She will agree."

"You mean you haven't asked her?" the prince snorted. "A lady *must* be asked, Tiverton."

"I...er...informed her that we were to be wed... this morning."

At Darius's reluctant admission, the prince rolled his eyes, and Warren shook his head in disappointment.

"*Informed?* My dear Tiverton, what on earth is to be done with you? Someone cannot be *commanded* into marriage, even if they are compromised. Will she be ruined? Yes, most certainly, but a man cannot force a woman into marriage. A woman must be wooed into it."

"Sir, if I may interject," said Warren. "Tiverton has never had the necessity to woo a young lady. They tend to fall into his arms at the slightest provocation. Perhaps you could offer him a few suggestions as to *how* he should go about wooing?"

Darius shot his friend a quelling look.

The prince puffed up with pride at being asked for such

advice. "Isn't it obvious? Flowers, sweets, hand-holding, walks in the garden. Recite some poetry, for God's sake, Tiverton. *Woo* her, and when she has informed me herself that she has accepted you, I shall tell the Archbishop you have my permission to receive a marriage license."

"But Sir—"

"Do not argue with me," he said flatly, his tone clearly ending the argument. "Now sit down, have a cup of tea and collect your wits, Tiverton. You will need them, it would seem."

Darius slumped into a chair and woodenly accepted a cup from the footman. Warren began an animated discussion with the prince on the latest fashions from the continent, and the prince was more than happy to provide his opinion on the newest ways to tie cravat, as well as patterns and cuts for trousers.

Darius listened to none of this. His frown deepened on his face as he tried to figure out how he was going to marry Meredith without going against the Crown.

He took another sip of tea, not tasting it at all, and continued to worry over his situation. Meredith would have to be tricked or cajoled into accepting his proposal, that was the simplest solution.

Woo her? Flowers? Sweets? Poetry? The very idea was ridiculous to him. It was performative art, and to him that felt akin to falsehood. The truth was that marriage was the logical thing to do, and one did not approach a truth with lies. Even if he did give into his more romantic tendencies and try to woo her, would she even believe he truly wanted her and cared about her, especially after he had commanded her earlier?

When their audience with the prince concluded, they left Carlton House and returned to their coach, pressing past the gathered onlookers once more.

Darius glared at his friend as he opened the coach door. "Do not say a word."

Warren grinned like a jackal as he settled into the seat opposite Darius. "Wasn't going to, old boy."

Warren was right. He didn't know how to woo. But he *did* know how to seduce and perhaps that was a place to start. Seduction, at least, was honest about its intentions.

With a renewed sense of determination, Darius stared out the coach window, planning how best to seduce his ward. Because he *was* going to marry her, even if he had to defy the monarchy to do it.

14

Meredith stepped out of the coach, carefully lifting her skirts and accepting the footman's offered hand. She had changed into a promenade dress of blush pink with long tailored sleeves. Silver embroidered plumes decorated the hem of the gown and the bodice.

It was a more sedate gown. Meredith had chosen it out of a desire to blend in, rather than stand out. Most of the dresses Darius had bought were stunningly beautiful works of art that would catch the attention of any man and the envy of any woman. But today, that was exactly what she wished to avoid.

Mrs. Petersham shared a glance with Meredith as they noticed with regret how crowded Berkeley Square was at this time of day. She'd wanted to get out and distract herself from the thought of Darius acquiring a special marriage license, but she hadn't given thought to being around other people. After Lady Mary Raikes' stinging words, she felt strangely exposed whenever strangers looked at her.

"It's just ice cream. I'm sure we'll be fine," Mrs. Petersham said.

They headed toward Gunter's, the famed confectionery shop at number seven in Berkeley Square. The shop had been founded by an Italian pastry cook, Domenico Negri, who specialized in a wide range of sweet and savory foods. Darius had once said that Negri was one of the first confectioneries in England to establish ice cream and water ices as a delicacy. When James Gunter had taken over the business, he renamed the shop and soon all of London's ladies were eager to have Gunter's cater their large dinner parties with fine pastries, sweets and ice creams.

As they entered the shop, Meredith felt dozens of eyes on her. All of the ladies and gentlemen in the shop were watching her. Unfortunately, Meredith recognized one of the women as one of those who had kept company with Lady Mary last evening at the ball. Had Lady Mary's cruel words last night traveled so quickly?

"Chin up, dear." Mrs. Petersham took Meredith's arm in hers and they approached the countertop to examine the confections and pastries on display. A waiter stood ready to take their order. Meredith stared at the collection of pewter molds and whimsical shapes that hung on the back wall.

"We freeze them in flavored ices," the waiter explained to Meredith when he caught her examining the various molds that were in the shapes of animals or fruits.

"How delightful!" said Meredith.

The waiter's face reddened at her reaction.

"I would like a flavored ice of jasmine and rose," Mrs. Petersham told the young man.

"And may I try the orange flower?" Meredith added.

The young man accepted Mrs. Petersham's payment and told them to find a table and he would bring the ices to them in a moment. There was a single empty table in the center of the room and Meredith hated how she felt like she was on display. Meredith sat down and placed her reticule on her lap.

Her chaperone leaned forward to whisper. "So we must get your note to Warren, that is our next task."

Meredith nodded. She had been thinking the same thing. But her eyes caught two men looking her way and whispering as they ate their desserts. There were gentlemen, judging by their dress, but Meredith didn't like the way there looking at her as though they *knew* something intimate about her. One of them smirked at her.

"Meredith?" Mrs. Petersham spoke her name in a quiet question.

"Two men are watching me," Meredith whispered as calmly as she could to her chaperone. "Do not look."

The waiter came to deliver their ices. Meredith tried hers, wishing she could enjoy it more without worrying. Several women started whispering nearby. It was hard for Meredith not to overhear some of their conversations.

"... some by-blow, I heard ..."

"... likely entrap Tiverton in marriage..."

"...well, who wouldn't? I heard..."

"...Nonsense. No gentleman would take..."

"...except as a mistress, I suppose..." The men who had eyed her before stood and came to her table. They stopped directly in front of her and Mrs. Petersham.

"Good afternoon, Miss Montague," one of them greeted her, his lascivious grin twisting her stomach sharply in apprehension.

It was appropriate for single men and women to meet at Gunter's for ice cream, but a man was not supposed to approach a woman without an introduction. These two men were breaking the rules of propriety, and Meredith dreaded discovering the reason that made them so confident in doing so.

"Sir, we do not know you," Mrs. Petersham said sharply, though she kept her voice down. "*Kindly* walk away."

"Ahh, but I wish to know the young lady," the man said, his eyes still locked on Meredith.

His companion chuckled and added, "As do I."

Meredith's mouth fell open at what these men were suggesting about her.

"I believe I said *walk away*," Mrs. Petersham's tone was as cold as the northernmost sea.

Meredith glanced around, all too aware of the people now watching this encounter, but desperate not to show how much it upset her.

"Oh hush, you old dragon," the first man said his voice a little louder as he snapped at her. "Your charge needs no protecting, not when it comes to sharing her favors."

"Oh, I am a dragon ... but *old?*" Mrs. Petersham set her flavored ice down on the little table and stood up, glaring at the two men. Neither of them seemed to be the least bit frightened by her.

"Come now, Miss Montague. Why don't you join us outside in our carriage? We can make it worth your while."

Meredith gasped as she rose to her feet as well, abandoning her orange flower ice in its little glass cup. "How dare you!"

"Come now. You do yourself no service by playing coy," the second man said. "We know you are willing to keep us company."

"I am most certainly not!" She turned to Mrs. Petersham. "I believe it's time we left."

"Agreed," Mrs. Petersham reached for Meredith's arm, but one of the men stepped between them and grabbed Meredith's arm with a gloved hand. Mrs. Petersham swung her reticule at the second man who tried to block her from getting to Meredith. He grunted as whatever she had in her small bag obviously hurt when it made contact with his skull.

"Let go—" Meredith wrenched her arm free of the one who'd grabbed her. The man scowled and reached for her again, this time more forcefully.

A deep voice rose from behind Meredith. "The lady said to let her go."

The two men glanced up. One paled slightly, the other one laughed in defiance.

"This has nothing to do with you, Lord Grey."

"Is that so?"

Meredith could breathe again and recognized the voice now. Felix Hawkins, the Marquess of Grey. He would chase these horrid men away.

"She's not claimed by any man," the second gentleman said to Felix. "She's open to spreading her favors *and* her legs. We have a right to her."

At this, Felix laughed. "Oh, that's rich. You have a right to her? No, you do not, and your insults will deal you only one favor … from *me*. But I'm feeling generous today, so I will thrash you here rather than kill you in a duel."

"Hold on—" The first gentleman blustered as he backed away. "You wouldn't hit a gentleman in Gunter's."

"No, I probably would not hit a gentleman. Fortunately for me…you aren't one." That was the only warning that Meredith had for what came next.

Felix swept her to the side with one arm while he swung a balled fist at the first man's face with the other. The dull sound of flesh impacting against flesh made Meredith's stomach turn. Several women screamed as the man Felix hit flew over the table behind him, sending it toppling to the ground with a crash of glass.

The second man spun to face Felix with a snarl and tried to land a blow. But Felix was ready. He ducked backward, light on his feet as he taunted the other man.

"Come on now, Lauder. Show me what all those expensive boxing lessons have done for you!"

Lauder raised his fists as the two began to circle one another. By now, most of the shop patrons had fled in terror. Meredith and Mrs. Petersham rushed to get out of the way of Felix and Lauder.

The waiter waved his arms frantically, as if somehow that would gain their attention. "Sirs! Please, I beg you, stop!" He tried to get between them, but in his haste he slipped upon a sponge cake that had fallen from a nearby table and landed on some broken glass. The waiter cried out in pain, and Meredith hastened to the poor man's side with Mrs. Petersham to examine his injuries.

"Please, let me help you," Meredith told the man. He nodded shakily as Meredith fetched some clean cloth from behind the pastry counter and cleaned the man's wounds. She didn't know too much about wounds, but she did know the basics of bandaging after one of Uncle Ben's new grooms had been bitten by one of the horses. She tried to bandage his arm while staying out of the way of the fight.

The shop was all but empty of patrons now as Felix and Lauder continued to exchange punches. The man who had been knocked down earlier now got to his feet and prepared to lunge at Felix from behind.

Meredith screamed a warning, but was too late. Felix was hit in the back by the man, taking them both to the ground. They tumbled on the ground until the man was on top of Felix, hitting him twice and drawing blood.

Felix grinned through bloodied teeth and grabbed the man's head, driving his own forehead into the man's nose. It stunned the man, who rolled off Felix, clutching at his bleeding nose.

But the fight was far from over. Meredith and Mrs.

Petersham helped the waiter to his feet to get him out of the way before the two men grabbed Felix and tossed him into the glass display cases of pastries nearby.

The waiter groaned in despair. "Not the pastries…"

"Look out!" Mrs. Petersham pulled the waiter and Meredith away just as Felix dove past them back into the fray. But no sooner had he done so than he took another blow to the stomach and doubled over.

"They're going to kill him!" She had to stop the fight somehow. Meredith released her hold on the waiter so she could run to Felix's aid, only to be stopped and hoisted off her feet by someone. She squealed as she was set gently down next to a tall man's hard body.

"Stay here!" Darius shouted at her. He and Warren seemed to have materialized out of thin air, and now dove into the chaotic fight. They tackled the two other men, knocking everyone to the floor with another crush of bodies.

"Darius?" Meredith said and covered her mouth with her hands. "Oh no…"

The day had gone from bad to worse … *much* worse.

FIVE MINUTES EARLIER, DARIUS'S COACH HAD BEEN PASSING BY Berkley Square.

"Seems something strange is happening at Gunter's," said Warren, leaning closer to his window for a better look.

"They haven't resorted to some silly form of human

advertising, have they?" Darius asked. Ever since London started taxing advertising posters, businesses had been finding ways around it. Usually with a sign, but once he'd seen a man wearing a ridiculously oversized hat with the store's services written on it.

"Not unless their intention is to scare off customers."

"What?" Darius pushed the coach curtains back to get a look. Men and women were rushing out of the confectioner's shop in an obvious panic. Just then, a crash loud enough to be heard on the street caused the young ladies to scream.

Darius banged his fist on the coach roof, a sign for his driver to halt immediately.

"Let's see what's causing all the fuss." Darius opened the coach door and hopped out, glad he didn't need his cane for once. Warren followed. As they reached the confectioner's door, he saw a sight that chilled his blood.

Meredith and Frances Petersham were clutching an injured waiter by the arms, looking on in terror as two men pummeled a third. *Felix*.

His friend's face was bruised and bloodied, but he looked like the very devil as he grinned while he fought on. But Felix wasn't winning the fight. Not without help.

Warren cursed under his breath and looked at Darius. "What the devil's gotten into him?"

"We'll deal with that later," said Darius. "Ready?"

Warren nodded. "Ready."

As they rushed inside, Meredith left the safety of the corner and moved towards the fray, intending to help Felix.

If she got hurt…he'd *kill* those men. But first he was going to do his damnest to stop her from reaching Felix and the other men.

He ran up behind her and grabbed her by the waist, pulling her back and setting her close to the wall, keeping himself between her and danger.

"Stay here!" he barked before joining Warren's charge into battle.

Darius landed a blow on one of the men's kidneys, but he lost his balance a second later and fell. Broken glass and pastries now littered the floor, and a shard cut into his forearm as he landed, but he did not let the pain stop him. Darius got up and struck his staggered opponent hard in the jaw.

The man swayed on his feet briefly, then collapsed on top of his friend, who Warren had knocked out a moment earlier.

Felix struggled to sit up, spitting blood but still smiling. "Pleasant of you to join in," he said with a laugh, then winced and put a hand to his ribs.

"What the bloody hell happened?" Darius asked between hard breaths.

Felix glanced at the two unconscious men. "These chaps publicly propositioned Miss Montague. They did not take her rejection kindly."

"I see." Darius looked toward Meredith, who stared at him wide-eyed, her hands clasped over her mouth. He felt like a villain at that moment. She'd seen the worst of him, brawling like a dockworker in a tavern. She must be terrified of him. No woman should have to see a man be so brutish.

"Come on, on your feet." He and Warren helped Felix to his feet. Felix still held a hand to his ribs and walked with a limp. Darius turned his attention to the ladies. "Meredith, Frances, wait for me in my coach outside."

"We have a coach ready—" Frances began.

"Warren shall take Felix home in your coach, but Meredith shall accompany me in mine." He growled the command lest anyone thought to argue with him.

"Yes, Your Grace. Let me help you, Mr. Burville." Frances assisted Warren in walking Felix out to the other coach.

But Meredith remained where was, staring at him, her bottom lip trembling.

Blast and Damn!

"Your Grace—" she began, "It was all my fault. I—"

"It absolutely was not," Darius snapped. "Now wait for me in my coach, Meredith." With tears in her eyes, Meredith rushed out of the confectioner's shop.

Darius approached the injured waiter. He removed his card and presented it to the man.

"Tell Mr. Gunter I shall pay for the damages and any lost business. After you see a physician or surgeon, you are to have them send your bill to me."

The young man's hand shook as he took Darius's card. "Thank you, Your Grace."

"Will you be all right to get yourself to a physician? I can take you in my coach if you wish me to."

The young man shook his head. "Thank you, but it's not that bad. I believe I am more shaken than anything."

"Quite understandable," Darius said gently. "This is a genteel establishment, and you are not expected to see such violence, and for that I am sorry."

Once he was sure the waiter would be all right, he left the shop. The other carriage had already left. A number of women stood across the street, fans fluttering and sharing whispers that somehow managed to reach his ears, but he ignored them. He knew he must look frightful. Pastries, sugar, and melting ices mixed with blood on his coat and trousers. He could feel pieces of glass still sticking out of his sleeves.

What a damned mess!

His footman opened the coach door for him as he arrived, and Darius climbed inside. Meredith was alone on the opposite seat, which meant Frances must have accompanied Warren and Felix. He didn't care that she was without her chaperone. The damage was done and no matter what Prince George said, they would be married soon.

Meredith's face looked out the window, away from him. Her lip still trembled a little. One of her sleeves was ripped, and a glint of broken glass was visible in the crown of her hair. Only now did he realize that some of the blood on the floor of the shop could have been hers. Suddenly, Darius felt like he couldn't breathe. He struggled to fight off the wave of panic he felt.

"Meredith," he began, his voice a raspy croak.

At the sound of her name, she burst into tears. He moved to sit beside her and pulled her toward him. She struggled but then surrendered as he settled her on his lap and tucked her face into the crook of his neck. Darius rubbed his palm against her back until she stopped crying. He carefully removed the bit of glass from her hair and tried to still her shaking with his arms.

"Were you hurt?" he asked as he gently brushed his fingertips over her cheek.

"I don't think I am injured..."

"Then why the tears? Was it because of me? I never meant for you to see me like that. I know I must have frightened you."

She lifted her tear-stained face. "Frightened of you? Darius, you *saved* me," she whispered, her breath still unsteady. "I am upset because those men heard that I spread my favors. They thought I was willing to go with them to their coach and treated me like some lightskirt in front of everyone. Darius, I believe the Lady Mary Raikes words have ruined me worse than anything that happened in the gardens last night."

"All the more reason for us to marry."

Meredith set her head on his shoulder and was quiet a long moment.

Surely now she would see reason, he thought. Marriage to him would be the easiest way for him to protect her now that society had taken a disliking to her.

But her answer was as brief as it was absolute. "No."

Rather than anger Darius, that one word took all the wind out of his sails.

"I will not marry out of some silly need to be protected." There was no fear or anger in her voice now, just simple resolve. "I will only marry for love."

Was the protection of his name and the protection of her body not enough? Did she have to ask for something he feared to give her?

Say it. Say it, you fool.

But the words remained trapped on his tongue, unable to get free. When the coach finally stopped in front of his home, Meredith got out without another word and hurried to her bedchamber.

That was when Darius realized he was losing her. And he had only himself to blame.

15

Darius winced as the surgeon removed the last slender shard of glass from his arm. He dropped the piece into a towel that contained several other bloody fragments. The surgeon peered at Darius's arms closely and wiped wet cloths over the wounds.

"May I borrow some of your brandy, Your Grace?" the surgeon asked.

"Yes, of course. It's on the drink cart over there." He nodded at the elegant wooden drink cart against one wall in his study.

"Hold this tight, please." Darius kept the bloody cloth pressed tight to his arm while the surgeon retrieved the bottle from the cart and soaked a fresh cloth in the liquid.

"This will sting," the surgeon warned. He removed the cloth Darius had been holding in place and replaced it with the brandy-soaked towel.

"Bloody hell!" The burn had hit him like a runaway

carriage. He bit his lip to keep a second curse from escaping his lips. "That was a lot more than a sting," he muttered as the burn slowly subsided. The doctor nearly smiled. Darius felt like a child for overreacting, but damn, it *had* hurt.

"I've noticed that pouring brandy or scotch on a wound works far better than bloodletting."

Darius hoped the man was right. Bloodletting was an awful experience.

"Thank you, Dr. Bradburn," Darius said as the man bandaged his arm tight with strips of cloth.

"No bathing this arm for a few days. Change the dressing once a day, and soak the wounds in brandy or scotch if it starts to feel too hot or look too red. You'll have some scars, but nothing too terrible, I should think."

"No worse than any of the other scars," Darius said with a chuckle.

The surgeon studied Darius. "How are you feeling? The leg still giving you trouble?"

"Not as much. Perhaps more on the days it storms."

"Possibly because of barometric pressure. I believe that one's body fluids and muscle tissues can be affected by changes in the pressure in the atmosphere."

"Interesting." Darius touched his bad leg absently. It was a habit he'd developed since the injury. He was more than a little relieved that his leg hadn't given in during the fight at the confectioner's shop.

"May I ask what caused today's injuries?" Bradburn packed up his materials in his black leather medical satchel.

"A minor disagreement with a few gentlemen who were

anything but," he said evasively. His felt renewed rage as he'd remembered Meredith telling him what those men had said, what they had wanted of her. "We made a mess of Gunter's."

"The flavored ice shop? I hope some of it's still standing. I rather like their cinnamon and clove pastries."

"I will be paying for the damages." Darius flexed his left hand, testing the strength of the wrappings around his forearm. They held fast. "Allow me to see you out."

He followed the surgeon into the corridor and escorted him to the entryway, where Mr. Chelsea handed him his hat and coat.

"Thank you again." He shook hands with the surgeon and Chelsea escorted him out.

The townhouse was deathly quiet as Darius climbed the stairs and headed for Meredith's bedchamber. Her door was closed. He lingered in front of it for a long moment before he finally decided to knock.

No one answered. He opened the door, whispering Meredith's name. She lay on her bed, curled up in a ball, facing away from him.

"Meredith, sweetheart," he said a little more loudly.

"Please go away," she replied in a raspy voice that suggested she'd been crying for some time.

His answer was as brief as it was absolute. "No."

His response tore a half-sob, half-laugh from her. He stepped inside and closed the door. Dusk was settling on the garden outside, and the muted light was a mix of purple and deep rose. The window was open, and a flowing breeze teased the air with hints of wildflowers. Something tight and painful in his chest eased when he breathed in that scent.

Darius came around the far side of the bed to see Meredith. Her face still shone with drying tracks of tears, her nose was red and her eyes puffy. Yet she looked beautiful to him. She always did. But he *hated* that she had cried, and that he was at least partly responsible for it.

He sat down on the bed beside her. "Do you want to hear something amusing?"

Her vacant, weary gaze drifted from the distant window to his face. He saw a faint glimmer of interest in her hazel eyes.

"The Prince Regent says I'm *not allowed* to marry you." Darius gave a half-smile as her eyes widened. "Not until you notify the Prince yourself that you have agreed to it."

Meredith's lips parted in shock. "He said that?"

"Oh yes." Darius chuckled, though he felt little mirth at the thought of their monarch having put him in his place. "Warren and I were told by the Archbishop of Canterbury that any special license for you to marry must be approved by the prince first. You *specifically*. I had no idea what that was all about. So naturally we went straight to Carlton House to seek answers."

He paused a moment, reflecting on how much effort the Prince Regent had gone to over this matter. "You must have made quite the impression the night you met him," said Darius. "I was forced to suffer a lecture about how I simply *cannot* command you to marry me."

"Well, he's right. You cannot force me." Meredith sniffled and sat up a little, bracing her shoulder against the carved wooden headboard and pillows.

Darius tried to change the subject. "Do you wish to talk about what happened today?" He placed a hand on hers, meshing their fingers together.

"No."

He smiled sadly. "Very well, then I shall speak. I was frightened today. When I saw you in danger from those men, it terrified me. Had anything happened to you, Meredith, I would have ..." He cleared his throat. "I could not bear it. If I lost you ... I would want to burn the world down. As someone who prides myself on my self-control ... being with you makes me feel *wildly* out of control."

Her eyes grew luminous. "You truly feel that way?"

Darius nodded.

"I didn't mean to cause any trouble," she said in a quiet voice. "Mrs. Petersham and I believed a little outing would be fine."

"And it should have been. I fear Lady Mary's anger at me has sent her spreading rumors about you. But that is not your fault, it is mine. Warren and I were rude to her, which made matters far worse for you."

He raised her hand to his lips, kissing the backs of her fingers. Her lashes fluttered. His heart skipped a beat as a surge of intense feelings deepened within him.

He felt as though he was standing at the edge of an ancient wishing well, feeling the stones beneath his palms as he gazed deeply into the magical waters below. The chance to love Meredith would be like casting a coin into that enchanted pool and having not one, but *every* wish granted.

It frightened him to feel so much for one person. He had lost so much in his life. He lost his mother as a boy, his father as a young man, and now his uncle. What if he lost Meredith? He could not bear such loss. Yet he had no words to tell her what lay in his heart. Those words were birds with wings of gold flying high into a glorious sunrise escaping his lips. At times he felt distanced from those he loved because words of affection were not easy for him to say, not because he didn't mean them, but stating such a thing felt like playacting, when he preferred to show his friends by his actions how he felt. And with Meredith...he didn't know where to start in showing just how much he adored her.

She touched the edge of the white bandage covering his left arm. "You're hurt."

"It doesn't hurt," he lied, but was moved by her compassion for him. "I know that I must have frightened you today with such a display of violence. But you must know that I would never hurt you."

"I know," Meredith said. "And as I said before, you didn't frighten me. You saved me."

How could she think of him as some noble hero when he'd done nothing more than fight like a brute? The mad thing was that he *wanted* to be her hero. To save her when she needed him, to keep her from harm, to give her everything of himself.

"Perhaps I should check you for injuries?" He tried to tease her, but his voice was too low and husky to be teasing.

She raised her chin, her lips parting as she held his gaze. "Perhaps you should."

He hummed softly as he set her feet across his lap. Darius began to unfasten the ribbons at her ankles that tied her slippers on. He stroked her stockinged feet as he slid the ribbons free and removed the slippers one at a time.

He traced the delicate arches of her feet and brushed his fingers around her toes before they slid up her skirts to her knees, where he loosened the ribbons that held her stockings up next. She didn't move as he rolled the stockings down off her legs and explored her soft skin.

"No sign of injuries here," he murmured.

"Then you'd better check elsewhere, just to be certain."

Meredith's teasing sent a thrill through him. She slid her legs off his lap and got off the bed.

"Indeed, I should," he agreed."

She turned her back to him as she pulled her hair out of the way so Darius could unbutton the back of her gown. Her breath caught as his fingers slipped along the skin of her upper back, and he was glad he had enough control not to rush this exquisite moment. The gown fell into a puddle of fabric at her feet. He leaned in, kissing her bare shoulder and neck as he undid the laces of her stays.

He bared her body in slow, gentle moves, stroking and kissing a dozen sweet places that drew soft and dreamy sighs from her.

Outside, a soft rain began to fall, enhancing the scent of

the flowers that drifted in from the garden, perfuming the room with a floral enchantment. Meredith peered at him over her bare shoulder, her hair tumbling down her back as she raised her hazel eyes to meet his.

"Find any injuries?" she asked, her voice soft, breathless.

"None at all. You are perfection itself," he replied. His hands trembled with the depth of his desire to pull her into his arms.

"Then perhaps I should check *you* for injuries now?" she asked with a seductive huskiness.

"Well, the doctor was just here," he said, raising his bandaged arm as evidence. "But it is always wise to garner a second opinion in such matters." He chuckled and held his breath as a deliciously naked Meredith turned to face him. Her hand slid over his waistcoat and began to free the buttons. It was the sweetest of tortures to allow her remove his clothing.

Once his chest was bared to her, she kissed his chest, his shoulders, his chin, exploring him in ways she hadn't had a chance to in the gardens the night before.

His body grew hard and hungry for her, but his heart refused to let him rush this moment with her. This wasn't a moment of lust to be slaked, but something more to be savored. She sat back on the bed and beckoned him to her with a curving finger. He had no desire to refuse, and crawled over the bed until he covered his body with hers.

Their mouths met in soft, fervent kisses that were sweeter and hotter the longer their bodies pressed against each other. She parted her legs, and he settled in the cradle of her thighs. It felt like coming home. *This* ... this was where he belonged. Here, loving this woman until nothing else existed and empires crumbled, and new stars were born in the night sky.

"You are *everything* to me," he whispered against her lips. "*Everything*." These he knew, were the right words to say, because they were so very easy and so very true to how his heart felt. He sank into the welcoming heat of her body, and Meredith moaned in pleasure against his mouth as they kissed.

Darius became lost in her—the taste, the feel, the intoxicating magic of all that Meredith was. He would have forsaken his sight to hear her laugh in delight again, and he would have surrendered years of his life for one last lingering look upon her face.

Meredith lifted her hips, meeting him in a gentle rhythm. They were unhurried in their lovemaking. He taught her how to love with his body, to let their heat and passion burn like a fire on a dark night, unable to be blown out by even the strongest of winds. Even if he could not find romantic enough words for it, he showed her in every kiss, every caress, every gentle thrust in their joining what it was to *love*.

She cried out his name, her legs tightening around his hips, and he released himself inside her, breathing her name in a soft chant. If ever there was a moment perfect enough to create a new life born out of love, he prayed this was it.

This was the simple truth of it. He wanted a life with Meredith, a future of endless wonder and adventure at her side. He would show her the world, teach her to take up space in it, and never again feel like she had to cower or that her voice was silenced because society didn't think she mattered.

"Marry me, Meredith." He nuzzled her nose with his own before sealing his question with another kiss. "Please marry me...because I cannot live without you."

She opened her eyes and looked up at him, their bodies still joined so intimately.

"Are you *asking* this time?" She arched a brow, and he wanted to laugh and kiss her senseless.

He nodded.

"Do you love me?" she asked, her gaze solemn.

He nodded.

"Say the words, Darius. I *need* the words." She said this so earnestly that he knew she did in fact need the words, the words that until now had been so hard to say because of what he feared would happen if he admitted loving her. But he'd gone too far now down this path to deny her what she deserved to hear.

"To say the words in a way that conveys all that I feel for you would take years to speak, and to say them in their simplest form would sound woefully inadequate," he replied honestly.

"All that matters is that the words come from your heart, Darius. That's the only thing that's ever mattered to me."

He knew he had to speak the words that mattered more than anything as simple as they were. "I love you," he whispered, praying that was enough for her to know how much he loved her.

Her gaze searched his for a long moment. "Yes, I will marry you. But what if you regret your choice? Lady Mary will not let her slight be forgotten."

Darius stole another kiss. "She will not make it easy, but now that we are both prepared for the coming storm, we can weather it together."

What he did not add was that he planned to visit Lady Mary and warn her that if she said another word against Meredith, she would make a very powerful enemy. What happened at Gunter's today would never happen again.

"Will you write to the prince tomorrow and tell him that I *asked* for your hand in marriage, and that you accepted?"

Meredith smiled at him. "Yes."

"Good. Now let's get beneath the covers. I want to hold you."

Darius held Meredith until she was fast asleep. He waited until the shadows of night settled over her face before he slipped out of bed. Darius put on his trousers and retrieved his dressing gown from his room, wrapping the belt around his waist. Moving through his house barefoot, he headed for the kitchens to retrieve some food. To his surprise, he met Mrs. Petersham on the stairs coming up. He had forgotten that she hadn't returned with them.

"Frances. You're back late."

"I was watching over your friend, Lord Grey until half an hour ago."

Darius nodded. "How is he?"

"Far too glib for a man who has taken so many blows. You'd almost think the man had enjoyed himself." Frances replied with a frown.

Darius chuckled. She might not have been far from the truth on that.

"How is Meredith?" Frances asked as if she'd been aware where Darius had been, but was polite enough not to mention it.

"Better now." He paused, then smiled. "She's finally agreed to marry me."

Frances's serious gaze filled with the light of hope. "Has she?"

"Yes."

"That's wonderful news, Your Grace. This makes me so very happy but ..." Her face fell.

"What is it, Frances?"

"In the short time I've lived here, I've grown to love this house, and love you and Meredith as my family. I will be sorry to leave. Would you permit me to visit you often? I would like to find a place to live that isn't too far away by coach so that Meredith and I could have tea each week."

Darius took the woman's hands in his. "Frances, you've become family to us as well. You do not need to leave."

She shook her head. "I would only be in the way of a newly married couple."

"Nonsense. You are staying, and that is the end of the matter."

Frances's eyes shone with happy tears. "Then I shall bid you goodnight on such happy news."

"Good night," he said with a chuckle before continuing down the stairs to the kitchens.

MEREDITH WOKE TO FIND HERSELF ALONE IN BED. HER FIRST thought was that Darius hadn't been there at all, and that what they had shared had just been a dream. Her eyes filled with tears, and she covered her face with her hands.

She didn't hear the door open, nor the rush of footsteps until they were right next to her. A pair of strong hands caught her wrists and she looked up into Darius's concerned face.

"Meredith, what's the matter?" His dark hair fell in his beautiful blue eyes that seemed to peer straight to her soul.

"It's rather silly. I thought ... When I woke and found you gone, I thought perhaps I dreamed everything that we..." She choked on a sob.

He sat down beside her. "Sweetheart, you didn't dream it. We did do that, all of that. You also agreed to marry me. After you fell asleep, I went to scrounge up a late supper." He nodded toward the tray of food he'd set at the foot of the bed.

"Oh ..." She felt even more silly now.

"Now, if you will permit me, I will fetch us some wine. I

will be back." He promised with a kiss that made her swoon before he left again.

Meredith pulled the sheet up around her body as she slipped out of the bed and walked over to the window overlooking the gardens.

It wasn't a dream. She was going to marry Darius St. John. He *wanted* to marry her. He *loved* her.

The world became filled with wonder and possibilities. It was like a dream come true, one that she hadn't even dared to dream for herself. Such things belonged in the realm of fairy tales.

But as Meredith's gaze drifted to the darkened Crell house beyond the garden wall, she remembered that not every tale had a happy ending. For a brief instant, she thought she saw the shape of Minerva Crell standing just beside the heart-shaped hole in the wall, but the figure was nothing more than shadows.

Meredith had the terrible sense that something was about to shift. She was standing on the edge of the cliff knowing that she would have to jump, but to what ultimate fate?

16

Waking up next to Darius was like a lovely dream, made even sweeter because it was real. Meredith cuddled against his body and savored the warmth of him. In the soft morning light, she had a chance to caress his body with a longing gaze. With a soft smile, she brushed her hands over his chest. A faint patch of dark hair was framed by his pectoral muscles, and another faint trail of hair below his navel led to…

Oh heavens…

With a little smile, she slid her hand beneath the sheets and gasped when her hand touched his male hardness. Darius groaned, and his eyes opened. When he realized who was touching him, his lips curved into a sensual grin.

"Good morning," she said. It should have been terribly embarrassing to be caught holding his cock, but she was too startled at having been caught to let go.

"It certainly will be if you keep touching me like that, love." He slid a hand under the sheet to join hers, showing her how to grip him but covering her fingers with his own, and urging her to stroke him. "Like that."

The roughness of his fingers over hers and touching the hot, hard part of him that had always been forbidden to her gaze was nothing short of erotic. But more than that, she loved that their hands were touching, that they were experiencing this moment of his pleasure together.

With a bit of practice, she learned how to squeeze him at a certain pressure as she moved her hand up and down.

"Yes, that's right…"

Meredith glowed with pleasure as his eyes closed. He threw his head back with a gasp of her name, and then a sudden wetness coated the sheets, and her hands.

"Ahh, God, what you do to me!" He relaxed into the bed. After a moment, he turned toward her, a hint of red high on his aristocratic cheekbones.

"You must know by now that you own me, Meredith. With just the touch of your hand, I lose myself so easily with you."

A rush of delight and joy swept through her at the thought that she had the power to bring this man, this god in bed, such pleasure. Even with his essence still coating her wrist, she felt as though she was his equal, a goddess of pleasure in her own right.

He leaned over to kiss her, the experience slow and seductive before he slipped out of bed. He returned with a wet cloth and he wiped her hand clean with tenderness. It humbled her to feel such affection and care in such a small thing.

Darius set the cloth aside and pulled her into his arms, kissing her senseless. That never-ending desire was stirred up inside her again, like embers coaxed into a healthy blaze once more. She let go of herself and fell into that kiss with everything she had.

A long, delicious time later, he rolled her onto her stomach, covering the backs of her shoulders with languid kisses. God, she wanted him, wanted that wildness that building within her to be unleashed again. Eager for more, she pushed herself up onto her hands and knees and looked over her shoulder at him. Her body was hungry to feel that intimate connection to him.

"Trust me?" he asked.

"Always," she replied without thought.

"You will enjoy this." He knelt behind her as he said this. He moved the blunt head of his cock against the waiting wetness of her sex, then pushed into her, filling her. It felt so good, and she was so wet and ready for him. His hips pressed against her bottom as he sank all the way inside of her. They both shared a soft shudder of pleasure at the deepness. There was no part of her that felt unfilled and untouched by him.

"That's it. Take me all the way, love." Darius encouraged as he held still. She could feel her body relax around him in this new angle of penetration. She experimentally moved away from him and pushed herself back, delighting in the sound of his moan as he slid in and out of her.

"Are you ready for me?" he asked with a husky chuckle.

She looked over her shoulder at him again. "Ready?"

"Yes." He grasped her hips, his fingers tightening. He withdrew and slammed back into her hard. "Ready for that?"

She nodded frantically. "Please, yes *please...*" She was thrilled by how Darius pushed her to her limits and showed her just how wild she could be when she was with him.

He leaned forward, fisting his hand in her long hair and gently tugging it. A spiral of excitement swept through her. A second later he began to drive into her in earnest. Their bodies slapped together as he showed her a rough side to lovemaking that made her mad for more, mad for him.

She was so close... So close to that pinnacle of pleasure. But before she peaked, Darius moved his hand underneath her to slide between her legs. He caressed that sensitive pearl until it was too much to bear. She wriggled her hips to escape his touch, but Darius was too strong and held her fast, continuing to tease that bud until she screamed in pleasure. She collapsed onto her forearms on the pillows as exquisite sensations rolled through her.

Darius continued to drive deep into her, his fingers still caressing her. Meredith wanted to weep at the overwhelming sensations that continued to roll over and over her. Meredith's body twitched with pleasure, her sated limbs heavy with exhaustion, but he didn't relent in his sensual assault.

She couldn't do more than cry out with ecstasy as Darius continued to take her, his hands holding her down when she felt like she might float away. When she was convinced she couldn't take any more, that she was going to sink into her bed and never move again, Darius thrust in hard and bellowed her name before they both collapsed on the bed together.

Darius lay half on top of her, his cock still buried inside her. He panted hard as she struggled to catch her breath, her body still twitching around his cock.

"You feel like heaven." Darius kissed her shoulder, then her cheek as he gazed at her. "I need to move, but I can't find the will."

She reached up behind her to catch his right buttock in her hand, holding her close to him.

"Then stay." She replied, knowing she sounded far too seductive. The man had turned her completely wanton, but she didn't care.

He closed his eyes and circled his hips as his cock moved inside her. They both shared a groan.

"If I don't move all, I shall take you again and we might *never* leave this bed."

"And is that a bad thing?" she asked with a contented yawn.

"No," he laughed. "But you have a letter to write to Prince George, and I have a wedding to plan."

My wedding. To Darius.

She was starting to believe that she was dreaming all of this, no matter how real everything had felt.

Darius eased out of her and then lay down beside her in the bed, sharing a pillow with her as he brushed his thumb over her cheek.

"Are you all right? I was rather rough."

She closed her eyes and nodded. After a moment she said, "Tell me the truth. Do you want me as your wife? Or is this simply to protect me?"

"Yes, I want you as my wife," Darius said without hesitation. "If you want the truth, from the first moment I saw you, I wanted you in my life. But then I learned what my uncle expected of me, and I didn't feel I was allowed to want you for myself. The issues of society did not help matters. But through it all, I still wanted you with me, and the thought of losing you to one of those damned suitors only made me realize I was a fool for not listening to my heart. I never want to fail you, not in any way."

"You haven't failed me. I was wrong to say that you hadn't stood up for me with Lady Mary."

"*That* will never happen again," he promised, a vengeful gleam taking hold in his piercing blue eyes.

"You cannot promise that."

"I certainly can. I intend to visit Lady Mary today and make it clear to her that *anyone* who comes after my wife will be dealing with me."

My wife. Why did that sound so wonderful even uttered as part of a growling threat?

"You do not need to threaten her."

"I'm afraid I do. The damned woman won't take me

seriously otherwise." Darius sat up a little. "And believe me, I shall enjoy it. That woman has ruled London's ballrooms with too much unchecked privilege." He leaned down and kissed her again. "Now, rest if you wish, but I must rise."

He slipped out of bed, delightfully naked, and she sat up to better see his backside and muscular thighs. His body was a work of art that would make any sculptor weep. Darius collected his clothes and dressed, then flashed her one more smile before he slipped out of her bedchamber.

Meredith covered her face with her hands to hide her giddy smile as she flopped back onto the bed. Being in love was quite wonderful.

DARIUS SENT WORD TO HIS FRIEND TO MEET HIM AT HIS townhouse for dinner, then called for his horse. Once his groom had his horse ready, he rode to the Raikes's townhouse and presented his card to their butler. He had only to wait a few moments before he was ushered into the drawing room. One did not leave a duke waiting after all.

Lady Mary smiled demurely as she and her mother greeted him at the entrance.

"Your Grace, we are delighted to have you pay a call, even if it is a bit early," Lady Raikes said. "Dare I hope that means you are here out of an eagerness to see my daughter?"

Darius smiled coolly at Lady Mary and her mother.

"Eagerness is not the word I would use. *Determined* would be a more appropriate choice."

"Determined?" Lady Raikes glanced between her daughter and Darius in confusion.

"Yes, you see, your daughter has done something quite foolish." Darius held Lady Mary's gaze as he continued. "She chose to make an enemy of me."

Lady Raikes tried to intervene. "Your Grace, I'm certain my daughter would never—" Darius held up a hand to silence the woman, eyes locked on his target.

"You spoke ill of my ward, Miss Montague, two nights past. I suspect you said even more to other people, including a number of gentlemen who have no honor. Yesterday, my ward was approached by two such men who had heard rumors about her and was attacked."

"She was unharmed, surely?" Lady Raikes asked, her eyes wide. Darius suspected she was not fully aware of her daughter's poisonous words.

Lady Mary, however, did not ask after Meredith's health. Her eyes gleamed with triumph and that made Darius furious. He could have strangled the woman for that evil joy so clearly showing on her face.

"She was thankfully unharmed, thanks to the efforts of myself and others, but the damage to Gunter's confectioner's shop was severe. Given that your daughter has put Miss Montague in danger"—he paused, looking at both women —"I have decided to finally act upon my feelings and marry Miss Montague."

The fire in Lady Mary's eyes grew hot enough to burn. "You're *marrying* her?"

"Yes, and I wanted *you* to be the first to hear the good news. I have you to thank, Lady Mary. Your lack of kindness and your petty jealousy have done what you wished would not happen." Darius took great satisfaction at the way the blood drained from Lady Mary's face.

"But you cannot!" Lady Mary insisted. "You are a duke, and she...is no one. A bastard. A—"

"Take care how you speak of my future wife, Lady Mary. Any word or deed done against her I will consider to be done against me. And you may ask anyone who has done me wrong that my retribution does not come lightly."

"But—" Lady Mary sputtered.

"Hush, you *stupid* girl," Lady Raikes hissed. She turned to Darius, humble and apologetic. "My daughter will not bother you or the future Duchess of Tiverton again."

"Good. See to it she doesn't," Darius warned. "Because if she does, my justice will be swift and unforgiving."

Lady Raikes nodded frantically in acquiescence to his command.

"Now that my point has been made, I will take my leave." He collected his hat and coat from the butler and left the Raikes townhouse. Once outside, he mounted his horse and headed to his next destination, the dressmaker's shop. He wanted Meredith to have a gown befitting the future Duchess of Tiverton. He would also order several sheer negligées for her trousseau to take on their honeymoon.

As he rode down the street, he felt his spirits lighten at the mere idea of Meredith as his bride. His wife. His *forever*.

What a fool he had been to deny himself the joy of being in love.

THAT EVENING, MEREDITH WORE HER FINEST EVENING GOWN, A dark blue silk decorated with peacock feathers in bright gold and green that led into a long train that mirrored the plumes on the magnificent bird that the dress was inspired by. When the dressmaker had mentioned such a gown, Meredith had thought it too bold to wear. But Darius had overheard, and insisted on her having it.

Tonight she felt brave enough to be bold, to wear a gown that would attract attention. For once she wanted the attention of others, rather than to hide behind potted plants. Her reflection in the tall cheval looking glass presented a striking image. She turned about, admiring the way the peacock-feathered patterns shimmered in the light.

"You will make quite an impression tonight," Nell said as she put the finishing touches on Meredith's coiffure. "As you should, seeing as how tonight is your engagement dinner."

"I do hope I make a good impression." Meredith's nerves left her feeling edgy and unsure of herself. She knew she looked beautiful, but would she be enough for Darius's friends? Would tonight garner support for Darius's choice of bride, or would she come across as silly for trying too hard?

Tonight Darius would tell his friends that they were to be married, and she could only pray that they would accept her, not for her sake but for his. It was one thing for them to accept her as his ward, but his wife? That was an entirely different matter. They hadn't given her any reason to think they wouldn't accept her, but she was so used to being unwanted, a burden even to those who loved her, like Uncle Ben. It was still hard for her to break that pattern of believing she was not enough.

Her bedchamber door opened. Darius was there, waiting for her.

"Are you ready?"

His gaze swept over her, the heat in his eyes an approving one. That settled part of her nerves. She was enough for Darius. That was all that truly mattered. She could see it so clearly in his eyes that it melted her heart.

"You look *magnificent*." He cupped her face in his hands and kissed her so soundly that only Nell clearing her throat broke them apart.

With a bashful grin, Darius tucked her hand in his arm, and they met Mrs. Petersham, who was waiting for them at the top of the grand staircase.

"Congratulations, my dear. This is the happiest of news." Her chaperone kissed her cheek and wiped away a stray tear.

"Thank you, Frances," Meredith replied with tears in her own eyes.

The others waited for them in the drawing room, all busy talking. But upon her entrance, the room went silent as they took in the sight of her and Darius with their arms linked.

"Well? What news have you to share with us?" Vincent asked.

Darius looked to Meredith, a teasing smile in his eyes before he replied. "Meredith and I are to be married."

"To *each other*?" Felix asked with a devious chuckle. Lionel whacked him on the back of the head with the newspaper he'd been holding.

Darius seemed torn between laughing and scowling. "Of course to each other."

"Well, in that case, bravo!" Felix said. Soon, everyone had surrounded them, offering cheers and well wishes.

Meredith noticed poor Felix was still a bit bruised from the fight in Gunter's. When he came toward her, she embraced him and whispered a thank you. The rogue looked utterly embarrassed if the red tips of his ears were any indication.

"I would destroy Gunter's for you anytime," he promised.

She hugged each of Darius's friends in turn and came at last to Lord Kentwell and Suzannah, who was wiping her eyes.

"This is quite wonderful, isn't it?" Suzannah said with a delighted smile.

Lord Kentwell offered one of his rare smiles to Meredith. "It certainly is."

"Thank you, Lord Kentwell," Meredith said.

"Kit, please. I insist. You will outrank me upon your marriage."

"I..." She couldn't think of what to say in response to that, and Kit laughed at her obvious discomfort.

"Trying to scare off my future wife?" Darius asked his friend as he joined them.

"Not intentionally, I assure you." Kit shook Darius's hand. "I simply reminded her that she will soon outrank me. I daresay she hasn't given that part of your arrangement much thought."

"Nor should she," said Darius. "At least, not amongst friends."

Meredith's face heated in embarrassment. Darius put an arm around her waist and kissed her forehead.

"Shall we go in to dinner?" Darius asked everyone.

The chorus of agreement, followed immediately by someone's stomach growling so loudly everyone could hear, and it made Meredith laugh.

Warren stepped up beside her and gently pulled her away from Darius. "I would like the pleasure of escorting the future Duchess of Tiverton to dinner." He informed Darius, who rolled his eyes but allowed it.

As Warren led the way, he leaned in close to her. "I felt this would attract less suspicion than asking to speak to you alone in another room."

Meredith nodded in understanding.

"Crell might not be at his new home much longer," he continued. "I heard he might be planning a trip to the continent. I imagine Darius's visit with Doyle has spooked him enough to think he must leave the country. If you wish to make a move, it should be soon."

Meredith pulled out the letter, which had been tucked away into her skirts. "I have the letter here. Deliver it tomorrow after Darius has left."

Warren answered with a single nod. Feeling confident in her plan to catch Crell in a confession, she enjoyed dinner immensely. She felt as though she *belonged* here. Everyone included her in their stories and teased her almost as much as they did Darius. She was thankful to have so many wonderful friends in this room.

Suzannah was seated beside Meredith. Her soft smile warmed Meredith's heart as they shared a miniature toast between the two of them by clinking their glasses of wine together.

"I believe Darius will make you very happy," said Suzannah.

"And I hope to make him happy."

"My dear, he already is, can't you see?" Suzannah nodded ever so slightly toward Darius. He was laughing at something Vincent said, but whenever he glanced Meredith's way, his eyes grew bright and his grin infectious. She grinned back at him.

"You two are clearly besotted with each other," Suzannah said. "And I, for one, cannot be happier for you."

Meredith agreed. It was impossible to believe one could feel so deliriously happy.

And yet she was.

WARREN LAUGHED. "LOOK AT THAT SILLY GRIN."

For once, Darius didn't care how silly he looked. Dinner had ended, and now he swirled a glass of brandy as he lounged in a chair in the billiard room with his friends. Life was good.

"You had better stay away from them, Warren," Felix warned. "This marriage business seems to be catching." He pointed his billiard cue at Kit and Darius, who sat next to each other. Kit shared a look with Darius that was reserved for only the happily married men in the room.

"You don't have to look so smug, you know," Vincent added as he leaned over to take his shot. Balls clacked and scattered in every direction.

"We're not smug," Kit said. "We are merely content in our happiness."

"We should celebrate with a shooting party. Felix, what say you?" Warren asked. "You have the best woods for pheasant hunting. Why don't you, Lionel, and Vincent go hunting with Darius?"

"What about you and Kit?" Darius asked.

"I would, but I fear I have a business meeting tomorrow morning. Rather urgent. I could join you in the afternoon. As for Kit, I know better than to speak for a married man. His will is his own, so long as his wife allows it."

Kit chuckled. "I'm sure Suzannah will not mind missing me for a few days."

"Excellent," Warren said. "Our shooting party is settled."

"Shall we leave early in the morning?" Felix asked. "My country house is ready for visitors."

"Yes, let's leave at half-past eight," Lionel suggested. "We would then have the afternoon to shoot."

Darius was quite excited at the prospect of a shooting expedition. It had been quite a while since they'd gone shooting together, and certainly not since Kit had come home.

Once they had finished their drinks and a round of the billiards, they left in search of the ladies. Chelsea informed them that, given the late hour, Suzannah had been escorted to her home across the street by a footman, while Mrs. Petersham and Meredith had gone up to bed.

Darius bid his friends farewell and told Chelsea to have the valet pack his valise for two days of shooting at Felix's estate. Then he went upstairs to Meredith's chamber.

He found her asleep in bed. With a soft chuckle, he removed his clothes and slipped under the sheets beside her, pulling her into his arms.

"Darius?" she murmured sleepily.

"Yes, sweetheart?"

She yawned and rubbed her cheek against his chest.

"I love you."

His heart clenched. "You and Frances may make any additional arrangements for the wedding you like, as well as choose your wedding gown. I will be leaving early tomorrow to go shooting with my friends at Felix's estate.

I've given Chelsea orders that you are now the lady of the house and shall defer to you on all things, and he is to help you with everything for the ceremony. I thought, perhaps, we could get married here in the gardens."

"That sounds lovely," she murmured. "*Simply lovely.*" A moment later, she drifted back to sleep.

For the first time in Darius's life, he was more than content.

He was truly happy.

17

"It shouldn't be long before we reach the house," Felix said, his attention shifting between the other occupants of the coach. They had shared a coach so they could talk, but Darius found himself to be strangely quiet. They'd been together for nearly five hours now, and he had barely said a word. Something didn't feel right given how his friends were acting.

Perhaps he was merely being overly anxious at the thought of leaving Meredith alone after what had happened at Gunters. But still, he couldn't shake the sense that something wasn't right.

And it seemed he wasn't alone in that regard. Lionel was frowning, his arms crossed, and Vincent looked ruffled. Felix seemed more on edge than usual, and Kit looked uncharacteristically baffled.

Darius had had enough. "All right, what's the matter with all of you?"

"Nothing is the matter." Felix's answer came too quick, and his smile was a little too forced.

Darius glared. "Something is most certainly the matter."

"No, it isn't," Felix protested. "You're simply nervous about your engagement."

Kit, who sat next to Darius and across from Felix, leaned forward, resting his elbows on his knees.

"Even after all these years, I can still tell when you're lying, Felix," Kit said. "And we *never* lie to each other." To hear this coming from Kit woke old memories in Darius. The vows they had made as young boys had sustained Kit through seven years of living as a convict laborer in Australia. He took their vows more seriously than any of them.

Lionel sighed. "He's right. We've been through far too much to lie. Felix, tell him, or I will."

Felix's gaze dropped to the floor of the coach, before he finally raised it again. "I did genuinely wish to celebrate your nuptials, but this all came about as a favor to Warren."

Darius frowned. "A *favor*? I don't understand."

"He needed you to be away from London for a few days."

"Why?" Kit asked sharply.

Felix glanced between Kit and Darius nervously. "Because he and Meredith have a plan to get Crell to confess that he murdered his wife."

"*What?*" That single word came out as a roar. Even

Lionel flinched. Darius banged his fist on the coach roof, then leaned out to shout at the driver.

"Turn around at once and take us back to London. Lives depend on it!"

The coach began to make a turn on the road, far too slowly for his liking. Darius flung himself at Felix, grabbing his waistcoat and pulling so their faces were but inches apart.

"Darius, steady on," Vincent began, but Darius ignored him.

"You will tell me *everything*, and you'd better pray nothing happens to my future wife."

Lionel put a hand on Darius's arm. "Before you blacken Felix's other eye, give him a minute to explain." His friend's calming influence only just reached him through his haze of emotion. "You know full well that none of us would put Meredith in any real danger."

Lionel was right. The man had taken a beating for Meredith, quite a bad one, and he still looked the worse for wear.

Darius released Felix and forced himself to clear his head. He trusted the men in this coach with his life, and now he was trusting them with Meredith's.

"Very well. Explain."

Felix described Meredith's scheme to catch Crell, and Warren's foolish role in it all. Terror gripped Darius's heart at the thought of her waiting in the gardens to meet a murderer. He hadn't forgotten the way she'd looked when she'd first told him about the scream she'd heard, or when told him later she believed it had come from Mrs. Crell.

Why hadn't she come to him? Why hadn't she trusted that he hadn't given up in his pursuit of Crell? But then, he hadn't told her that he'd gone underground with his investigation.

"You knew all this?" Darius snapped at Lionel. "Who else knew?"

"Not me," Kit said, scowling at the others.

Felix sagged. "Because you're *married*, Kit. Warren knew you wouldn't hide this from Darius because you think of Meredith's safety just as you would Suzannah's."

"He's damned right I would." Kit's face was full of storms. "I'm sorry, Darius. I would have stopped this nonsense had I known."

Darius glared at Lionel, Felix and Vincent. "You three just agreed to help them?"

Lionel matched Darius in his displeasure. "I did not *agree*. I only learned of the matter before we departed. I was debating whether to tell you when we reached Felix's country house."

"I have no doubt regarding Meredith's safety," Vincent replied honestly. "Warren will be there, along with Mr. Doyle. Crell would have to be a fool to act against her once they announce themselves."

A fool... or desperate, Darius thought. He knew how easily *everything* could go wrong. And a man could snap Meredith's pretty neck in an instant before help could arrive. But as he tried to calm down, he realized there was blame to lay at his own feet.

"I should have been honest with her about what I was doing," Darius said as he stared bleakly at his friends. "She must have thought I'd given up trying to catch Crell, and that I was focused solely on our wedding. I fear that might be what motivated her to act."

"You didn't tell her about the inquiries I have been making into Crell's finances?" Lionel asked.

Darius shook his head. "I was planning to, once we had something worth sharing."

This surprised Lionel. "I had thought *that* was the reason she decided to act, since it would have given leverage to get a confession."

"You mean you've found something?" asked Darius.

"I have. I had planned to tell you what I'd learned at Felix's estate. I managed to find the barrister who handled Minerva Crell's affairs. You were right in suspecting that she'd had the control of the money, and that most of it was still tied up in a trust that her husband had very little access to. At the time they married, there was a miscommunication between the couple. Crell believed he would be given control, when rather his wife's money was neatly tied up and protected by an outside trustee."

Lionel paused a moment. "This created some strain between them over the years, at least from what the barrister could tell during his infrequent visits with Minerva. Then, in the last few months, money requests started to increase from Minerva. So I looked into where the money was ending up. I spoke with all of the fashionable tailors, the best jewelers and dressmakers."

"Well, don't leave us in suspense," Felix replied.

Lionel cleared his throat and continued. "Crell was spending lavishly, and I don't think any of it had to do with his wife. There were dinners in hotels, jewels being purchased in large quantities, and he'd completely redone his wardrobe in the last month and there were custom dress fitting bills, box seats at the theater. But as I understand it, Minerva could barely leave the house and hadn't attended any dinners, nor the theater."

"He was spending time out with his mistress," Vincent surmised. "That would certainly cause a vast increase in his expenditures."

Darius digested the information. It was all valuable information, but didn't prove much, though it seemed quite obvious as to what must have happened. Minerva learned what her husband was doing and likely confronted him about it. The only way for him to keep access to her money was if the mistress took his wife's place. Thus the move outside of London, where all future contact with the barrister would be handled by letters and forged signatures would enable him to keep drawing on her accounts. But Minerva would have known and therefore she would have to have been killed.

But a man could not be convicted of murder on common sense guesswork.

With his questions answered, Darius fell into an

anxious silence for the next several hours it took to return to London. He could only pray they wouldn't be too late.

BY LATE AFTERNOON, MEREDITH'S NERVES WERE FRAYED. SHE paced in the drawing room, waiting for Warren to return from Crell's country house.

Darius and his other friends had left earlier that morning. She'd only had dim, sweet memories of him kissing her goodbye before he'd slipped out of bed. That tender parting had left her feeling strangely bittersweet, perhaps because she now wished she had told him about her plan to trick Crell into confessing.

They had started this investigation together, and now it had all become twisted up. She'd pulled away from Darius to handle this on her own because she feared he would not let her do something simply because it was dangerous. But she had to do this. She had ignored the signs that Mrs. Crell was in danger. Flashes of the woman flinching as she'd moved in the gardens, and her mention of being clumsy...it was so obvious now that Mr. Crell likely had a hand in those bruises. Sadly a man had a right to beat his wife, at least in a court of law, but that didn't mean he had the right to murder her. Still, she hadn't felt she could push Darius to let her assist him, and it had become clear he no longer wanted to be involved in catching Crell, not after his failure to find evidence with Doyle.

He may have given up, but I cannot. I must press on, even if it means keeping this from him until I've seen it through. I owe it to Minerva.

Meredith turned that memory of Darius's goodbye kiss over and over in her mind, remembering the feel of Darius's lips upon her throat, her cheek, her forehead as he murmured he would bring her back a gift from the jewelers before coming home. But the real gift had been the way he made her feel before he had left. She felt loved and cherished, and that only twisted the knife deeper into her chest at the thought that she had been the one to keep this a secret from him.

She could have let this all go and focused on her marriage to Darius, but she couldn't get Mrs. Crell's face out of her mind. That poor woman had been so excited about an afternoon tea with Meredith, and Mr. Crell done something to her. Meredith knew it deep in her bones. And she could not let such a wretched injustice go unpunished.

Mr. Chelsea appeared in the doorway and announced Warren's arrival. Meredith instructed him to be shown in at once.

Warren soon entered the drawing room, passing his hat and gloves to Chelsea. His usual teasing smile was gone, and in its place was a somber expression that made her feel uneasy.

"Did you deliver the letter without being seen?" she asked once Chelsea had left them alone.

Warren nodded solemnly. "I hid in the woods and saw Crell receive the letter from a footman at the door."

She absorbed this new information, her plan was coming together.

"What is next in this dangerous plan of yours?" His tone wasn't exactly disapproving, but clearly he had his concerns.

"If he read the letter, he will be in his garden at seven o'clock tonight," she explained, twisting her fingers nervously in her skirt. "Next, I will send a note to Mr. Doyle, asking him to wait in Darius's garden, by the..."

She paused as a flash of a memory hit. Darius stood shoulder to shoulder with her, trying to discern what was transpiring on the other side of the wall. "By the heart-shaped hole in the wall. Then he will hear Crell's confession."

"Ideally," Warren murmured.

"Yes," Meredith agreed, reaching out to touch Warren's arm briefly before asking, "And you will be hiding nearby, just in case things do not unfold as I hope they will."

Warren nodded in understanding, but he did not look pleased.

"Good," Meredith said. "Then I believe we may just catch a murderer tonight."

Meredith felt no joy at the thought, but she was determined. She had to do something for Mrs. Crell, and whatever fate befell her. Like Minerva Crell, Meredith had felt alone for many years. Even though Uncle Ben had given her a wonderful home, she'd always felt like a guest there. She wasn't Ben's daughter, no matter how much she'd grown up wishing she was. A woman alone in the world deserved to have someone care about them, and Meredith cared about Minerva Crell. Even if no one else did.

"Meredith, why does it need to be you who meets with Crell? I would readily take your place."

"I appreciate that, but it must be me, Warren. As a woman, he will underestimate me. He will be more likely to confess to me, because he will think I have no power to prove his guilt."

"He will *also* think that he can easily remove you if you are a threat to him," Warren countered. "You are exposing yourself to far too much risk, even with Doyle and myself nearby to protect you. Trapped men become desperate, and desperate men are dangerous. Is catching this man worth your life?"

Meredith rubbed her arms and looked toward the drawing-room windows. "It might make little sense to you, but I believe that Mrs. Crell and I are similar creatures. She was alone, unwanted, and I believe her husband erased her for the crime of being *inconvenient*. She did not deserve that. Women are often overlooked, hurt, and erased from life by the violent desires of men." She held her head high as she met Warren's gaze. "I don't want Mr. Crell to get away with whatever he's done. If he killed his wife, he shouldn't be at liberty to live his life, not when he stole Minerva's."

"You really believe he killed her then?" She studied him as he asked this, and she found a hint of uncomfortable resignation mixed with the barest hint of admiration which steeled her spine and her resolve to defend what she was certain had happened.

"Isn't is possible that, rather than reconcile, they agreed to live apart? He stays with his mistress, and she with relatives? No one wants to draw attention to a broken marriage."

She shook her head. "The scream I heard the night of the ball was *human*. I know it was. There's been too much I've seen, too much I've heard coming from that house to think that whatever happened between Crell and his wife was innocent. I saw her flinch when she moved and she mentioned bruises. I should have known something was wrong."

"No one wants to assume something terrible has happened to someone. You cannot take that blame upon yourself."

"I must catch him...I owe it to her. You believe me, don't you? That he truly did it?"

She saw a hint of uncomfortable resignation mixed with a hint of admiration when she asked him this, which only steeled her resolve.

Warren took a deep breath. "I believe you." She hadn't realized until that moment that she needed to hear those words.

Warren stepped up to the window next to her, his expression full of unexpected tenderness, like that of an elder brother, or what she'd always imagined having an elder brother might feel like.

"And, might I add, you aren't alone. Perhaps you were once, before you came here. But now? Even if you weren't marrying Darius, you would always have a home at Devil's Square with all of us."

Those words were everything to her. She finally believed she could have the life she'd always dreamed of having, with Darius at her side and in her heart. The thought sent another pang of guilt through her chest, knowing she'd betrayed his trust by keeping silent on her plan.

"If you haven't learned by now, we protect our own. And you most certainly are one of us." He gently squeezed her shoulder in that same brotherly way, which melted her heart. "Never doubt it, Meredith." His smile returned as he winked. "I should be back at dusk."

Meredith spent the remainder of the afternoon discussing her trousseau with Frances and assisting Mr. Chelsea with wedding arrangements.

"Do you think we should hire a housekeeper for the townhouse?" she asked the butler, wondering if he might take offense at the idea.

"I would quite appreciate that, Ms. Montague," the butler confessed in a rare show of openness. "Your Grace has Mrs. Ledbetter in the country, but I am on my own here and not getting any younger. After his father died, our previous housekeeper left, as she did not wish to take care of a young bachelor duke, believing that his title and wealth would go to his head as it does many young men. It did not however, as you can see, His Grace is the epitome of good manners and does well with economizing. But we could certainly use a housekeeper's expertise now that I imagine we will be entertaining with a lovely young duchess in the house."

She blushed at the butler's sweet compliment.

"Then I shall ask Darius to hire one. In the meantime, Frances and I can assist you in whatever is required."

"I would like to have charge of the menu for the wedding breakfast and the dinner reception the night before the ceremony," Mr. Chelsea replied, and began to describe what he thought would be enticing courses.

Not for the first time, Meredith felt truly accepted by Darius's staff. When she first arrived, she had only hoped to be tolerated by them, yet they had been as welcoming as Darius's friends. Mr. Chelsea trusted her and agreed with her decisions, just as any good butler would for the future mistress of his household.

I will make this home even more wonderful for Darius and everyone else, myself included, she thought with pride. She'd had a decent amount of practice helping Uncle Ben's housekeeper run a household and believed she would do well here.

WARREN AND MR. DOYLE ARRIVED SHORTLY BEFORE SEVEN o'clock. It was time to spring her trap and catch a murderer. Doyle listened patiently as she explained her intentions and, with a nod to Warren, took up position by the heart-shaped hole in the wall. Warren climbed over the garden wall and caught Meredith when she followed him, setting her gently on the ground.

"Where would you like me to hide?" he asked as he searched the gardens for a prospective hiding spot.

"Perhaps inside the shed? I know it's a ways off, but everything else is too exposed, and you can see through the window without being noticed."

"Very well. Be careful," Warren said.

Meredith held her breath, her fingers twisting against each other as she waited to see if Crell would come. She paced in a tight circle, then stopped, stared up at the evening sky, feeling stiff and a little cold as an evening chill settled in the air. Surely it was half past seven o'clock now. The light was fading, and the gardens were now wreathed in purple shadows.

In that seemingly endless span of time alone, doubts began to creep upon her. What if Warren was right? What if Mrs. Crell was alive and living somewhere else to keep their separate discrete?

Darius had abandoned trying to catch Crell, and had gone on with his life. Should she have done the same? What if this was all some fevered dream she'd had after first meeting Minerva Crell in the gardens? What if the fighting she'd overhead and the unhappy marriage she'd witnessed through the windows of the Crell house had been a violent fantasy she'd conjured when peering through those opera glasses and not the truth?

No. The memory of that scream she'd heard was too real to be imagined. The circumstances of Crell's move away from the city too suspicious. Something terrible had happened to Minerva. She couldn't let herself be convinced otherwise.

But what if Crell didn't come? She had no other way to catch him without finding evidence, evidence he had certainly disposed of given that Doyle's search of the gardens had come up empty.

A soft step on the path jerked Meredith from her inner thoughts. She strained to see the figure that emerged from behind a rhododendron bush at the far end of the garden.

Crell was tall, almost as tall as Darius, but a little more thickly built around the middle. There was a cold cruelty that corrupted his otherwise handsome features into something harsh and off-putting.

He came toward her. "So, *you're* the one who sent me that letter? I thought it might be Tiverton."

"I know what you did to your wife."

Crell's brown eyes narrowed. "Do you, now? And just what did I supposedly do?"

"You murdered her. The woman at your country home pretending to be her is your mistress." Meredith hoped he would say something to confirm this. Doyle needed some concrete bit of proof before he could arrest the man.

"Your letter mentions proof. What proof do you have? I am innocent of any crime."

Her voice grew stronger. "An innocent man wouldn't have come here."

"Oh no? And what if I'm here to clear up a misunder-standing? Perhaps I want to know what it is you plan to reveal so I can defend myself."

"Come now, Mr. Crell, we both know what you did. Why don't you simply admit it?"

"I admit nothing." He glanced around. "And you've made a terrible mistake attempting to blackmail me."

Crell's words gave Meredith a sudden burst of inspira-tion. "Of course it's a mistake."

That threw him for a loop. "Pardon?"

"Blackmail is never a one-time thing, is it?" said Mered-ith. "Blackmailers demand regular payments, and even when they say a payment is the last one, you never truly know if that's the last you'll hear of them. It's a prison, Mr. Crell."

Crell frowned, not knowing where Meredith was going with this. Chances were Mr. Doyle and Warren were equally baffled, but she pressed on.

"And you've only just escaped one prison, haven't you? Life with Minerva couldn't have been easy for you. Always requiring attention. Unable to care for herself. Even when you had staff to take care of her for you, the extra cost must have been draining. All for a woman you didn't even have feelings for, and who taxed your patience every single day.

"But you found a way out, didn't you? One small act, and you could finally escape from your prison. You could finally be free. Have you enjoyed your freedom, Mr. Crell? Or have you found yet another prison? One of your own design?"

Crell looked uncomfortable, his teeth braced in rising anger. Meredith was on the right track. "Do you still see her face at night, Mr. Crell? Is it one of shock and horror? Does she call your name? Does she ask you *why?*"

Crell lunged for her. Meredith leapt back, but not quickly enough. He latched onto her left arm and yanked her toward him. She screamed as he wrapped his hand around her throat. Crell slammed her against the garden wall and began to squeeze the life out of her.

"Stupid woman, you couldn't leave well enough alone, could you!" he snarled.

Meredith clawed at his hands, her vision dotting with stars as her lungs screamed for air. Crell loomed above her, his face twisted with a violent sneer. It was so hard to think, so hard to keep struggling against the hands that were squeezing the very life out of her, until her mind blurred with a torrent of memories.

Uncle Ben walking with her in the gardens. Her mother laughing in the sunlight as she chased Meredith along the beach. Her first sight of Darius in the doorway. Darius making love to her in the gardens. Darius smiling at her, holding her, telling her that she owned him body and soul. Darius loving her...

All went dark.

THE MOMENT THE COACH ARRIVED AT KNIGHTLEY STREET, DARIUS leapt from the coach while it was still moving and ran for his townhouse. Kit and the others were right behind him as he burst through the front door, nearly knocking Chelsea over as he hurried to the back gardens.

A scream pierced the air, followed by shouting. Darius ran blindly, madly toward the direction of the scream. When he reached the back garden wall he leapt onto the bench and vaulted over the garden wall just as Frances stood frantically beside the bench trying to see what was happening. Darius landed in crouch, pain shooting up his bad leg, but that pain paled in comparison in comparison to the sight that met his eyes.

Warren and Doyle had Crell's arms and were attempting to pin him down on the ground, but the man was struggling, nearly tossing them off. Meredith lay inert a few feet away, her face was an unnaturally dark color and her eyes closed.

Oh God...

"Darius!" Warren shouted. "See to Meredith! This bastard is stronger than he looks—" he grunted as Crell threw his body up, nearly tossing Warren onto his backside.

Darius knelt by Meredith's body, lifting her up into his arms and cradling her against his chest.

"Come on, my darling, breathe," he gasped. It felt like he couldn't breathe either, like he was dying just as she seemed to be.

No...please no... He choked on the thought that he might have lost her.

He should have been here with her, protecting her, loving her, proving that he believed in her, not keeping secrets from her.

Suddenly Meredith gasped and descended into a fit of coughing, her body curling up in a ball.

"Thank Christ." He held her even closer, oblivious to everything else around him. All that mattered was that she was alive. "Easy, sweetheart, just breathe."

"Help us lift him up." Doyle's voice intruded on Darius's focus. He turned up to see Felix help Warren and Doyle get Crell onto his feet.

"Louis Crell, you are under arrest for the attempted murder of Miss Montague. But rest assured, that won't be the only charge." Crell was barely conscious now, wavering on his feet. Then the man was escorted away, but Darius did not care. All that mattered was the woman he held in his arms. Meredith's lashes fluttered as she gazed up at him.

"D—Darius?" she wheezed. "I didn't think...I'd get to see you before..."

"Hush darling," he said, noting the deep red marks around her neck. "You need to rest. That man nearly killed you. Your vocal cords will likely be damaged." He stood up, lifting her in the cradle of his arms.

"Take me home," she whispered, and slipped into unconsciousness again.

Kit joined Darius, looking around warily as if expecting more men to jump out of the shadows. "Is she all right?"

"I'm not sure. She's passed out again. We need the doctor to see to her at once."

"Of course." Kit left and Darius carried Meredith home, just as she'd asked.

The doctor arrived shortly after Darius settled Meredith in her bedchamber. She hadn't opened her eyes, but she seemed to be resting peacefully. The bruises that had started to darken along her neck, a sight that drove painfully into Darius's gut. He left her side reluctantly when the doctor asked, so as to allow the man enough room to examine her.

"She woke for a moment and then lost consciousness again," he informed the doctor.

Dr. Bradburn nodded as he began his inspection. He checked her breathing first, then lifted her lids and peered into them.

"She will have a sore throat and her eyes will be blood-shot, but I believe she will heal without any complications," Dr. Bradburn said. "She is likely exhausted from the struggle. I will give her some laudanum for the pain. That will also help her sleep."

Darius could only nod and hold Meredith's hand as she rested. The doctor poured some laudanum onto a spoon and parted Meredith's lips. She stirred slightly, frowning and licking her lips as she took the medicine. Satisfied, the doctor took his leave.

Frances brought Darius dinner, but he didn't touch it. He had no appetite. He kept replaying that moment of finding her limp and nearly lifeless. She had almost died. The woman he loved so much he was going mad with it. His future wife.

And for what? To catch a murderer, because she hadn't trusted him. She'd gone to Warren instead. His own friends had kept him in the dark. He was left with an empty feeling inside. He'd believed they'd trusted one another, and that there would be no more secrets. Yet she'd kept one that had almost killed her. And so, after a fashion, had he.

Holding her hand, he brushed the pad of his thumb over her skin.

"Why didn't you trust me?" he whispered. "We were going to catch him. I just needed more time."

They had started this investigation together, but somewhere along the way, she'd stopped confiding in him. Would their marriage be like that? Would he lose her trust as a husband someday, just as he had in this matter? He couldn't imagine doing anything that would drive her away, but now that fear grew inside his chest, making him ill at the mere thought of it.

He sat at Meredith's side until his body ached from the bent position. When the moon rose high in the sky, the bedchamber door opened.

Warren's voice pulled him out of his bleak thoughts. "How is she?"

A crimson veil descended over his vision. Darius leapt up and charged at Warren. He struck a blow against his friend that sent Warren reeling back into the corridor.

"*How is she?*" he hissed. "She almost bloody died!" Darius's fear exploded through him, turning into a molten rage. "You nearly killed the woman I love, and you expect me to just sit here and—"

"Darius I—"

"She chose to confide in *you* over me. How could you let her do that? And because she trusted you, she nearly died!

"Darius, I—" Warren lifted his hands in surrender. "It was a sound plan—"

"*That was not your decision to make!*"

"No, it was hers," Warren said. "She blames herself for the death of Crell's wife."

That stopped Darius, but only a moment.

"This was something she believed she *had* to do," said Warren. "Because she did nothing when it might have mattered."

"That woman's death is *not* Meredith's fault," Darius growled.

"I know," said Warren. "But she's never believed that. It was tearing her up inside. That's why I agreed to help her. I never—"

"*Get out!*" Darius snarled. "Get out before I do something I will regret."

Warren's face shuttered as he turned and walked quickly away.

Darius's body was still shaking as he went back into Meredith's bedchamber. He closed the door and sank down with his back against the wood, then covered his face in his hands and wept.

All of his life, he'd endured loss. As a boy, he'd lost his mother's loving compassion, and as a young man when he'd needed the loving support of his friends most, he'd lost Kit to the penal colonies for a crime Kit hadn't committed. For seven years he'd believed that he might never see Kit again, a man that was as close as a brother to him. And when he held his head up, and carried on despite the pain raging like a tempest in his heart and soul, he'd lost his father, the kind, generous man who'd taught him to be everything he had become. He'd quarreled with Uncle Ben and never had a chance to make things right before he died.

Through it all, Darius had held his head up. Maintained appearances. But now he was breaking. Because the one person he could not afford to lose, the one person who held his heart like no other, had almost been lost to him.

Tears soaked his hands as he tried to calm himself, but he still felt like he couldn't breathe. He could not lose Meredith. He would never survive if he did.

18

M inerva Crell reclined in her rolling invalid chair in the garden next to the little table where Meredith had laid out the tea. A contented sigh escaped Meredith's neighbor.

"It is quite lovely this evening, is it not?"

Meredith added two lumps of sugar to her teacup and stirred it with a dainty silver spoon.

Meredith agreed. "Quite lovely... *Perfect,* in fact."

It was just as she'd hoped it would be to have her new friend over for tea. There was a gentle breeze, and the night was pleasantly quiet with a nightingale singing in a nearby tree. She took a sip from her cup, relishing the way the tea warmed her throat. But it left a strange taste behind... something like laudanum.

From the far end of the garden, Darius walked toward their tea table, pausing a moment to take in the scent of roses that bloomed amid the wildflowers. He shot Meredith a smile that made her belly tingle with warmth and excitement.

"You'll be happy with him," Mrs. Crell said. "I know it."

"You think so?" Meredith still feared that she would not be enough for Darius, that someday he would find her lacking and regret marrying her.

"They say opposites attract. But in truth, love is a calling, and like calls to like. You and he are so similar, at least in the ways that matter, the ways that *heal*. You need each other. There is no greater destiny than one loving heart finding another."

Meredith studied Mrs. Crell's face. "What went wrong... with you and your husband?" It was an intimate question to ask, but Meredith sensed her new friend would answer. "Were you ever actually in love?"

"I had been enchanted by his looks and charm, and he by my sizable inheritance. I thought in time it would become something more. But as the years passed and my illness set in, no foundation of love had grown between us. Money and desire will never be enough to sustain the flowering of true love. But I was too young and foolish to know that. And now..."

Meredith reached out and curled her fingers around Mrs. Crell's hand, squeezing it gently. Her hand was strangely cold the touch. She let out a soft little sound, almost a choked sob, before she turned to Meredith again.

"Perhaps in time I can rest. But you... you've rested far too long."

"What do you mean?"

"I have taken up too much of your time. You must wake up."

"Wake up?"

Mrs. Crell shook Meredith's hand, her eyes wide and suddenly fearful. "Wake up, my dear!"

Meredith jolted awake. She tried to swallow, but her throat was painfully tight. She was in a darkened bedchamber. Comforting images of ocean waves greeted her upon the walls. She was in the Seaside room of Darius's townhouse, not in the garden with Minerva Crell.

A dream… just a dream.

Minerva Crell was dead. Meredith touched her throat and winced. Mr. Crell's hands around her throat. She'd been trying to get him to confess what he'd done. She'd goaded him until he'd attacked her.

I was such a fool to think that would work.

Vague memories of Darius holding her surfaced. Had he been there, or was that a dream too? Darius was supposed to be in the countryside with his friends on a shooting party. It must have been Warren who'd come to her rescue. But Darius must have been there. She remembered his arms around her, his masculine scent filling her nose. She recalled only brief flashes of seeing Crell pulled to the ground by Warren and Doyle before she blacked out.

She pushed back the covers and walked around the room. Her body was stiff and sore, and she had a sense that she'd been asleep a long time. She poured herself a glass of water and drank, though her throat protested each time she swallowed.

Moonlight bathed the bedchamber with a pale, milky light, and she took in the night as she drank the water. She looked out at the lonely dark Crell house. How long had she been asleep? A few hours? Days? She found her dressing gown draped over the back of a nearby chair and slipped it on, tying the sash tight around her waist. Then she slipped her feet into her mule slippers.

She opened the bedchamber door and peered into the corridor, finding a quiet, darkened house. Darius's bedchamber door was closed. Just then, a shadow emerged in the hall and moved towards Meredith. She held back a strangled scream but then a lamp was lit and Frances's face appeared in the darkness at the end of the hall as she held the lamp up.

"Meredith? I knew I heard something. What are you doing out of bed?" Frances said in a hushed tone. She also wore a dressing gown, her hair pulled up in a messy knot atop her head.

"I needed to move about a bit. I'm dreadfully stiff. How long have I been asleep?"

"A little more than a day." Frances put the back of her hand to Meredith's forehead to check for a fever and then searched Meredith's face with a motherly eye. "The doctor gave you laudanum. He warned us you would sleep for a while. How are you feeling?"

"Everything aches, and I'm still tired, but I didn't want to stay in bed." Her voice was a soft whisper. It was all she could manage with her throat hurting as it did. Her belly suddenly grumbled.

The corners of Frances's eyes crinkled. "Oh dear, you must be hungry. Let's sneak down to the kitchen. The cook has some rhubarb pie left over from dinner."

They snuck downstairs to the quiet, darkened kitchen. Meredith slid onto a stool by the large countertop as Frances produced two glasses of milk and a slice of pie from the cold cellar. As they shared the dessert and enjoyed the silence, Meredith was grateful that her friend understood she was still processing what had happened and did not want to speak of it right away.

"How does your throat feel?" Frances eventually asked. "We were told it would be a while before you would recover."

"It is quite sore," Meredith replied, her voice raspy. "What happened? The last thing I remember was Mr. Crell attacking me."

Frances's face paled. "I heard you scream, and saw Mr. Doyle climb over the wall. He and Warren pulled Crell off you, just as Darius arrived. He carried you up to bed and called the doctor."

"Darius? I didn't dream him, then?" Meredith's heart leapt, then panic took over. "Oh no. He must be *furious* with me." That image of his bedroom door firmly closed against her was proof enough. If he hadn't been angry with her, he would have been in bed beside her, as he had the last few nights.

Frances set her fork down on her plate and sighed. "Yes, he is quite angry. But I believe it is because he was afraid for you."

"What happened to Mr. Crell?" Meredith asked, hoping to distract herself from thinking about how angry Darius must be with her.

"Mr. Doyle took him into custody. It is over. He will face justice for what he tried to do to you, and no doubt a fuller investigation into the fate of his wife will come of this. Lionel provided Doyle with a bit of information about Crell spending his wife's money in ways that clearly weren't for her use but for himself and his mistress. Doyle said he will likely be sent to the penal colonies in Australia at the very least for what he's done to you, and he'll be hanged if they find him guilty of murdering his wife."

Meredith flinched. Lord Kentwell, Kit, had suffered a similar fate, though he had been wrongfully accused. But he had managed to return to England. Would Crell return here someday? Seek revenge? She shivered and prayed that he would be found guilty of murdering his wife, or else she might not be safe ever again from Crell's desire to get revenge on her.

"The penal colonies might be justice for me, but not for what he did to his wife."

"No," Frances sighed. "But we can hope that Mr. Doyle has enough financial evidence to open a larger inquiry into the wife's disappearance now and that might lead to a murder charge." She took their dishes to the sink to wash them, and Meredith helped. It was soothing to do such a simple task.

"Off to bed now," Frances said when they were done. "You still need rest."

She put an arm around Meredith's shoulders as they headed back up there to their chambers. Once back at their chambers, Frances bid her good night and disappeared into her room. Meredith opened her own door after a lingering look at Darius's closed door. So he *was* here, but he hadn't slept in her bed with her. Was it because she was injured or because he was upset with her? Either way, she wasn't going to wake him in the middle of the night. She wasn't prepared to face his anger, because it would be entirely justified and she already felt quite wretched. Facing Darius's disappointment on top of his anger would be too much to bear.

She stepped into her bedchamber and halted in shock. Darius was there, silhouetted against the window, moonlight outlining his figure. He gazed out the window toward the Crell house. Her desire to avoid him until morning evaporated. Now she only wanted to curl up in his arms and close her eyes, forgetting everything that had happened in the last day.

She came up behind him, wrapping her arms around his waist and pressed her cheek against his shoulder. He tensed briefly, then relaxed. She took in a deep breath, wanting to steep herself in the comfort of his scent, but he didn't smell as he usually did. Instead, he smelled of sweat, leather and hay. Had he been riding earlier and not changed?

"Darius, I am sorry," she whispered. "I didn't mean to keep my plans from you because I didn't trust you. I do trust you. It's just that well...I thought I could catch him. I had to...I owed it to Mrs. Crell because I failed to save her when I should have known he was hurting her. That's why I kept my plans a secret, because I knew you would say it was too dangerous."

"That's because it was *dangerous*," a deep voice growled.

A voice that did not belong to Darius.

The man turned around and in a brief moment of illumination, she saw the face was not that of the man she loved, but the man she *feared*.

"Crell!" she gasped. Terror the likes of which she'd never known before dug into her chest, making it impossible to breathe.

He struck her across the face with the back of his hand and she collapsed to the floor. Her head swam as her head throbbed with pain.

"How did you know what I'd done?" He hissed above her as he stood looming over her. "*How?*" He grabbed her by the hair and wrenched her head up to look up at him.

"The w—window..." She tried to point, but her left arm ached from her body landing on it.

"I suspected as much," he snarled. "Not that it matters now. If I'm to be banished to some foreign bloody continent for attempting to kill you, I might as well finish the deed." He hauled her up to her feet, her neck imprisoned within the grip of his large, powerful hand. He dragged her toward the open window.

"No!" She struggled as he tried to force her out of the window.

Meredith fought to free herself of Crell's hold. She tried to scream again, but her vocal chords were too bruised to manage anything above a soft cry. Her grip on his arms slipped and she started to fall. She scrambled to catch at something, *anything*. Her fingers caught the lip of the windowsill. Meredith jerked to a sudden stop hanging above the terrace, pain shooting through her shoulders

Crell leaned over, his face painted by moonlight as he stared at her.

"No..." she rasped. "*Please...*"

A demonic fury lit his eyes as he leaned over her, his hands digging at her fingertips to pry them away.

She tried to move her hands away from him, but it was no use. She couldn't hang here forever, and sooner or later, he would pry her fingers loose. She tried not to think about the fact that in a matter of moments she was going to fall...

A roar shook the windows and disturbed the lonely nightingale in a nearby tree that had been watching these events. With a look of terror on his face, Crell was jerked away from the window and dragged into the darkness. It could only be one person.

"Darius!"

Meredith clawed, trying to pull herself up in the window, but she was too weak. Her fingers began to slip...

DARIUS'S FIST STRUCK CRELL HARD IN THE JAW, BUT THE MAN HAD come prepared for a fight. He pulled a long blade from his waistcoat, which flashed in the dim light.

"You'll hang for this, Crell," Darius growled. "No matter what."

"Do you think I care?" Crell snapped. "I won't be trapped in another prison, my marriage was prison enough!"

Darius feinted left, then dove to the right as Crell lunged, swinging his blade. Taking advantage of his now exposed side, Darius buried his fist in Crell's stomach. Crell staggered, but a strangled scream from Meredith snapped Darius's focus away from the fight. She was hanging from the window, barely keeping her grip.

Darius leapt toward the window just as Meredith's fingers slipped from the edge of the sill. abandoning the fight with Crell even if it meant leaving his back exposed. He had a mere instant to realize Meredith was falling. He grabbed her by the wrists just as her fingers let go of the edge of the sill. The weight of her body jerked his shoulders roughly, but he held fast.

A sudden, blinding pain nearly made him to let go of Meredith. Darius heard Crell's cold, breathless laugh just as his blade pierced Darius's back.

"I say, can *anyone* join in this dance?" Another voice called out. Crell was pulled off Darius, but he didn't dare look to see what was happening for fear of losing his grip. The strength was bleeding out of him, and he was unable to pull Meredith up.

"Meredith... I can't... I can't lift you..."

"Let me go," she said, her eyes beginning to fill with tears. "It's all right...just let go..."

"*Never*," he vowed, even as his vision began to turn black.

Bang! The report of a pistol nearly deafened him. There was a hard thud near Darius, but he dared not break his concentration. He had to hold on.

"Steady, old boy, let me help." Warren appeared at his side, reaching past him to grab Meredith's arm. A flood of relief gave Darius that extra bit of strength he needed to not let go.

"Hold on," Warren called to Meredith. He and Darius pulled her up the side of the house and back through the window. She stumbled on her dressing gown as she tried to put her feet down on the floor. Darius moved to catch her and steady her.

"Are you hurt?" he asked, ignoring how hard it was to breathe. All that mattered right now was Meredith.

She shook her head, her hazel eyes now swimming with tears.

Darius pulled her into his arms, cradling her against him, never wanting to let go of her again. "Oh, sweetheart."

Darius glanced down at the floor. Crell lay dead next to them. His sightless eyes reflecting the moonlight from the open window. "How the devil did he get inside? I thought Doyle took him away."

"I have no bloody idea. It's a damn good thing I didn't leave. I was wandering around the gardens trying to think of a way to apologize to you, old boy, when I saw Meredith and Crell struggling at the window."

Darius met Warren's gaze, a friend who had always

been there for him, yet he had chased Warren away in a fit of anger. If his friend had listened to him and left his house...he and Meredith would both be dead. A well of deepest brotherly love surged within him for this man he called his friend.

He almost choked with emotions as he spoke. "Warren, I'm sorry I spoke to you as I did. I wasn't thinking clearly. I shouldn't have—"

"Yes, you should have." Warren didn't look away from Darius. "I was a fool. I should have convinced Meredith to tell you about her plan. Instead, I let her put herself in danger. You can be angry at me for the next century if you need to."

"Right now, I'm glad you are so bloody stubborn that you didn't leave after I threw you out."

"What's happened?" Frances's panicked voice at the door, drew his attention.

Frances and Mr. Chelsea, along with the rest of the house servants now appeared in the doorway.

"My goodness, is that Mr. Crell?" Chelsea asked.

"Are you all right, Your Grace?" a maid asked.

"Warren, send for Doyle. Chelsea, see that Meredith is looked at by the doctor. I must..." He took a step forward and his legs gave out beneath him.

"I *must*..." he repeated slowly as his vision spiraled and the light shrank into darkness.

"Darius!" Meredith tried to catch him as he fell, but he was too heavy. She collapsed with him on the floor. Darius didn't move.

"Damnation." Warren cursed as he pushed Darius's waistcoat and shirt up to examine the bleeding puncture wound on his lower back. Then he noticed the blade on the floor by Crell which gleamed red with Darius's blood.

"Was he was stabbed?" Meredith nearly choked on the words, terrified by the thought of losing him.

"Don't give up on him yet," Warren said as if he could read her thoughts. "It doesn't look deep. And it looks too low to have pictured a lung, that's the true danger, that and organs being pierced.

Meredith's stomach convulsed at the thought of all that could have gone wrong and that Darius wasn't out of danger.

Chelsea and Frances helped Warren and Meredith get Daruis on Meredith's bed, laying him on his stomach. Meredith used a wadded up cloth and pressed it hard against the wound to slow the flow of blood.

It took an age for the doctor to arrive. Meredith was forced to get out of the man's way so he could treat Darius's wound. Frances held up a lamp for the doctor as he got to work.

Doyle arrived just as the doctor finished stitching up the wound. Warren wasted no time in confronting the man.

"What the devil was he doing here, Doyle? You had him in custody!"

Doyle rubbed a weary hand over his stubble-shadowed jaw. "He escaped."

"That much is obvious," Warren countered. "And you didn't think to tell us? How did he escape?"

"He feigned illness and attacked the guard who entered the cell to check on him. Roberts is a new lad who only just started with us. Almost got himself killed. We'd been scouring the coaching inns of London and the docks, thinking he meant to flee the city. I never imagined he would come back here."

"The man knew he wouldn't escape his fate," said Warren, looking down at the body. "So he set his hopes on revenge."

Doyle gave Meredith an apologetic look. "I am sorry for all that you suffered, Miss Montague. But it is ended now."

"Is it?" Meredith whispered. "We'll never know what became of his wife."

"I think we might have a chance to find answers still," Warren said. "His mistress is in the country and so is that blasted butler. They must know at least part of this tragedy."

"I had that same thought the moment Crell escaped. We are sending men to his country house as we speak."

The doctor cleared his throat.

"Well?" Warren's tone went quiet. "How is he?"

"I believe he will live. Tiverton has the devil's own luck, I will say that much," said the doctor. "This is the second blade wound which has missed his organs."

"Devil's own luck indeed," Warren said with unconcealed relief. "I shall have to tell the others, but it can wait until morning."

Meredith knew he meant the other rogues in the square. They would of course want to know what had happened, but he was right. There was no need to wake them if Darius was going to be all right... She prayed that was true as she walked over to Darius's bed. Warren joined her, putting an arm around her for comfort. Doyle's men came to remove Crell's body, but Meredith paid them no attention. Crell was in the past now. Meredith's future lay here on the bed.

"The wound must be cleaned daily and fresh bandages applied. If it turns angry and swells, send for me at once." He placed a bottle of laudanum in Meredith's hand. "One spoon a day for the pain, no more. He's already had a dose for tonight."

The doctor left and Meredith sat on a chair that Warren had set beside Darius's bed. He was breathing evenly now. The white bandages wrapped around his stomach seemed so stark in the dim light.

Frances and Warren checked on her throughout the night to see that she was all right and to beg her to use one of the other beds to sleep. But Meredith refused to leave the room. At last, her weariness was too much for her to fight. She leaned back in the chair to rest...to sleep...

She was once more in the gardens and Mrs. Crell was there. This dream felt different somehow than the first. Mrs. Crell was no longer sitting in that rolling invalid chair.

Or was it because she looked somehow younger than before? Happier?

"Mrs. Crell?" Meredith walked toward the woman.

"Minerva...I am *Minerva* once again, thanks to you." She smiled. "He has no hold over me anymore. I am myself once again."

"I don't understand," Meredith confessed.

"You don't have to," Minerva said. "What matters is, you set me free. It feels like I am flying once more." She spoke a swirling trio of brightly colored butterflies danced around Minerva and she laughed, holding her hand out to them. "Simply flying..." Minerva said more softly and wistfully. She took one of Meredith's hands in her own. "I have only one regret, that you and I had so little time to get to become friends." She squeezed Meredith's hand. "You will tell everyone that I once lived here?"

Meredith's lips quivered as she understood Minerva's question. She did not wish to be forgotten.

"I shall never forget, and I won't let anyone else either." The promise left a deep ache in her throat as she fought off tears.

Minerva leaned in and embraced Meredith.

"It will be all right, my dear. That man you chose will let you be free to fly...so spread your wings."

The garden was suddenly filled with thousands of butterflies, and once they had cleared, Minerva was gone. She closed her eyes within that sad and beautiful dream, but could still smell wildflowers and distant rain.

And as she did so, she felt the kiss of a thousand butter-flies wings upon her cheeks.

Minerva was right. She was free to fly.

DARIUS WOKE TO THE TENDER TOUCH OF THE WOMAN HE LOVED, who was wiping his brow with a cold wet cloth. He did not feel feverish, but the cool cloth felt good upon his skin.

"Meredith..." he said, and she gently shushed him.

"I'm here, Darius. I'm safe. All that matters now is that you get better, so that we might get married."

He found himself relaxing. That simple statement had assured him that all was going to be well. "Married...yes. I want that more than anything."

Meredith smiled down at him. "As do I. Now, while I have you at my tender mercy, there are things I must say."

He reached up to cup her cheek with his palm. "These things must be quite serious."

"They are," she agreed, her tone solemn. "I kept my need to catch Crell from you, and I shouldn't have done that. I feared you had given up. Lionel explained to me that you and he had been investigating Crell's finances."

He stroked her cheek with his thumb. "I planned to tell you what I'd found, once I found something worth sharing. There was never a moment when I planned to give up on catching him," Darius insisted.

"Lionel told me that too. I'm sorry I thought you had."

"I suppose I shouldn't have kept my intentions from

you, either. But I didn't want you to worry before I had proof."

Meredith nodded. "I was just so accustomed to being alone or kept at a distance—even if that distance is of my own making. I'm not used to the idea of sharing my entire life with someone. You will have to be patient with me." She stroked her fingertips along his arm, which felt simply wonderful.

"You aren't the only one used to doing things alone. We must both endeavor to share things with each other. That is what marriage means, that we lean upon one another, *trust* one another."

Meredith kissed the backs of his fingers of his hand. "I couldn't agree more."

"Lord, I don't feel much pain, did you give me laudanum?" Darius chuckled at the thought for some reason. Right now it seemed anything could be amusing.

"Absolutely. Doctor's orders," she said with a soft laugh.

"Good. Because I wish for you to lie beside me, so that I can feel you, and hear your soft breath in the dark."

She carefully climbed into bed beside him and tucked herself against him. He let out a breath as the last knot of tension uncoiled within him. Her hand settled just above his heart, the heart that had belonged to her the moment he'd first laid eyes on her standing on his doorstep. He drew in a deep breath, one that thankfully held no pain, and gazed up at the ceiling with a bright sense of wondrous clarity.

Loving someone was the most exquisite thing he had

ever experienced in his life, and he would have the honor of loving Meredith for the rest of their lives. Through the window that faced the gardens of his home, the morning light pierced the window at just the right angle to cast a shower of rainbows and diamonds upon the walls in the room

And, for just a single instant, he saw a figure wreathed in morning light...it was a woman, a woman whose face he might have recognized, had he seen it but a second longer.

Then it was gone, and he was drifting back to sleep knowing that his future with Meredith was just as glorious as the dawn.

19

One month later...

MEREDITH HELD A BOUQUET FULL OF HUNDRED-LEAVED ROSES, their soft pink hue contrasting sweetly with the bright green satin of her wedding gown. She lifted up the roses to inhale their scent and smiled. Warren had said that Darius chose those flowers because they meant sincere love.

Tucked amongst the roses were apple blossoms, which meant he preferred her above all others, and red tulips, which meant he declared his love. Learning the language of flowers had captivated her. She remembered the look on Darius's face when he had been forced to carry one of the bouquets of her suitors and smothered a giggle.

She took one final moment to check her appearance in

the wall mirror of the drawing room. She'd had the modiste design her gown with a beautiful shade of emerald silk that matched the stems of the flowers in Darius's garden.

"Are you ready?" Warren asked. He waited with her in the drawing room while Darius and the guests had gone outside to the gardens.

"Yes." She smiled up at Warren. "You are so sweet to give me away."

"I am delighted by the honor." He winked at her. "Though I almost had to duel Felix for the chance. He wanted to give you away as well."

Someone knocked on the drawing room door and Warren called for them to enter. Meredith expected it to be Mr. Chelsea to inform them the ceremony was about to begin, but she gasped at the sight of Prince George standing in the doorway, bedecked in his finest clothes.

"Mr. Burville, I understand you've been looking forward to this moment, but would you allow me to have the honor of escorting Miss Montague down the aisle? It would allow me to put to rest anyone else's poor opinions of this darling woman. If a prince gives her away to Tiverton in marriage, then none can challenge such a union."

Warren exchanged a glance with Meredith, and she nodded her agreement.

"Yes, of course. I quite agree." He kissed Meredith's gloved hand, then walked her to the Prince. "I will be outside with the others."

The Prince of Wales eyed her dress with approval. The pink roses on her sleeves and the flowers embroidered along the bottom half of her gown made it look as though a garden was growing up her skirts.

"Quite an exquisite design," he said. "I expected nothing less for the Duchess of Tiverton." It was high praise from a prince who prided himself on his taste in fashion.

Prince George took her hand and tucked it on his arm as they left the drawing room. A footman was ready to open the doors for them to the back terrace. Meredith's eyes filled with tears as she saw all of Darius's servants lined up on either side of the terrace. They wore their Sunday best, and more than one woman dabbed a handkerchief at their eyes, as did one of the footmen. Meredith murmured a thank you to them as they passed into the gardens.

A crowd of forty guests had formed rows on either side of the petal-drenched aisle toward and archway of flowers. All of her suitors were present, including Jordan Evers, who beamed at her as she walked past him. He had sent her a note expressing his delight that she'd ended up with the man who held her heart.

Darius waited for her under the archway of blooms, his eyes soft as he took in the sight of her. Meredith no longer felt shy or out of place in his bold, beautiful world, because it was *her* world too.

She had come to London without family, connections, money, or even a sense of value in herself. But all that had changed. Her new friends had shown her that even without money and connections, she was valued and cherished. It had taken a little time to believe it herself, but she did now.

I belong here. I belong with Darius.

Had Uncle Ben known that it would come to this? That the letter he had charged her to deliver to Darius would result in such wonderful happiness for them both? Somehow she suspected Uncle Ben might have known that they would belong together.

"This may be a small wedding by some standards," the prince whispered as they approached Darius, "but I believe all the people who matter are here."

Darius bowed to the Prince and accepted Meredith's gloved hand in his own as she joined him and the clergyman. Prince George retreated to the first row of guests as the ceremony began.

Meredith spoke her vows of love to Darius, and he spoke them in return, his eyes never once leaving her face. At last he leaned in to kiss her, and the world faded away beneath the tender press of his lips. It was their first kiss as husband and wife, and it held such a sweet fire that Meredith's soul would never be cold again.

When Darius raised his head, his grin was so seductive and yet so tender that she knew she would always be loved, always be wanted.

"I belong to you, forever," he whispered before stealing another kiss. The clergyman cleared his throat and Darius's friends cheered in the waiting crowd.

Meredith giggled and Darius smiled against her lips before he turned to face their guests.

"My wife and I would like you all to join us in the drawing room for a wedding breakfast."

She and Darius led the crowd indoors, where Mr.

Chelsea had arranged for the wedding cake to be cut and plated ahead of time. Meredith had insisted that the servants would be able to join them for the breakfast as guests. Everyone dined on cake and the breakfast meal that Frances and Meredith had carefully planned out a month ago. By the time everyone was finished, Meredith's face hurt from so much smiling.

After the breakfast had concluded, Meredith and Darius saw everyone off. The last to leave were Warren and Felix, who had indulged in a bit too much champagne. They were singing and weaving their way across the street toward Kit's house, where the rest of the rogues of Devil's Square were going to continue to celebrate Darius's good fortune. Vincent had even dragged along Jordan Evers to join the other bachelors, insisting the poor man deserved a drink.

Meredith flinched when Felix and Warren barely avoided a coach rumbling down the street before reaching the steps of Kit's townhouse. "Do you suppose they will be all right?"

"It's not the first time they've been foxed, my dear. Kit will handle them." Her husband then grinned mischievously. "However, I have a wedding present to show you. I believe it should be installed now."

"Installed?" She echoed as he led her back out into the gardens.

"Yes. They started the moment we went inside for breakfast. I wanted to give you something special."

"I don't need anything special. I have you."

He turned to silence her with a kiss. Then, when she

was good and breathless, he stroked his thumb over her bottom lip. "You must let me give you things, sweetheart. I fear it is the terrible price you must pay being mine."

"Oh, all right, if I *must*." She sighed dramatically, which made him laugh. She leaned against him as they walked down the aisle of petals upon the grass toward the back garden wall. When they were close to where the heart-shaped hole was, Meredith gasped.

A statue had been placed in the gardens, right next to the heart-shaped hole. It was of a tall woman dressed in a Roman robe and helmet. She held a spear in one hand, and an owl sat on her shoulder. A battle shield rested against the woman's legs.

"This is Minerva, the Roman goddess of wisdom and strategy."

"Minerva…" Meredith covered her mouth with her hands. "You did it for *her*."

"And for *you*," Darius said. "Without you, we never would've known what Crell had done, nor would we have caught him. I don't ever want you to forget how brave you are. And I don't want anyone else to forget her, just as you wished."

Wildflowers and roses had been planted around the base of the statue. The wildflowers would attract dozens of butterflies in the spring and summer. This part of the garden would become full of them.

"How are you so perfect?" she asked Darius.

"How? By loving you." He pulled her into his arms, kissing her. His lips were soft and eager against hers, making her belly quiver in anticipation of their wedding night.

"Now, what say you to celebrating our newly married state in my bed?"

Their wedding night was to become a wedding afternoon...and she had no complaints at the change in plans.

"*Our* bed," she corrected. "I want to share rooms with you."

"I want that as well." They raced back to the house hand in hand, their feet flying upon the ground and their laughter echoing off the stones of the house.

WARREN SIPPED HIS BRANDY AS HE WATCHED THE BOW STREET Runner bend over the billiard table and line up for his shot. "Answer me a question, Doyle."

Doyle was unfazed by the interruption, focused on his present task. "Ask away, Mr. Burville."

"How did he do it?"

"Who?" Doyle struck the cue ball, which shot across the green baize surface and connected with several other balls. One dropped neatly into a corner pocket, and another rolled perfectly into place for his next shot.

"Crell," Warren said. "Did you ever learn of his wife's fate?"

"Oh yes. The mistress told us the whole of it in order to escape the noose." The other men in the room stopped talking. Several gathered around the Bow Street Runner to hear him speak.

"It was planned. He tried to smother her with a pillow, but she was stronger than he expected. She escaped the bed and tried to flee. She made it to the mews before he caught up with her and stabbed the poor woman. He cleaned up the blood with the clothes Darius dug up in the garden. He also hid the jewels in the same hole in the garden, hoping to sell them in a year once he'd convinced everyone his wife never planned to return to London and didn't need her jewelry."

"What about the servants? Didn't someone see the struggle?"

"He let go of his entire staff, except for the butler, a week before he killed her. That man was paid handsomely for his silence and assistance in concealing what happened. He's the one who dug up the bloody clothes and jewelry after Darius found them."

"And what about her body?" Warren pressed.

Lionel groaned. "Christ, Warren. Let the poor woman rest in peace."

Doyle sighed and leaned on his billiards cue. "They put her body in a trunk and buried it in the country. She was given a proper burial in her family's plot in Kent."

"A *trunk*? You mean to say he traveled with it when he went to the country?" Warren asked.

"Yes, I believe so."

"Christ," Warren muttered. "I might have helped lift that damn trunk down with the man's hired footman. All that time, the poor woman was right there, and I didn't know." That was going to haunt him a long time. If he'd looked in that trunk, he would have found Mrs. Crell and caught her husband right there, and avoided the events that led to Meredith and Darius being attacked.

Vincent clapped a hand on Warren's shoulder and gave it a squeeze. "A damned shame what happened to her, I know. But you and Meredith caught the man," he told Warren. "You did all that you could for that woman."

"Yes," Warren said softly. The entire incident had left him with a sinking melancholy. But Vincent was right. Crell was dead, and his wife was avenged. It would have to be enough.

"Your turn, Warren," Felix announced. Warren set down his brandy and took up his cue, leaning over the billiard table to take his shot.

IT WAS EARLY EVENING WHEN MEREDITH CAME DOWN THE STAIRS to see about dinner being sent up to her and Darius in their bedchamber. She was tiptoeing down the stairs on bare feet, wearing nothing but her chemise and dressing gown when she heard strained voices. Mr. Chelsea was in the drawing room, arguing with someone.

"Let me see her! I know she's here," a man's voice snapped.

"No," Chelsea replied firmly. "I'm afraid she is unavailable for visitors."

"Mr. Chelsea?" She pushed the door open and froze as she saw who was arguing with their butler. It was Harry St. John.

"Aww, Merry dear, tell this fool that you will see me." Meredith pulled her robe more firmly around her body and crossed her arms. Other than her bare feet, she wasn't improperly dressed for her home, but with Harry she sensed any amount of clothes would not be enough to make her feel safe.

"I would ask that you please leave."

"Not unless you accompany me. My father wanted me to care for you, after all."

Meredith blinked. He was here to *retrieve* her? But that would mean...

She looked to Chelsea and said quietly, "He doesn't know?"

"He does not." Chelsea, being the consummate professional he was, said it without smiling, but the implication was clear.

Harry ignored their private exchange. "You know it took me bloody *ages* to figure out where you'd gone? You didn't even stay for the funeral. That is badly done, Merry, badly done indeed."

That struck a chord. She had hated missing Uncle Ben's funeral, but had had little choice in the matter.

"Come now, pack your things. I have a coach waiting for us."

Meredith betrayed nothing as she looked to the butler. "Mr. Chelsea, would you—"

"Yes, of course." The butler nodded and hastily left the room.

"I have no idea what got into your silly little head," Harry said, exasperated. "Imposing yourself on the my cousin's goodwill like this, after he and father had such a falling out. It's a miracle he didn't throw you out on the street.

"And you intend to take me back home?" Meredith said evenly.

"Of course. Oh, I know you ran off because I was a bit *forward*. But honestly, such an overreaction is unbecoming. My conditions for your upkeep are not at all uncommon, I assure you."

What sickened Meredith most was the feeling that he might not be wrong.

Harry looked up at the ceiling as if weighing her fate with a heavenly expertise. "You can't expect my cousin to pay to keep you forever, my dear. Charity can only go so far. I, however, shall buy you pretty frocks and all the trinkets you could—"

"Good evening, Harry," Darius said coolly as he appeared in the doorway behind Meredith. He was fully dressed, his face a mask hiding all emotion.

"Darius." Harry's scowl was replaced by a nervous smile. "How are you?"

"Quite well. And you?"

"Well enough." Harry cleared his throat. "I didn't mean to disturb you. I only just learned of Meredith's imposition upon your hospitality, and came at once to take her home.

I'm sorry she's been a burden to you. I promised my father on his deathbed that I would see to her care, but the silly girl left before I could tell her that."

Darius's gaze flicked momentarily to Meredith before settling back on Harry. They both knew that Uncle Ben had *never* said such a thing on his deathbed.

"I see," said Darius, feigning understanding. "Well, I must say she has not been a burden to me. Far from it."

There was a glint in Harry's eye as he misinterpreted Darius's words. "Come now, Darius. You have your pick of women, fashionable courtesans far more worthy of you. You don't need her. Send her home with me, otherwise she'll start putting on airs."

Darius looked at Meredith in mock disapproval. "I say, have you been putting on *airs*?"

Meredith feigned shame. "Well, I did ask Harry to leave before you arrived."

"Oh I'm sure that's forgivable," said Darius, his lips twitching ever so slightly as if he fought off a smile.

Harry rolled his eyes. "Stop playing games, Darius. It's what's best for her, and you know it. It's not like she *belongs* here." Harry snorted. It was clear he believed Darius would agree with him.

Darius crossed his arms over his chest, but his tone remained calm. "Ahh, but she *does* belong here, cousin. You see, Uncle Ben sent her to me to help her find a husband among my peers."

"A husband?" Harry said in disbelief. "But who would marry her? She's a bastard."

"Well, it just so happens that we did find her a suitable match, didn't we?" Darius looked to Meredith, who nodded.

"Oh yes, the most splendid husband."

Darius looked at Harry. "Yes, I'm afraid you just missed the wedding. I regret that you didn't get an invitation, Harry, but, you see, I do not *like* you."

Harry's eyes bulged. "What? You don't...?" he was at a loss for words. "Then who did she marry? What fool would take the wretched chit?"

"This fool," Darius interrupted as he pointed a finger into his own chest. "I adore her so much so that I married her this morning. The Prince of Wales himself gave her away."

Harry's eyes bulged slightly. "What?"

"I am Meredith's *husband*, Harry. Now, tell me again what you called my wife." The conversational tone was gone, replaced by a dark, furious growl. Darius waited, standing perfectly still but Meredith could sense her husband was an instant away from unleashing all that raw power coiled so tightly up in his hard, beautiful body.

"Darius, tell me you're joking," said Harry. "Meredith? A duchess? She is nobody, she—"

Poor, stupid Harry never saw the blow coming. Darius hit him hard enough to send him flying into the wall. He slumped to the ground, out cold.

"She isn't nobody. She is the love of my life," Darius said to the unconscious man on the floor. "Chelsea?" Darius called out.

The butler appeared behind them in the doorway. "Your Grace?"

"Please take my cousin out to his coach and have the driver return him to Yorkshire. Pay the man handsomely to see it done at once."

"Yes, Your Grace." Chelsea called for a footman to help him lift Harry up and carry him out of the room.

The moment they were alone, Darius gently pulled Meredith into his arms. All of the violence and coiled rage inside him was gone. He was *her* Darius again.

Darius lifted her chin so she looked up at him. "I'm sorry he said what he did."

"I'm not," she replied. "Hearing him say those words, it tested me rather than break me. It made me realize that such words have no power over me. Not anymore." She curled her arms around his neck. "You taught me to be brave, to fight for what mattered, and damn the rest."

Darius chuckled. "Tell me Harry is included in *damning the rest?*"

"Most certainly," she said with a giggle.

"He will never hurt you again, now that you're my duchess."

She smiled up at him. "I shouldn't love it so much, but I do."

"Love what?" His eyes grew soft in a way that made her knees weak.

"You calling me your duchess." She let her gaze drop to his sinfully perfect mouth, which she desperately wanted to kiss. "It's not because I like the title. It's because I'm *yours.*"

"You *are* mine," he promised. "Until the stars fall from the skies and an eternity beyond."

Then, with all the perfection of a fairy tale duke who'd longed his entire life for love, he leaned in and kissed the woman he adored with every breath in his body. His duchess. His *wife*.

Warren Burville was deep in his cups, which was a very dangerous thing. His vision swam as he left the coaching inn and staggered toward the waiting vehicle. It wasn't a public mail coach, but it was not *his* coach either. He had foolishly forgotten to notify his driver of his plans to travel to the country, where he was to attend Darius and Meredith's first country house party as a married couple. His driver, Mr. Leeds, had apologized profusely when he explained that his coach was unavailable while a broken axel was being repaired.

It was a damned nuisance to hire a private travel coach like this. Still, he was too foxed to ride a hired horse. He couldn't take the chance that he'd fall asleep and slip off the saddle.

The moon was high in the sky, illuminating the ground outside the inn. The coach driver loaded Warren's travel trunk and valise onto the back and strapped them down on top of another two trunks.

"Are we ready to depart?" Warren asked as the driver finished the task.

"Yes sir. The other passenger is ready to depart."

Warren halted, his hand on the coach door. "Other passenger?"

"Yes. When the innkeeper heard your destination, he asked to book another passenger who was traveling in the same direction."

"But I requested a *private* coach," Warren growled.

"It *is* a private coach, sir," the driver replied flatly. "But as you are both headed to the same destination, I was able to take the additional fare."

"Fine." Warren muttered. Perhaps it was another of the house party guests. His head was pounding again, and the driver's voice was like a knife to his skull.

He wrenched the coach door open none too gently and climbed into the vehicle. He could just make out another figure in the dim confines of the coach. Figuring he should greet the fellow, he held out a hand. But before Warren could say a word, the coach jolted into motion, sending him crashing into the other person.

He grunted as he landed on something soft and most decidedly feminine. So, not a fellow then.

"I beg your pardon!" the woman hissed, shoving hard at his shoulders.

He grinned as his body pinned hers in the coach seat.

"Darling, *beg* all you wish, and I will endeavor to deliver." She seemed warm and inviting, this mystery creature.

A palm connected with his cheek, and the pain, however temporary, was like a bucket of cold water, providing much needed clarity on the situation.

He pushed away from the woman and collapsed on the opposite seat, groaning as the world tilted. He tried to get a clear look at the woman facing him, but all he could make out was a dull frock and the pert bonnet with ribbons tied into a massive bow at the base of her chin. Who the devil wore a bonnet at night? The woman's features were too shrouded in shadow from the bonnet for him to see her clearly, but he was definitely seeing *double* of her.

"I say, do you perchance have a twin?" He teased. "Because I'm seeing *two* of you."

"Are you drunk?" The woman demanded. He found the tone of feminine anger oddly arousing. He had never cared for fussy woman in general, but he was genuinely intrigued by this particular midnight mystery.

"Oh yes, quite foxed, darling. Have *you* ever been foxed?"

"Of course not! Only a fool would drink so much that they'd lose control, as you so clearly have."

Warren grinned. The moonlight entering the coach was lighting up his face, which meant it also lit up his smile. Even drunk, he knew what effect his smile could have on a woman.

"I was in the midst of a card game. It was hard to lose, so had to drink to make sure that I did, in fact, *lose*."

She scoffed. "You *wanted* to lose a card game?"

"Oh yes." He continued to grin, because he knew she had to ask another question.

"Why?" she finally asked.

"Because life is not interesting unless you dare yourself to lose a little."

She didn't immediately reply. Instead, she made a sound like a *harrumph*.

"So..." He left the single word in the air a moment before continuing. "I wonder, are you hiding a passionate heart under that awful dress? Or are you some dour woman who despises passion?"

The callous question got the exact reaction he was hoping for. She leaned forward to smack him again. Warren caught her wrist and jerked her to sit across his lap, then used his hand to tug at those ridiculously long ribbons until he pulled the bonnet free of her head.

He saw a rather plain face of a woman in her late twenties, but her lips were quite *exquisite*. He kept her prisoner on his lap as he cupped her neck and closed the distance between them to kiss her.

Her lips parted in a gasp of shock and he slipped his tongue inside her mouth. She tasted sweet, like lazy summer days full of ripe strawberries and lemonade. He inhaled deeply as he kissed her more urgently, drunk now on the taste of her. Her scent, a light floral aroma that came from no bottle but from time spent kneeling in a flower bed, wrapped itself around him, completing the masterful dream. The mystery woman's lips softened and she melted into him.

Christ, what luck he had!

The coach suddenly hit a rock on the road. They rose up and crashed down with a loud bang. The impact jolted him and his travel companion apart.

With a little curse, the woman jerked away from him and retreated to the seat opposite, hastily putting her bonnet back on her head. He watched her try to pull her loose tresses back under the shelter of that silly bonnet. It was intensely satisfying to know that because of his vigorous kissing, she failed to put her appearance back to rights and tossed the bonnet on the seat with a frustrated growl.

He stretched out his legs and crossed his arms over his chest. The alcohol was catching up with him and, as much as he wanted to steal another kiss, he simply wasn't able to stay awake.

"So sorry, darling, but I'm afraid I must sleep now." He chuckled as he closed his eyes.

The woman did not yell or shout or do anything that a woman would normally do after being kissed by a stranger. A more sober version of himself would question why, but sober Warren was hours away and that version of himself would no doubt believe this was all a dream. The best kisses always were.

J OAN H ENLOW, THE ONLY DAUGHTER OF THE LATE E ARL OF R IVERS touched her tingling lips with a trembling hand. She stared at the man who had kissed her like his life depended on it and then promptly fell asleep.

She knew this man, and the second she'd seen that devil-may-care smile her knees had buckled.

Warren Burville.

The last time she'd seen him she had been a young debutante. He had danced with her only once, but once was all she had needed to lose her heart and once was all he needed to walk away and never turn that smile upon her again.

That been six years ago. He'd been a young buck of twenty and she a girl of nineteen, eager, hopeful and ready for love. She'd seen Warren, danced with him, and knew no other man would ever make her feel the way he had.

Later, she learned that he was entirely unsuitable. He was too young to marry at the time and was quite reckless and wild. Now she was twenty-five, several years past those bright and eager days of her debut. She had never married, much to her parents disappointment.

After losing her father and her mother in quick succession to illness, she had thrown herself into managing her father's estate and her own inheritance. The hope was that she would marry and produce a male heir to take her father's title before the next male relative was located by the solicitor, but she suspected that day might never come.

And now, just when she had given up on love and happy

endings, the man who'd stolen her heart with one dance, had stolen a kiss and upended her quiet and controlled life.

"Damn you, Warren Burville," she whispered. "Damn you."

THANK YOU FOR READING *THE DUKE'S CARRIAGE WINDOW*! IF you haven't read Kit and Suzannah's book get *The Scoundrel of Drury Lane* HERE! Be sure to sign up for my newsletter and follow me on social media to get the latest news when Warren's book releases!

ABOUT THE AUTHOR

USA TODAY Bestselling Author Lauren Smith is an Oklahoma attorney by day, who pens adventurous and edgy romance stories by the light of her smart phone flashlight app. She knew she was destined to be a romance writer when she attempted to re-write the entire *Titanic* movie just to save Jack from drowning. Connecting with readers by writing emotionally moving, realistic and sexy romances no matter what time period is her passion. She's won multiple awards in several romance subgenres including: New England Reader's Choice Awards, Greater Detroit BookSeller's Best Awards, and a Semi-Finalist award for the Mary Wollstonecraft Shelley Award.

To connect with Lauren, visit her at:
www.laurensmithbooks.com
lauren@Laurensmithbooks.com

facebook.com/LaurenDianaSmith

x.com/LSmithAuthor

instagram.com/LaurenSmithbooks

amazon.com/stores/Lauren-Smith/author/B009L54KTC?ref=ap_rdr&store_ref=ap_rdr&isDramIntegrated=true&shoppingPortalEnabled=true

bookbub.com/authors/lauren-smith